All In

All In

A Novel

L.K. Simonds

NEW YORK

LONDON • NASHVILLE • MELBOURNE • VANCOUVER

All In
A Novel

Published in New York, New York, by Morgan James Publishing. Morgan James is a trademark of Morgan James, LLC. www.MorganJamesPublishing.com

Publisher's Note: This novel is a work of fiction. Names, characters, places, and incidents are either products of the author's imagination or used fictitiously. All characters are fictional, and any similarity to people living or dead is purely coincidental.

Scripture taken from the New King James Version®. Copyright © 1982 by Thomas Nelson. Used by permission. All rights reserved.

Scripture quotations are from the ESV® Bible (The Holy Bible, English Standard Version®). Copyright © 2001 by Crossway, a publishing ministry of Good News Publishers. Used by permission. All rights reserved.

Scriptures taken from the Holy Bible, New International Version®, NIV®. Copyright © 1973, 1978, 1984, 2011 by Biblica, Inc.™ Used by permission of Zondervan. All rights reserved worldwide. www.zondervan.com. The "NIV" and "New International Version" are trademarks registered in the United States Patent and Trademark Office by Biblica, Inc.™

The versions of the poems "In a Library" and "The Chariot" by Emily Dickinson reproduced herein are in the public domain. The copyrights for most, if not all, other versions of these poems are the property of Harvard University.

The poems "When You Are Old" and "The Heart of the Woman" by William Butler Yeats are in the public domain.

Andrew Lloyd Webber's musical *Cats* was adapted from T. S. Eliot's *Old Possum's Book of Practical Cats*, which has entertained children and adults since it was published in 1939. *Cats* played at the Winter Garden Theater in New York from 1982 to 2000, a total of 7,397 performances, according to *Playbill*.

ISBN 978-1-64279-291-1 paperback
ISBN 978-1-64279-292-8 eBook
ISBN 978-1-64279-293-5 hardcover
Library of Congress Control Number: 2018911509

Edited by:
Leslie Lutz
Elliott Bay Editing

Cover Design by:
Rachel Lopez
www.r2cdesign.com

In an effort to support local communities, raise awareness and funds, Morgan James Publishing donates a percentage of all book sales for the life of each book to Habitat for Humanity Peninsula and Greater Williamsburg.

Get involved today! Visit
www.MorganJamesBuilds.com

Acknowledgements

My deepest thanks go to my family and friends who believed in this novel. My heartfelt thanks to you too, dear reader, who are about to spend your valuable time with characters I created. You are the most important person in the business of writing, publishing, and marketing books.

I was sought by those who did not ask for Me;
I was found by those who did not seek Me.
I said, "Here I am, here I am,"
To a nation that was not called by My name.

Isaiah 65:1

Spring to Autumn
1998

Chapter One

Even after everything that's gone my way, I still feel like an outsider waiting for someone to open a door and let me in. I huddle over my writing desk—my refuge and the only furniture I kept from Arizona. It's situated to catch the morning light coming through the apartment's tall bay window. Its polished plane is uncluttered, an open space with room to think and work, a space on which my hands now fidget. Within easy reach are a manuscript, a Grand Canyon souvenir mug filled with number two pencils, and a steaming cup of Jamaica Blue Mountain coffee laced with cream. Everything is accessible. Familiar. Safe.

On the street below, the foot traffic has picked up with morning commuters. Ants marching into another day of toil. A few blocks down the street, brick and iron and asphalt give way to a green slice of Central Park. Crowded elm trees overhang the low stone wall that keeps park in and city out. Their new leaves flutter in a chill spring breeze, and the only cloud in sight is the one hanging over my head.

New York, so foreign from everything I knew, sent for me. The first siren song was a black-and-white photograph. The photographer captured a quintessential urban street in the smudged shadows of predawn. In the foreground, a portly grocer in a starched white apron leaned far over a bin of fruit, as if to arrange every apple perfectly, even on the back row. On the other side of the street, a young couple in evening clothes strolled toward the camera, each with right foot forward in midstride, their heads together in a private moment. A grainy glow reflected off a puddle with just enough detail to suggest neon and Broadway. The picture was in *National Geographic*, and the caption read, "A new day kisses the old good-bye in the Manhattan dawn." I spent hours dissecting it, and at twelve years of age, found myself seduced by a threadbare and world-weary city.

When I was twenty-six and experienced enough to hold my own, I moved to New York. After a few months, I was no longer awed by the city's magnificent architecture or overwhelmed by Manhattan's sprawling human reef. I no longer heard the constant roar of taxis and buses and speech, and the city's arrogant pageantry no longer turned my head.

Eventually, I saw past the shell game, the sleight of hand. Expectations that had been disappointed far too often hid behind facades of calloused boredom. Eyes averted in clichéd New York apathy were feeble defenses protecting a glimmer of hope that trust, one day, might be found. Even the brashest up-and-comers, if caught alone in unguarded moments at corner tables, wore hesitant expressions that belied their confidence. They would be broken too, soon enough, and they knew it.

I wasn't afraid of being broken, so I braved the city's indifference and bared my tender pale throat in the hope I would be taken in. I endured many lonely nights in my newly purchased Upper West Side apartment, accepting with humble gratitude the occasional favors New York sent my way.

I reel in all the reminiscing over what brought me to this town and tighten the terrycloth robe around my thinning body. At times like these, I feel I could just melt away to nothing, and I curse Joel for bringing on this black despair. Last night, my latest boyfriend—if you could call him that—anyway, Joel suddenly told me that even after a year and a half together, he still feels like a stranger with me.

"What does *that* mean?" I asked as I propped on one elbow and pulled up the sheet.

He leaned back and sighed. Joel is drop-dead handsome, with fair skin that contrasts with his dark hair and eyebrows—perfectly formed eyebrows. Stunning. His eyes are that rare aquamarine, as clear and warm as Caribbean seas. And his smell! Clean and musky, a mix of aftershave and his body's essence. Sometimes, when he comes to me after a show, he carries the sharp odors of spirit gum and sweat and the hot energy of backstage.

I used a line in a story once with Joel in mind: Eat him up with a spoon. That thought flashed through my mind as I watched him rest his crown of thick black hair, messy from bed, against my headboard. His full lips, the shadowed chin that needs shaving twice a day—no doubt about it, Joel is easy on the eyes. I'm addicted to the side glances and double takes we get when we're out together, even in this town.

"I don't know, Cami," he said, his mouth drawing tight in frustration. "You're just so—what?" He shook his head. "Sometimes, sweetheart, it feels like I could be anyone—any guy—and it wouldn't matter. Sometimes, it feels like *I* don't matter to you. Me specifically, I mean."

My face flushed. "So I don't show you enough passion, or what?"

"That's not it." He sat up.

He thought I missed the point. Of course, I didn't miss it at all. I knew what he was talking about.

"It's just that sometimes I wonder what, if anything, you feel for me," he said. "It seems like we have this tight relationship, intimate, you know, but I don't think . . ." His voice trailed off, but then he quickly launched in again. "You keep me at arm's length. You don't let me in. Not really.

"What's important to you, Cami? Your work? Is that all? Do you care about your family? You never mention them or anything about your life before you moved here. It's like you came from outer space. And you never ask me about my family."

"That's not true."

"Oh, well, when I bring them up. What I mean is you never initiate it. Our relationship is in this capsule, separated from the rest of our lives. You don't seem interested in anything but what show we're going to or where we're going to eat, or whatever. Nothing important. Nothing that matters."

I swore and sat up. He watched me, as if waiting for me to defend myself. Or break.

"How *do* you feel about me?" he finally asked.

I bit my tongue and got out of bed without answering. I slipped into the bathroom to dress, because it's impossible to be angry and naked at the same time. Too vulnerable. Even when I was a kid, I hated to wear my pajamas when I was mad. If I had a fight with my parents at bedtime, I always had to put on my clothes again until the anger had worn off.

I went into the kitchen without looking at him and got a diet soda from the fridge. Then I rummaged around in the cabinets and drawers until I found a squirreled-away pack of Marlboro Lights. I sat at the kitchen table and lit up. Joel, fully dressed, came in just as I was stamping out the first one in a saucer. He sat down across from me. "I thought you quit."

"Shut up."

"Look, Cami, I really care about you." He paused, and I lit another cigarette. "But I'm tired of wondering where we're going. Tired of wondering how you feel, if you feel anything at all. Sometimes, it seems like you're kinda—this is a terrible thing to say—but it seems like you're kinda dead emotionally. Your characters feel all kinds of things, but do you? It's almost like you're putting up a front all the time."

His voice was gentle, but every word was a sharp blade right into my soul. Fear pounded in my ears, and my only instinct was to circle the wagons. Slowly and deliberately, I drew down on the cigarette and asked in a smoke-choked rasp, "What do you want from me, Joel?"

He reached across the table and took my hand. Wrapped around mine, his fingers were warm and dry. "I care about you, Cam. I just want to get inside you—"

I snorted and exhaled the smoke in a thick jet. It was abusive, I know. A cheap shot. But it was out before I could stop it.

His hand withdrew instantly. "Touché," he said. He slapped his palms on the table and stood. "You know, I have a friend who sees a really good therapist. You should think about it. Her name's Wortham. Sylvia Wortham."

All of that happened last night, and this morning I woke up with a grunge mouth from all the cigarettes I smoked after he left. I'm obviously in no mood to work, so I pull back my hair and throw on my sweats to go for a run. My lungs are heavy, resisting the abuse, but I run the full five-mile circuit of my regular route anyway. Afterward, I walk to the corner of Fifty-Ninth and Fifth, where I sprawl on a bench.

Head back. Eyes closed. Nothing but the morning sun on my face and the sounds of the city. Cars. Buses. Horns. Voices everywhere. Carriage horses snort and knock their shod hooves against the asphalt. The cool temperature mercifully mutes the odors of horse dung and the stench of urine when a homeless guy passes too close.

I don't have to look to visualize the people on the street. Manhattan lays out a daily smorgasbord of humanity. Old and young, rich and poor, bourgeois and Bolshevik. Shuffling lunatics. A courier or two. Tourists and locals speaking every language and dialect on the planet. All together, they form a single living organism, a New York amoeba, shaping itself to its sidewalk container, shrinking from the overflowing wastebaskets and ubiquitous vendors. When the light changes, its tentative pseudopod reaches forward and spans the street in a long skinny stretch. Then the organism reforms on the next corner. I can be part of that, a bit of DNA that's different from the rest but definitely connected to the strand. I can almost imagine myself whole again, centered.

Until I get an overwhelming sense of someone's attention fastened on me.

I open one eye and squint at the well-groomed silhouette of Hillary Bachman, my publicist.

"Cami? Cami Taylor? Is that you?"

Of course she barely recognizes me. No makeup. Dirty hair. Why her, today, of all people?

"Hi, Hillary."

She sits primly on the bench beside me in her size 2 Chanel suit. I'm the thinnest I've been in my life but sitting next to Hillary makes me feel fat.

"So," she says, "have you been out for a run?"

I'm so self-conscious that I can't even feel superior about her asking such a stupid question. I'd give anything for my sunglasses right now. "Yeah. I was just cooling down."

"Well, dear, you certainly picked a good spot. I'm on my way to meet a client at the Plaza. It's such a beautiful morning that I decided to walk."

"How's Ethan?"

"Oh, he's fine. He's fishing upstate this week."

Hillary's husband, Ethan Bachman, is the senior partner in the law firm of Bachman, Strauss, and Leichmann. This prestigious station in life affords him and Hillary a Park Avenue address and a summerhouse in Bar Harbor, Maine. I spent a week at the Bar Harbor place last year. It sits on a hill overlooking the town and the bay. Every morning, I sat on the front porch and watched an enormous ferry depart for Nova Scotia. I wrote a story set in the little town and sold it to a New England literary journal.

Hillary works as a diversion. She's good at what she does when she does it, but she doesn't mind canceling an appointment for something more important, like a bridge game. I don't have any complaints though. On my modest publicity tour, she put me up at the best hotels and allowed as much free time as she could manage for sightseeing, no small feat on the budget allotted to an emerging author. The only thing that really bothers me is that I get the impression she feels sorry for me.

Not long after I moved to New York, I let Hillary fix me up with her nephew Paul. Paul was all right—a little self-absorbed, but decent company for dinner or whatever. We dated long enough for me to let things go too far. I didn't have any strong feelings for him one way or the other, but we drifted into an affair because, well, let's face facts, it was no big thing to me.

I'm sure I sent a lot of mixed signals, depending on how much he was getting on my nerves at any particular moment. Eventually, it got weird between us and he stopped calling. That was that, or so I thought. But afterward, it seemed as if Hillary and her husband thought they had discovered some gaping need in me. Nothing was ever said, but they looked at me differently after Paul. It wasn't my imagination either. I actually *saw* pity in their eyes. It made me wonder what he'd told them. He didn't even know me, for God's sake.

"He asked how you were the other day," Hillary says.

"Who?"

"Why, Ethan, of course." She looks at me curiously. "I told him it's been ages since I've seen you."

"Oh. Sorry for being preoccupied. I'm afraid my mind is full of my novel this morning."

She checks her watch and stands. "Well, I should go anyway. Let's have lunch soon."

"Yes, let's. I'll call you."

My solitude is sweet as I stroll home through the park. I walk slowly, savoring the fresh air. The sun is high and growing warm. The light, the chattering birds, and the cheerful faces I pass buoy me enough to make me believe this day might be salvaged, even though thinking about Paul is a sucker punch to my already bruised ego.

I pass a vacant kiosk, and my image in the dark window stops me. I have stared at my reflection in mirrors for as long as I can remember.

Not admiring my appearance, but wondering what I'm doing on the planet, a question that still hangs unanswered in the happy morning air.

I turn away and finish my journey home, stopping in the lobby to retrieve a bundle of mail from the box. Speaking to no one. My gaze pushes along the floor, then up the stairs as I haul myself to the second floor.

The hallway is deserted. At the door to my apartment, I fumble with the key. Before I know it, my breath catches, and the pieces of mail slip away, falling to the floor. I close my eyes and rest my forehead against the doorjamb. Tears rise from my belly and splatter onto the bills and advertisements as I slide to my knees.

Chapter Two

I t's after three in the morning when I reach a decision about seeing the psychiatrist Joel recommended. I'm standing at the kitchen counter, throwing down a shot of Jack Daniel's. I'm not much of a drinker. I seldom have more than a glass of wine with dinner or an occasional aperitif. Joel drinks wine like water, so I keep the makeshift liquor cabinet above the refrigerator stocked with good cab. But the situation at hand calls for stronger medicine. I've counted all the punched-tin ceiling squares I care to for one night, and tomorrow's another wasted day if I'm fried from no sleep. The bottle of Jack was pushed to the back of the cabinet, the forgotten leftover of a forgotten guest.

The first shot doesn't go down easy. I gulp it in a hot sluice that feels like it has no business in my throat. I pound down a second and grip the counter, considering whether or not my stomach will hold up. My gut finally warms to the job, so I move to the table with the bottle and the glass and get serious. First thing in the morning, I'll look up Sylvia Wortham and give her a call. But was Sylvia the therapist or Joel's friend? I can't figure it out.

◆ ◆ ◆

A sudden, head-shattering clanging startles me out of my coma, and I swing and swipe in the direction of the nightstand. The Big Ben windup clatters to the floor, but the ringing doesn't stop. I kick and flail myself free of the bed's cotton tentacles and stumble blindly around the apartment until I locate the telephone in the kitchen.

"Hello?" I croak as the machine picks up. The recorded greeting competes with me in a discordant clamor. I slump over the table, waiting for it to play out. The sight of the open whiskey bottle brings on a stabbing headache. I push away a pink Fiestaware saucer filled with cigarette butts, every one smoked down to the filter, testifying that I resorted to relights. Oh, God.

The greeting finally ends. "Hello?" I say.

"Hello, Ms. Lingo?" says the caller. A solicitor. My telephone number is listed under my birth name in the Manhattan phone book. Well, close to it anyway. L. C. Lingo, not the cumbersome Leona Camille. This was Mom's idea in case of a family emergency, but I only get nuisance calls.

"I don't want any," I say.

"Excuse me? I'm so sorry to bother you. Did I wake you?" The woman's accent is definitely Southern.

"Yes, as a matter of fact, you did."

"Oh, I'm *so* sorry. Please forgive me. Is there another time when I could call you back?"

"No, there isn't. Like I said, I don't want any. And put this number on your no-call list."

"Can I just—"

"God, lady, are you deaf?" Is she an idiot or what? I pull the phone away from my ear and am about to end the call when I hear her say something about family.

Has dad had another stroke? Or something worse, something so bad that my mom can't call? Sourness pushes up from my stomach. "Are you calling from Phoenix?" I ask. "Is it my dad?"

"Oh, no. It's nothing like that. I'm just down the street at the Essex House. I don't—forgive me—I didn't mean to startle you so."

I exhale slowly. The day won't be spoiled by a family crisis. "What then? Why are you calling?"

Silence.

"Are you there?"

"Maybe it would be better if I call back another time."

"No, no. Just wait a minute. Let's take this from the top again, and maybe we can stop talking past each other. How can I help you?"

The caller laughs. "I'm afraid you're going to think I'm a nut after all of this. My name is Kate Davis. I'm here in New York for a couple of weeks with my husband. He's here on business. Advertising. Anyway, I got out the phone book this morning to see if there were any Lingos. It's just a silly thing I do sometimes when I visit other cities. Lingo is my maiden name, you see. I found you listed in the book, and you're the only Lingo. Your address isn't far from the hotel so, well, I just had a wild hair and called to see if we might be related."

She has one thing right. She's a nut. I shuffle back to the bedroom and collapse on the bed.

"I'm from Dallas," she says. "Well, Fort Worth originally."

"Uh-huh."

"Did you grow up in New York?"

"No, Phoenix."

"I see. Well, do you—"

"Do I think we're related? No, I don't."

A pause while she gets the message. "Oh. Well, as I said, it was such a silly impulse to call. I'm so sorry for waking you."

"No problem. Enjoy your stay in New York."

"Thank you."

"Good-bye."

I toss the cordless phone to the foot of the bed and snuggle down into the embrace of feather pillows and Egyptian cotton.

The city sun leaks through the loosely drawn blinds and bathes the room in milky light, but the sunlight in New York is never as pure as in Phoenix. In Arizona, long before the fiery beacon actually ascends, the horizon grows luminous, and deep violet pushes the velvety black nighttime sky toward the Pacific. Clouds of crisp white stars race away, chasing time itself. I ache for the beauty of a western dawn.

In the half hour or so between first light and daybreak, the desert holds its breath. Nothing moves. Not air. Not cactus flower. Not thermometer. Then the sun, in full bloom, crests the lumpy red mountains, and the birds abandon their night roosts with trills as clear as the air itself. By noon, you can grill tortillas on any sunny sidewalk, but the early mornings are perfect.

Those who live in Phoenix a long time eventually turn as brown as cockroaches. My father's one of those, a golfer in spite of a gimpy hobble from a stroke a few years ago. Patrick Earl Lingo. He was born in Fort Worth, from roots that support a Lingo tree as big as Texas, for all I know. But I wouldn't know because Dad strayed as far away from his family as a man can. He joined the Air Force, married an Illinois girl, and never went home again. By the time I stumbled on the scene in their middle age, both of my parents had dried to rootless tumbleweeds. I have never spoken with even one of Dad's people. Until today.

I have no doubt my morning intruder belongs to the old clan, but she didn't arouse any familial longings in me. She did pique my curiosity, though. A person who calls a stranger in a strange city on a whim is a little bit different, a little bit interesting. The seed she unwittingly donated goes into the crowded incubator where my characters gestate. I wriggle deeper into bed, close my eyes, and let my mind slip into well-worn fantasies.

◆ ◆ ◆

I'm standing in front of the stage door of the Winter Garden Theater with a big lump of pride in my mouth. This is the follow-through for my

Do Everything Right Day. It started with a phone call to Dr. Wortham's office. That felt good. Actually, it felt fashionable. Afterward, I marveled that I hadn't tried therapy sooner. That done, I shoehorned my mind into my novel-in-progress.

It was slow going at first, and my thoughts darted away to Joel every time I let my guard down. I kept shoving my imagination back into the manuscript until the distractions finally caved. By two o'clock, I'd knitted a couple of thousand words into a pattern that worked. My celebration was a late lunch from the café across the street: organic salad and ahi tuna as rare and firm as steak.

I reach for the battered stage door, glancing up in time to see a passing businessman watching me. He smiles and mouths the word "nice" before turning the corner. What does he like about me? My rich—and expensive—auburn hair? My hairdresser keeps me in a short, textured do that brings out my cheekbones—my best feature. Did the clothes I selected so carefully this afternoon catch his eye? My short-sleeved sweater is almond-colored silk that clings in all the right places, and my slim Levis, well, they're a hard-to-beat bargain for showcasing miles of running and hours of exercise. Whatever caught the man's fancy, his compliment is just what I need at this moment.

I insert the key Joel made for me and descend into the catacombs of his world. My timing is perfect. I've missed the crowd. Cast and crew don't hang around and waste time between rehearsal and makeup, but Joel checks and rechecks the costumes. He's always the last to leave. I weave my way past heavy curtain lines and hunks of manufactured garbage. The presence of the dancers lingers in the heavy smells of greasepaint and sweat. Somewhere, an actor sings a strain from the finale, and in the backstage silence, his baritone rings out as clearly as a brass horn.

I search the dressing rooms for Joel and find him sitting on a stool, bent over a costume. His left hand dips and pulls a needle and thread. He looks up, and I give him my best self-deprecating smile.

"Cami," he says.

I open my mouth to say how hot he looks when he sews, but what comes out is, "No break?"

He holds up the ginger fur shot through with black, yellow, and white. "Macavity caught his tail on the set during rehearsal."

"Poor cat."

"Yeah." He smiles, a kind of weary, sad smile. "So, how've you been?"

"Not great."

I pull up another stool and sit very close. On impulse, I lean forward and kiss him. I couldn't have come up with a smarter move if I'd planned it for three days. Physical communication is our strong suit, and it doesn't take long before he's kissing me.

After a moment, I pull back. "I'm making lasagna tonight," I say. "Maybe you'll come over after the show. We could look through the family albums."

He laughs. "You have family albums?"

"Well, no, but don't you?"

"At my mom's," he says, reaching to kiss me again.

I place my fingertips against his lips. "It's a long subway ride to Brooklyn. Maybe we can find something else to do."

"Maybe," he says, and he smiles that sad smile again. He takes my hand. "What am I going to do about you, Cami Taylor?" He's about to say something else when his gaze shifts toward the door.

"Sorry. Didn't mean to interrupt," says the baritone in a languid drawl. "Just let me get my cold drink."

"It's okay," Joel says quickly. "Cami, this is Willie. He's our new Rum Tum Tugger, for how long? A couple of weeks now?"

"Fifteen shows," Willie answers, "but who's counting?"

Willie is huge in bicycle shorts and a Mississippi State tee shirt. When he crosses the room, the well-defined muscles of his bare limbs flex and glide under the inky skin.

"Nice to meet you," he says.

I extend my hand. "Your voice is wonderful."

"Thanks." He takes my suddenly tiny fingers and gives them a shake. "Well, let me grab this." He reaches for a bottle of water on the table. "Sorry again to interrupt. See you later, Joel."

The actor leaves, and an awkward silence fills the space between Joel and me. He's about to decline my invitation, a move that could leave us hopelessly uncoupled. "I called the therapist you recommended," I blurt. There. My last morsel of pride down the hatch. It's my final offer, take it or leave it.

"Really? I didn't think you would."

"I was a little surprised myself. Anyway, it can't hurt."

Joel says that everyone needs help from time to time. I watch him talking, not knowing how to answer and hoping he'll interpret my silence in a favorable way. "I like spending time with you, Cam," he says.

"Then come over tonight."

"I want to, but I want more too. What are we doing?"

"Let's just take it step by step."

"What's the next step?"

"I don't know." Exasperation swells inside me.

"We need to talk about what we want out of life."

I know what I want, and he's not going to like it if I tell him. "Maybe I just need more time," I say. "Maybe talking to this doctor will help."

He smiles again, a real smile. "Maybe so."

I sense a fragile truce, a willingness on his part to let the status quo prevail a while longer. We stand together, and I press myself against him. "Will you be there tonight?"

"I'll be there."

Once again, all my hard work pays off.

Chapter Three

"**D**r. Wortham will return shortly," the receptionist says. She hands me a clipboard filled with forms. "Please make yourself comfortable and complete these. Would you like some coffee or a soda?"

"No, thanks."

"I'm Virginia. Let me know if you need anything."

"Thank you, Virginia."

"Dr. Wortham shouldn't be more than fifteen or twenty minutes."

Virginia closes the door. I'm glad she showed me into the office rather than leaving me in the waiting room. The doctor's tardiness gives me a chance to get my bearings.

Sylvia Wortham's professional space is tastefully understated, no doubt designed to calm the demons that are her stock-in-trade. The whole of it can be taken in with one calming sweep, and no single element competes for attention. But I've trained myself to notice details, and my survey tells me there's a lot more going on than meets a casual glance. For example, one muted painting at first seems dull, maybe even mass-produced, but when I look closely, I see it's an original, a beautifully intricate watercolor of Carnegie Hall.

The bric-a-brac tucked between the books on her crowded bookshelves turns out to be pretty nice stuff. I recognize some of the pieces, and they're expensive. I put down the clipboard and browse the spines, finding *The Catcher in the Rye*, *A Clockwork Orange*, *The Mosquito Coast* hiding among dozens of textbooks. I'm leafing through an over-my-head volume of *Man and His Symbols* by Carl Jung when the doctor breezes in.

"Ms. Taylor, please forgive me. A colleague needed my assistance, quite unexpectedly." The doctor reaches out, and we exchange a firm handshake. "I see you found my passion. Are you familiar with Jung's work?"

"Only from brief references in a psychology book or two that I've read. Is your passion for books in general or Jung in particular?"

"The former," she answers brusquely. She glances at the clipboard and its empty forms. "We'll get this information later. Please, sit down."

She waves in the general direction of a circle of wingback chairs. I choose one of the chairs in front of her desk instead. I want to see if the doctor takes the other chair or gets behind the desk, where she belongs. She takes the seat beside me, with only a small occasional table between us. It's a move intended to take away the barriers of rank and authority. I've had editors pull this on me too, and I always wish they'd stay behind their hard-earned mahogany, where they really want to be anyway. It's more honest that way. I said as much once to a peach-faced magazine guy. After that, he got flustered and couldn't come up with a comprehensible sentence. I was cruel, but at least I taught him to think about what he was doing.

"So, Ms. Taylor, why are you seeking professional help?"

"Depression, I suppose."

"Nope," she says. She reaches for a notepad and pen on her desk. "Nope" is not her word. She chose it to put me at ease, another move to get down on my level.

"Excuse me?"

"Depression is too easy. Too vague. Why, specifically, did you seek therapy?"

"Okay. To pacify Joel, actually."

"Joel is . . . ?"

"My boyfriend."

"So you're here for Joel?"

"I'm not here *for* him. I'm here to *pacify* him. Big difference."

"Please explain."

"He's pushing me, and I'm stalling."

"So . . ." She makes a note on her pad, but a vase on the table between us blocks my view of what she wrote. "You're starting therapy as a stall tactic to . . . ?"

"To keep Joel from—" What's about to come out of my mouth, that I've started therapy to keep Joel from breaking up with me, sounds either codependent or more manipulative than I care to admit. I can't think how to finish the sentence.

The doctor looks at me over her glasses. "To keep Joel from what?"

"Just so he'll back off while I—I just need to buy some time."

"Time for what?"

"I don't know. Time to figure out what *I* want, I suppose."

"What you want from what?"

"What I want out of my relationship with Joel, of course."

Now I'm just making stuff up.

"So, you aren't depressed?"

"No."

"Are you happy?"

"For the most part. As much as the next person, I suppose."

"How happy is that?"

"What?"

"How happy is as happy as the next person?"

God! This is the woman who'll straighten out my life for $275 an hour?

"I have no idea," I say.

"Ms. Taylor, may I call you Cami?" I nod, and she continues, "This first session is a kind of orientation, a chance to see if we both think therapy is the right course of action for you."

"Okay."

"So let's take a different tack. What bothers you?"

"That's pretty broad."

"What bothers you about your life? What would you change if you could change anything?" She pushes her stylish glasses up on her nose.

I'm eager to answer this question. It gives me a chance to brag. "I've worked hard to make my life into what I want it to be," I say. "I wanted to be a writer, and I am. I wanted to come to New York, and I'm here. I have a handsome boyfriend and plenty of money. I look better than I ever have in my life."

"Sounds perfect."

"Doesn't it?"

"I'm sure a bright woman like you isn't spending a fortune on therapy just to keep her boyfriend happy. There are other boyfriends."

"Yes, there are." My mind drifts to Willie. I've seen him twice more at the theater since our first encounter when I was groveling to Joel, and he's becoming a mild obsession. Could the answer be as simple as changing horses? If so, what am I doing here? If I were honest—entirely, brutally honest—I'd admit that I could use a real answer, an answer to the problem of me. But there isn't an answer to that problem. "There's probably more to it than Joel," I say.

"It would seem so."

The doctor writes on her steno pad. She looks like a favorite teacher or a trusted aunt, an amalgamation of innocuous mother figures. Her face is gentle, neither pretty enough for her to be vain nor homely enough for her to be self-conscious. She has an air of command to make me believe she knows just what she's doing. She'll lead me to freedom in her bobbed gray hair and Donna Karan glasses. Go ahead, honey, spill your guts, and I won't hold anything against you. Why shouldn't I? I'm giving the doctor a fortune—as she put it—for this little powwow. I might as well get my money's worth.

"My first novel," I say, "*Double Down Blues*, is about a woman who deals blackjack. Not in Vegas, but at a Native American casino in New Mexico."

"I read it after you made an appointment."

"Really? Wow. I'm impressed, and thank you."

"It was my pleasure."

"Then you know the character, Jackie. She always feels as if she's on the outside looking in."

"Jackie believes everyone else feels the same. They just don't show it," Dr. Wortham says.

"Yes."

"Do you share Jackie's belief?"

"Pretty much."

"I see. What if there's a chance that isn't the case?"

"Why would I be different from everyone else?"

"You aren't."

"Well, if I feel I'm on the outside, and everyone else feels they're on the inside, then I am different. But if everyone feels the same way, then my emotions don't mean anything."

"Emotions are never meaningless," Dr. Wortham says. "Life is filled with emotions. Love. Anger. Ambition. Fear. They drive most of what we humans do. Our feelings define us, Cami."

"Do they? I'm not sure I agree with that. What about you, Doctor? Do you feel as if you're on the outside looking in?"

"No."

"Would you admit it if you did?"

She laughs. "Good question. I don't know. Did you seek therapy on the chance there may be a way to get rid of that feeling?"

"Would that be a good enough reason?"

"It's a starting point. It's something we can work with. Tell me, do you have trouble functioning? Or working?"

"No."

"When was your most recent physical examination?"

"Five or six months ago."

"Any problems?"

I shake my head. For the first time since we sat down, I really see the glass vase on the table between us. It's an exquisite piece.

"Are you taking any medications?" asks Dr. Wortham.

"No. Tri-Cyclen, is all."

"Do you use recreational drugs?"

"No. No drugs."

"Alcohol?"

"Very little. This piece," I say. "May I?"

"Of course."

I carefully lift the vase and turn it. The light from the big window plays on the pear-shaped body, which curves inward to a slender neck, then flares again in a delicate lip. The silhouette reminds me of a lily. The interior is clear crystal, but it's overlaid with milky ribs so deeply colored at the base that they appear almost black. The colors bloom to deep blue, rose, and lavender as they rise up the sides, finally fading to pale pastels at the lip. It looks like a primordial flower, whose graceful motion has been frozen in time.

"It's Venetian crystal," Dr. Wortham says. "Nineteenth century."

"The artistry is incredible. I noticed it when I came in, but until now, I didn't see how really beautiful it is. I can't believe you keep it here where one of your patients might break it."

"I want to enjoy it every day."

"Where'd you get it?"

"It was a gift from a friend, many years ago."

"Must've been a good friend," I say. I gently set the vase back on the table.

"A trusted friend."

I suddenly feel empty. I'm tired of bantering with the doctor, and I want to go home.

"I need a copy of your last physical," she says. "Give Virginia your doctor's name on the way out. And we need to run some profiles for a baseline. Virginia will set that up too."

"Okay." Apparently I've decided to do this.

"I recommend weekly sessions."

"What's your plan?"

"I don't have a plan. It isn't that canned. We'll run the tests. You and I will get to know each other. Basically, we'll work through the things that have a negative impact on your happiness." She glances at her watch. "We have about ten minutes left. What's your current project?"

"The next novel. I'm still composing the first draft."

"Tell me about it."

"I never talk about a book or a story in progress."

"Oh?"

"No. It releases the creative energy to talk about it. I work better if I keep the lid on until it's finished."

"So you don't let anyone read your work?"

"No. No one."

She makes another quick note on her pad. "Wouldn't feedback be beneficial early in the process?"

"I'll get plenty of critique from my editor when I'm finished. It's his opinion that really matters anyway. His and my readers'."

"Yes, but wouldn't it be nice to receive encouragement along the way?"

"Yeah, it would. If that's what you got. But I don't like explaining my work to people who don't get it and think they need to fix it."

"Did that happen with your first novel?"

"Sure it did, and I learned my lesson."

"I assume you're talking about amateurs reading your work, but what about professionals? Colleagues?"

"It isn't like I know a lot of writers. We're a pretty competitive bunch."

She makes a final note. "Do you mind if I record our sessions?"

"No."

"Very well." She smiles brightly. "I'll see you next week."

I leave Dr. Wortham's office feeling a lot more vulnerable than I expected.

Chapter Four

Joel's niece tugs my linen sleeve with her greasy fingers. "Cami! Cami! Watch this!" She leans forward and blows bubbles into her chocolate milk through a plastic straw.

"Impressive, Rachel. But maybe you shouldn't do that at the dinner table."

"Rachel, stop." Joel's sister, Jennifer, rolls her eyes at me, as if I understand all about how it is with five-year-olds. Then she resumes her conversation, and Rachel tugs at my sleeve again.

"Will you play with us after dinner?"

"Maybe later," I lie. "I want to talk with the grown-ups first."

"Okay. Mama, I'm finished. Mama, can I be excused?" She chants "Mama, Mama, Mama," until Jennifer finally notices and excuses her.

This little drama takes place in the dining room of the quaint Brooklyn house in which Joel was raised, where I always feel as if I've been plunked into of a revival of *Brighton Beach Memoirs*. Joel is Jewish, but his family isn't the least bit religious. His surname, Grand, doesn't give away the Jewish heritage either.

✦ ✦ ✦

I sneaked upstairs to Joel's bedroom tonight before dinner. I suppose some sappy part of me wanted a last look. Joel's mother, Ruth, cornered me there. "Jenny's boys love sleeping in here," she said from the doorway. I jumped guiltily. "Sorry to startle you."

Ruth is a tiny slip of autocratic maternity. It's no wonder Joel gravitates toward strongly independent women. His mother rules her world from the lofty perch of gracious servitude. No one seems to realize she's making all the important decisions. Hers is a craft lost to my generation. My sisters and I bulldoze through life, demanding what's ours.

"It's no wonder they like it," I said. "It's the quintessential boy's room. Bunk beds and"—I motioned to the window—"a tree to climb down. Or up. All that's missing are football pennants and a poster of a supermodel in a swimsuit."

She laughed. "Those are packed away." She crossed the room. "Yes, Joel went down that tree in the middle of the night more than a few times."

"Meeting girls or carousing with the boys?"

"Both, I suspect." She winked. "Joel is my serious one. He never gave me any trouble. He's a good man."

A mother bear's protective instinct. Actually, more like a wolverine. She smelled trouble and knew that I would hurt her little boy. I smiled to ward off further probing, and then I asked about the framed photographs she'd put up in place of Joel's things.

"My family," she said, "and Ben's. I kept them packed away for years, but as you get older, you appreciate the past more."

"Were some of these taken in Europe?"

"Yes, the oldest ones were in Belgium."

"Did you have family there during the Holocaust?"

"Oh, yes, of course." She took down one of the black-and-white photographs and handed it to me. "My parents and my brothers, and that's me." She pointed to a child in the woman's arms. "My father got us out. His family didn't want to leave, and they didn't want him to leave. They thought he was overreacting, that it would all blow over."

She took the photograph back and pointed to another one, a sepia tintype of a dashing, mustachioed dandy posing in front of a buggy-like automobile. "This was Alexander, Joel's great-grandfather, the first Grand. He changed his name. Did Joel tell you?"

"A little bit. Joel said he changed it because of persecution. What was his name before?"

"No one knows. There's a story for you. Alex was forty-two when he married, and they had five children. The youngest was Joel's grandfather. Alex brought no history to that marriage, only himself. He never spoke about his life before. That wasn't unusual back then. People were tight-lipped, and it was considered rude to press them for personal details."

"How do you know all this?"

"When Alex knew he was dying, he asked for a rabbi. He said he wanted to return to the God of his youth. At least, that's how the family legend goes."

"A deathbed confession?"

"Personally I've always thought it was a coward's way."

"What about the persecution? What did he say about that?"

"Well, I guess that's an assumption. Everyone assumed Alex wanted to escape the anti-Semitism that was so prevalent around the turn of the century. Jews, the Irish, Italians—all kinds of people changed their names to avoid discrimination. It was easy to do that back then."

"Reinvent yourself."

"You might call it that."

One of the tintypes was of two young men with the same black hats, coats, and side ringlets as the Orthodox Jews I see around town. The picture had to be from before World War II, but they could've had the same tailor as the guys in the Garment District. "What about these two?" I asked. "Who are they?"

"My uncles."

"Was your family religious?"

"They were, but I'm not. Neither is Joel's father. I married so young that my mother—these are her brothers—blamed my agnosticism on my husband. But my beliefs are my own. I just never saw much use in religion. Do you?"

"I never think about it."

"Do you believe in God?"

"Which god?"

She laughed. "Why, any of them."

"Like I said, I haven't given it any thought. But I have to say I don't see much evidence of anyone being in charge."

"No, it's a harsh world, isn't it? These two . . ." She touched the picture tenderly. "They were murdered at Auschwitz."

"I'm sorry."

"Thank you. It was a brutal time. Well, enough of this. Let's go finish making dinner."

I followed her down the stairs and into the kitchen, where I diced and dished with Jennifer and Joel's two sisters-in-law. Even if I loved to cook, which I don't, I couldn't enjoy slaving in the kitchen before and after meals, knowing the menfolk sat in the other room chewing the fat. I could've left these women and their kitchen work and deposited myself in the living room with the men, as I've done before. I could've made a statement, but it was my last night in this house, and I chose the high road.

Marrying Joel would mean marrying the entire Grand tribe. Having gone there mentally tempers my desire to stay with him, even though he's a perfect partner. We like all the same things, and I could put up with his companionship, well, indefinitely. But all it takes is one dinner at his parents' house to remind me that we can't last. I can't live that life. Joel loves the whole tight family thing, but I hate it. Everyone crammed together all the time. Joel will never walk away from them for any woman. Honestly, he shouldn't have to.

◆ ◆ ◆

"Cami, dear, would you like some pie?" asks Ruth, waking me up from my reverie.

"No thanks, Ruth. I'm way too full. That meal was delicious. Excuse me, please. I need to step outside and return a phone call."

I feel everyone's gaze on me as I get up and leave the table. I make my way to the front door, grabbing my purse from the sofa table on the way. On the porch, the night is crisp in the waning spring. I breathe in the fresh air and tell myself to calm down, that this is no big thing. It's how normal people live, all shackled to one another with the bonds of daily life. Why the anxiety? Why the overwhelming urge to bolt like a startled deer? The truth is simply that I don't want to lose my freedom, and no matter how you slice it, that's exactly what long-term relationships mean.

I pull my cigarettes and matches from my purse and light up. I enjoy simple things like the feel of a matchbox in my hand, the sound of the friction when I strike one, its yellow flare, the first rich drag. I glide back and forth on the swing, smoking and flicking ashes into Ruth's azalea bed.

This once affluent neighborhood is coming back from a period of decay, its resurrection underwritten by energetic young New Yorkers. The house across the street has plastic sheets stapled to gaping remodeling wounds. They flap in the breeze, sounding like the dull, repetitive crack of a bullwhip. The front door opens, and Joel steps out.

"Thought you might be here," he says.

"I'm just getting some air. Got a little warm inside."

He glances at my half-smoked cigarette but says nothing. He points to the space beside me on the swing, and I scoot over to make room for him. He sits and temporarily jars the rhythm, and then we settle into a new one: Joel's rhythm. His nearness stirs me, and I want to turn back the calendar and take him home.

He takes my hand. "I love you, Cami."

This isn't a fit of passion, going for a homer "I love you." Joel's sincerity and naked vulnerability send every fiber of me into rigor mortis.

"Joel—"

"No, Cami. This is it. I want to know, here, tonight, if we have a future together."

He leans toward me in the darkness, the face I've come to know so well indiscernible in shadow. He cocks his head, and a glimmer from the streetlight flashes across his eyes. In this moment, I wish I could be a different woman.

I squeeze his hand. "What's ahead for you, Joel?"

He sits back. "We've never had this conversation. In a year and a half of dating, you've never asked."

"I'm asking now."

"Okay, let's see, I don't guess my dreams are spectacular, but I'd like to have enough to be comfortable. I want to move to Long Island, eventually. It's nice out there, a nice place to raise a family. I think about having my own firm someday." He stops talking, and we sit in silence. Finally, he asks, "What about you, Cam?"

"I don't know."

"Well, what do you wish for?"

"Nothing, really. I can't say, but I know what I don't want."

"What's that?" His voice is flat, resigned, as if he already knows what I'm going to say.

"Two-point-five kids, a mortgage, and a life in the suburbs."

He lets go of my hand. The emptiness of my palm is nothing compared to the sudden void inside me. I didn't expect to feel this way. I didn't expect to feel anything except relief.

"That's it then, I guess," he says. "Now I know. Why didn't you tell me how you felt?"

"Why couldn't you just let things ride? We were having a good time."

"Is that what we were doing? Having a good time? God, Cami, you're one of a kind."

"Tell me something. Why is it that I could've told you exactly what you want out of life, but you didn't have a clue what I want?"

"How could I know?" he says. "You've never let me past that front you put up. You're a closed book, sweetheart. What are you so afraid of?" He pauses, and then he takes my hands again, as if he's snatching me from an invisible precipice. "Let me in, baby. We can work this out."

I pull away and wipe my face. Then I rummage in my purse for the cell phone. "Go back inside where you belong. I'll call a cab."

He gets up. Then he bends down and kisses me. So sweet. So gentle. The taste of him grieves me in its comfort. Oh Joel! Why couldn't you leave it alone? He stands before me a moment longer, but he's so far out of reach that he might as well be in Shanghai. He turns away, and I watch him disappear through the front door. He doesn't look at me again.

Chapter Five

*D*ay seven, uncoupled.

I was with Joel so long that I've forgotten my between-boyfriends routine. Work rushes in behind his departure like water through a breached dam. I hole up in my apartment, shuffling between the coffeepot and the computer and my sun-drenched desk, where I smudge neat, laser-printed sheets of manuscript with a number two pencil. I even have groceries delivered. My only escape from the apartment is my daily run through the park, which I perform like a methodically exercised animal. Or a convict.

I don't share any of this with Dr. Wortham. Instead, I give her a redacted version of our breakup, and she asks how I've felt since then.

"Productive," I answer.

She scribbles on her pad and looks up. "Anything else?"

The novelty has worn off our weekly chats. I looked forward to the first few appointments in her intimate space, which feels like a professor's well-used study, but feminine and bright too, with the sunlight coming through an oversized window that overlooks Broadway.

I'm not disappointed that I haven't gotten anything out of therapy. I never expected Dr. Wortham to exorcise my demons.

I glance toward her, and she smiles patiently. Right now, I can't even remember her question. In the beginning, I found her practiced attentiveness interesting, entertaining even, but now I'm bored with it. The constant probing and scribbling annoy me.

"I feel the same as anyone would feel after breaking off an eighteen-month relationship," I say in a fit of recollection. "Why would I feel differently?"

"You wouldn't, Cami, but I'd like to hear you express it in *your* words. You make your living putting words together. You're good at it. Tell me how you feel. Be specific."

"You know, I'd really like to get off Joel and move on to something else. I know I've had an emotional upheaval. I don't need to talk to a shrink to figure that out. Is this what we're going to do each week? Pick apart whatever happened between sessions?"

"We must have starting points. What do you expect to happen in these sessions?"

"I don't know. Magic, apparently." I spring from my chair and stalk to the window. "This is futile, really, when you think about it."

"What's futile?"

"You don't know me." I turn and glare at her as if all my problems are her fault. What am I, a teenager rebelling against her mother? Before I can look away, our eyes lock like the horns of two bull elks. Dr. Wortham's not one to shy from conflict. Neither am I, but I'm humiliating myself. I soften the stink eye and force a smile. "I'm wasting your time and my money. I can't expect you to show me how to be happy."

"That's true, but I can guide you. That's all I am, a guide with some experience in human behavior."

"Where are you guiding me to?"

"That's up to you. Whether or not therapy works is entirely up to you. Actually, whether or not you're a happy person is too. People can help in many ways, but you have to let them. Answer a question, Cami. Who do you trust?"

"Whom." The correction flies out before I can stop it.

"Don't be petty. Is there any other human being out there on whom you can rely?"

I turn away and look at the familiar scene on the street below. Probably a thousand people pass under this window during one of my appointments. They're strangers to me and to one another, yet every single one of them is wrapped in a complicated life that involves scores of other people. I wonder how there's room in the world for it all.

"Cami?"

"I'm starting to feel as if I know some of the people on the street outside your building, like the guy who has the flower cart at the corner of Eighty-Second. He's always there." I turn to her. "Do you know the one I'm talking about?"

"Yes, I've seen him."

"He has this little routine of bowing and touching the bill of his Yankees cap whenever tourists walk by. He's a pretty good ambassador for the city. Do you ever look at someone like that guy and wonder what keeps him going? What keeps him smiling, day in and day out, on that same street corner?"

"No, not really."

"I can imagine a whole life for him, and I bet I wouldn't be too far off the mark."

"Do you realize how evasive you are?" she asks.

"Oh, yes. It's an art form with me." I return to the chair, sit down, and face her. "How many sessions before we get around to my childhood, Dr. Wortham? That seems like a logical starting point to me. I thought all therapists jumped right into childhood."

"Okay, let's talk about your childhood."

I'm immediately sorry I brought it up because I really don't want to talk about it.

"When we broke up the other night, Joel told me that I put up a front," I say. "Do you think that's true?"

"You know it is."

"I would welcome someone getting to know *me*. Cami Taylor, not their idea of who I am or who I should be, but the way most people try to get inside your head feels like rape."

"That's an intense response."

I laugh at this. "It's an intense *emotion*. Joel thinks I only know about emotions. He said it's as if I don't have any of my own. That's how little my lover knew me." I wave my hand toward the bookcase. "All those volumes and volumes about human beings, and we still don't know what makes us tick. Even you, Doctor. Even you are grasping at straws."

"No, I'm not."

"Well, it seems that way from this side of the couch. I suppose that's only to the untrained eye."

"What's going on?"

"Nothing." I glance at my watch. We're only halfway through the session.

"Cami, no one can bear your pain for you, but it helps to talk it out."

Bear my pain? What's she talking about? "I'm not in pain."

"No?"

"I never said one word about being in pain. Is that how you see me?"

"I see a young woman who has it all and still isn't happy. Not really. I see a woman who's drowning in loneliness and, yes, pain. I see a woman who hasn't begun to live her life as fully as she can."

"My life is full," I answer, too quickly and defensively.

"No, it isn't."

"How would you know?"

"You're easy to understand. In fact, you're quite transparent."

"Transparent," I echo. The good doctor couldn't have found a more effective insult. "Then why all this probing? Why not give me some answers to take for a test drive? You could save me a lot of money."

"Because they'd be my answers, not yours. People will try to get in your head, as you put it, for the rest of your life. Get used to it. You'll want to let some of them in, and others you won't, but they'll always knock at your door. You mustn't hate them for it because you aren't any different."

"Why do they knock? Why are they always forcing their way into private places? I'll tell you why. To level the playing field. That's why people try to figure out other people. So they can outmaneuver and outmanipulate them."

"That's an incredibly cynical viewpoint, even from you."

"All right. Try this on. Some people are jealous of my independence. In some sick way, they want to conquer it—dominate the wild animal. I'm indifferent toward most people, and it drives them crazy, so they project all kinds of issues onto me. The way they see it, I could use some help, and they're just the ones to give it to me. It feels like they're using meat hooks to drag me down."

I lean back in the chair and take a breath. "*That*, Dr. Wortham, is what I think about people and their relationships with one another. I'll tell you what's important to me. The life I've built. My work. Who I've become. These are the things I'll fight for."

"Relationships demand give and take. There are compromises to be made, always. And yes, some people ask for too much, but that doesn't make all people users."

"Not all, just most."

"Is compromise so horrible if it doesn't mean giving up the really important things?"

"Giving up is the nature of compromise. It's a scenario that plays itself out over and over again, isn't it? I'm not just talking about women. It happens to men too. They meet someone. They get involved. Next thing they know, they're pinned to the mat with big-time responsibilities and they can't even remember their dreams."

"That happens, true, but the situation you describe isn't the norm," Dr. Wortham says. "It's the exception. Most people believe they get back at least as much as they give, if not more."

"I don't believe that. Besides, it all depends on what you want, doesn't it? If no one's buying what you're selling, then you're out of the market. I don't want to settle down and become Joel's suburban housewife and the mother of his kids, of his parents' grandkids. I love his company, and I miss him—" My voice breaks. I grab a tissue from the nearest box and swipe at my eyes.

"Take your time." Dr. Wortham doesn't seem as surprised by my tears as I am.

I collect myself and then say, "I feel a terrible sense of loss, and I'm lonely as hell, but what am I supposed to do? He doesn't want my life, and I don't want his. That's what's real, and I have to make the best of it."

It's Dr. Wortham's turn to take a breath. She puts down her notebook and rubs at the corner of her eye. "What are your parents like? Tell me about them."

I sigh. "They were older when I was born. By the time I came along, they were pretty wrapped up in their own lives."

"Are you an only child?"

"Yes. An accident, probably."

"What was it like, being the only child in the house?"

I think back to my first decade and a half on the planet, most of which I spent holed up in my bedroom. Mom planted herself in front of the television every night, and Dad stayed out with his drinking buddies. At least, that's how I remember it. Mom was chatty during the day, but she went quiet at night after a few glasses of wine. She always fell asleep in her chair with the TV going. I'd see her there on my way to and from the kitchen. Dad was Dad. He was pretty much the same all the time, drunk or sober.

"Being the only child was okay," I say. "My dad drank a lot, but he wasn't a mean drunk. He was a sergeant in the Air Force, but we didn't move all over the country like most military families. He liked Phoenix, and we stayed put."

"What about your mother?"

"Mom complained a lot. Not about me, just about life in general. They were good to me."

"Would you say they took care of you?"

"Definitely. I never did without."

"Were they nurturing?"

That word and my parents have never occupied the same thought. "Like I said, they were older. I wouldn't say they were available emotionally, even to each other."

"I see. Think about this, Cami. A child raised without the proper nutrition doesn't develop physically as she should. The same is true of emotional nourishment. A child who's raised in an emotionally bankrupt family loses something because of it. She might fail to develop appropriate responses."

My mind immediately conjures a picture of a withered me creeping along on skinny, warped limbs. It's a hideously comic image, an oddity, like the Rubber Band Boy at the state fair. People don't want to look, but they can't take their eyes off him. Arm bones and leg bones all bent at crazy angles above and below the joints. The limbs gyrate in unnatural "you have to see it to believe it" movements. The creature scuttles along the Midway, a Human Crab.

"So I'm an emotional cripple? Is that what you're saying?" The words shoot out, accusatory and caustic.

"I'm only suggesting there might be a logical reason for why you feel detached, for why you feel you can't depend on anyone. There are methods to help emotional dysfunction." She glances at her watch. "Until next time, I'd like you to think about your emotional responses. See if you can identify any patterns that seem counterproductive, and we'll talk about it next week."

She clicks off the recorder and ends our session.

Chapter Six

I know it's time to get out of the apartment when I've slept so late that my housekeeper has to wake me.

"Miss Taylor," she says. "Miss Taylor, are you okay?" Concern furrows the brown skin between her brows. Sleep has come more slowly with each night, but I've resisted falling back on Mr. Daniel's comforts. Result: I finally fell into a deep sleep around four, and I didn't hear her quick rap at the door or her key turning the lock.

"Estella, good morning. What time is it? I was up late last night."

"It's eight o'clock. Should I do another apartment and come back later?"

"No, no, I need to get up. Go ahead and get started. I'll be out of your way in a minute."

She brightens, clearly pleased with not having to disrupt her schedule.

I found Estella the week after I moved into the building, and she's been cleaning the place ever since. Hiring a housekeeper was a hedonistic move for me, one that agitated my mother to no end. "You're a single

40

woman who doesn't even have to go to a job every day," Mom said, "and you have someone come in to clean?" Bad enough I'd moved all the way to New York. Now this.

I did everything right when I hired this wiry little Cuban. My neighbors in 201B, for whom she also works, told me Estella was honest, reliable, and actually seemed to enjoy cleaning. When I interviewed her, I was cool and professional. I drew up a list of questions beforehand and fired them off to her one after another. I even asked her to sign a contract of responsibilities before I handed her the key. She took it all in stride.

About a month after I hired her, Estella began to leave small pamphlets in discreet places around the apartment. They were amateurishly printed, stapled booklets that bore titles like *The Four Spiritual Laws*, and *Do You Know Where You Will Spend Eternity?* I found one near the coffeepot, and another on the back of the toilet. At first, I thought she left them by mistake, and I tossed them in the junk drawer to save for her. But when I left them on the counter and she didn't retrieve them, I surmised she was trying—in a mysteriously silent fashion—to convert me.

This seemed to be oddly evangelical behavior for a Catholic, which I assumed Estella was. I didn't want to lose her for this minor anomaly in her otherwise stellar performance, so when she left a pamphlet beside the telephone titled *Who Jesus Christ Really Is*, I doodled a pointy mustache, horns, and a pitchfork on the Jesus face stamped on the cover and left it out for her to find on her next visit. My defacement did the trick. There was no more paper left around the apartment.

I change into some running shorts and a tee shirt and sweep my too long hair from my face with a cotton scarf. "Be back in about an hour, Estella," I call on the way out of the door. The weather is warm, and I break a sweat right away. My pounding feet carry me deep into the green of Central Park, and the sounds of the city give way to birdcalls. I near the pond and hear the ducks quacking and fighting over tourists' bread. My breath swells above it all, pumping its hard, familiar rhythm.

By the time I walk a cooldown to my favorite spot on the corner across from the Plaza, I feel as light as a feather. I am light—under 110 pounds. Eating alone isn't very satisfying, and I've been existing on a diet befitting my confinement to the nunnery. It's time to get my hair done, buy a new outfit, and face the world again. I've been sequestered too long because of Joel. He'd be surprised if he knew.

After the breakup, I threw myself into my novel's world and wrote with sustained fervor. I'm stretching myself artistically with this second book. At least I consider it my second. I don't count the half dozen lost causes that languish on the computer's hard drive and on steno pads, each better than the one before, and each chronicling my journey from blind groping to understanding my craft. I don't have a title yet, but that will come.

My heroine is Rachael Hunter. Her name symbolizes the contradiction that she is: innocuous, eccentric Rachael, a mousy clerk in a shop that sells rare books, and Hunter, a predator who lurks in the subtext until the end of the story. A double life may be a tired plot, but it's always intrigued me. Rachael Hunter's secret identity is a metaphor for everyone who says one thing but means another, which is just about every person on the planet, as best I can tell.

I'm writing from the perspective of Rachael's boyfriend, Jerome. Jerome is a socially awkward, clueless dolt, whose best trait is his absolute apathy toward others' opinions about him. He never internalizes, and he takes at face value everything that comes his way. By telling Rachael's story from Jerome's point of view, I'm trying a bit of sleight of hand to divert the reader's attention while Rachael's true identity unfolds.

By the end of the book, the reader will finally see Rachael for who she is: a mercenary who fronts herself as a harmless shop clerk and Jerome's lover. The exposure of her duplicity will be her undoing and Jerome's salvation, though he'll never quite understand what transpired. And so, the lesson that might've been learned will be lost.

Telling a woman's story from a man's point of view gives me a chance to stretch my skills without getting too far from my comfort zone. I look forward to writing the end, the culmination that ties everything together. That time is coming soon.

The sun is high when I walk home. I'm careful to look the other way when I pass the abandoned kiosk and my fleeting reflection. I jog up the stairs to my second-floor apartment. Estella has saved cleaning the bathroom until after I showered. She works around me on the rare occasions I don't get out of her way altogether. I suppose she likes to stay busy because she often spends time on unassigned tasks like polishing the apartment's oak wainscoting or cleaning my antique silverware. She's scouring the kitchen sink when I come in and grab a quart of Gatorade from the refrigerator. I sit at the table to rehydrate.

"Did you have a good run, Miss Taylor?" she asks.

"Yes, thanks. How've you been, Estella?"

"Very well. How's your new book coming along? I saw the papers on your desk."

"Pretty good. I'm almost finished with the first draft."

"I had a dream about you this week," she says. "Do you want to hear it?"

"Sure."

She rinses her hands and leans against the counter, facing me. Her black eyes sparkle with mischief and with more intelligence than I've ever given her credit for. "In my dream," she says, "you are working on a difficult book. You would say it's a complicated book. You look everywhere for the right ending, but it doesn't come, even though you work very, very hard at it."

"That isn't good, Estella. I'm glad I already know the ending."

"Yes, well."

"What happened?" I ask. "Did you wake up?"

"While you are trying to write this book, trying so hard because you're worried about how it will end, you go to a place. It's a new place for you, and there's a celebration there. You meet a man there, Miss Taylor. He's a stranger, but you fall in love with him anyway."

"I could use a new man in my life."

"This man is different. You want to be his bride."

"That is different. What did he look like?"

"I didn't see his face, but I know he's a good man." She looks at me as if she's looking right into my soul. I wonder what kind of exotic magic this Cuban has up her sleeve. Then she smiles and turns back to the sink.

"What about the book? Did I finish it?"

"Oh yes, yes. Of course. The ending comes to you, just like that. It was a simple thing all the time."

"Good," I say. "Well, I'll go jump in the shower so you can finish up."

"Okay, Miss Taylor."

Afterward, I wrap myself in my terrycloth robe and go directly to the computer. Estella and I don't speak again except to say good-bye.

Chapter Seven

My hairstylist, Gus, has a shop near the theater district. He always tells me, "Walk in anytime, babe. You don't need an appointment." Gus is a knockout gorgeous Greek, and his accent is as warm as sun-drenched islands. His eyes practically have stars in them, they're so black, and a woman could get lost in his eyelashes. He's a bodybuilder, bulked up through the shoulders and chest. I could sit in the shop all day just watching him. Never mind that he's crazy about his wife and daughter.

Another thing I like about Gus is that I never know what he'll say next. I've swiped so many of his one-liners that he teases me about getting a share of my royalties.

When I walk into the shop, he spots me immediately.

"Celebrity alert!" he calls out. Real celebrities are a dime a dozen in here, so no one bothers to look up. Gus pulls me toward him and busses my cheek.

"Help, Gus. I've turned into a hermit."

"You've come to the right place, babe. What's it gonna be?"

I run my hand through my shapeless mop. "Color, highlight, cut. The works. I'm thinking pedicure and manicure too. Are they busy this morning?"

"Check with Audrey. See what they have going, and I'll work around it."

I find Audrey, the lead manicurist. She's white-tipping the nails of a matronly Upper East Side socialite. I've seen the woman's picture in the society pages of the *Times* more than once. "Hi," I say, and she gives me a short nod. It isn't quite a greeting, but I'm sure she thinks it'll do for West Side riffraff like me.

Louise, my colorist, greets me with a hug. "It's been too long, sugar," she says. "Where've you been?"

"Holed up writing. I came to be pampered."

"You know we'll do that." She helps me into a smock and leaves to mix my color.

This place, the temple of my reinvention, is just what I need. I'm a writer of novels, a celebrated talent with a bright future. I'm a sexy, successful woman who has the world by the horns. No one here questions my motives. What you see is what you get. And here, I can modify what you see as much as I want.

A new girl who introduces herself as Darla says she can do a pedicure while the color's on my hair. "If you'd rather wait, Ms. Taylor, I'll work you in a little bit later," she says.

"That's fine, Darla. Thanks."

"Just come back to my chair when Louise is finished," she says.

Darla's chair is a high-tech wonder, with heated rollers that run up and down my back at speeds I adjust using a remote control. Darla fills the whirlpool footbath with warm water and therapeutic salts. She turns on the switch, and aerated jets massage my pavement-pounded feet. I close my eyes and let my entire body relax. While one foot soaks, she slathers eucalyptus lotion on the other, working it up to my knee. She spends ten minutes kneading my feet and calves. It's incredibly luxurious.

I'm practically dozing by the time Darla starts on my toenails. The cuticles are untended and thick, and when she goes too deep on a snip I feel the blade and let out a squeak before I can stop myself.

"Oh, no! Ms. Taylor, I'm so sorry! The clippers slipped."

"It's okay, Darla. I hardly felt it." I lean forward to look and am surprised at the small river of blood flowing from my toe into the water. "Looks like my foot's a bleeder."

"Warm feet bleed like crazy." She pulls the drain in the basin and blots my toe with the towel, making rows of red smears across the white terrycloth. I pull my foot up and rest it on my knee, and she hands me the towel. "I'll just hold it here until it stops bleeding," I say.

"I've got some antiseptic. Let me get it."

"It's fine, Darla. All your equipment is clean. Don't worry about it. Besides, it's stopping now."

"I feel terrible," she says. "I've never done that before."

"Forget it," I say. "It's no big thing."

An hour later, I settle into Gus's chair.

"How's my favorite author?" he asks.

"Writing like crazy. Joel and I broke up, and I've been working nonstop ever since. As a matter of fact, I'm sick of it."

"Sorry to hear that. Do you want the usual, or are you in the mood for a change?"

"What do you have in mind?"

"Maybe something fresher, more textured for summer. What do you think?"

"Work your magic."

"Are you dating again?" he asks. While he talks, Gus looks at my reflection in the mirror, lifting sheaves of hair with the comb and watching how they fall through the teeth. He takes the scissors and begins to snip.

"Not yet," I say. "Like I said, I haven't been out."

"You have to get out, babe. Get back in the game. You won't have any trouble meeting someone you like."

"You think?"

"Look at you. You can have your pick."

I smile at his reflection in the mirror. Make me feel good, Gus. Who cares if you mean it? "My psychiatrist says it's all up to me. Are you're telling me that too?"

"You're seeing a shrink? When did this start?"

"Oh, a few months ago. Have you ever been to one?"

"I'm a simple man, Cami. Way too shallow to be dysfunctional. Just give me the love of a fine woman and something to do with my hands." He holds up the comb and scissors and winks. "Add a good meal and a glass of wine at the end of the day, and I'm happy."

"My shrink says I'm transparent. Do you think I'm transparent, Gus?"

He turns my chair around and stares hard at me.

"What are you doing?"

"Trying to see through you. I know, I know. My daughter says I'm corny." He turns me back to face the mirror. "Who isn't transparent?"

"You're right. Who isn't?"

◆ ◆ ◆

I step outside the salon and don my sunglasses. I'm myself again, and I feel like being out and about. At times like this I miss having girlfriends in my life to fill the empty hours with shopping and lunch dates. I haven't had any girl chums since I was in school. I look down Seventh Avenue, thinking I'll walk to Macy's. A familiar form materializes within the crowd, Rum Tum Tugger in khaki slacks and a white pullover.

"Willie! Hi!" I call.

"Hey, I know you," he says.

"Cami Taylor. We met at the Winter Garden."

"Yeah. You were—" He grins. "You haven't been around for a while." His accent is as delicious as a bowl of warm, buttery grits. He looms over me like a work of art, every muscle on display, even under the knit of his brilliantly white shirt.

"How's the show?" I ask, suddenly breathless.

"Dunno. I've been down with my knee, but it's kinda nice to have some time off."

"Eight shows a week has to be grueling," I say.

"Yeah, it is." He glances across the street.

"So," I say quickly, "do you want to meet for a drink later?"

He looks at me sideways. "Sure, why not?"

"The bar in the Essex House is nice, up on Fifty-Ninth. Do you know it?"

"Yeah, I've been there," he says. "Six o'clock?"

"Perfect."

"Okay. See you at six."

I turn and walk away. I'm going the wrong direction, but who cares? There's a spring in my step, and I can feel his gaze on my back.

Chapter Eight

I hang the dress I bought at Macy's on the bedroom door and tear away the plastic bag. I'm a frugal shopper by anyone's standards. I hate to pay full price, even though I can afford it. Clothes are too perishable to be as expensive as they are, and I hate feeling wasteful when I box them up and ship them off to my mother's garage sales.

I found a prize today, a scoop-necked sleeveless little number in sienna jersey. The color really pops with my hair, and the dress drapes in soft folds over my bare legs, with a hemline that exposes enough calf for Willie to appreciate. Since our first meeting at the theater, he has starred in my fantasies with increasing frequency, enough to make me tingle in anticipation of the real thing. In my new dress, I expect to feel bright, feminine, and seductive.

I conduct the predate ritual without haste. Every part of this preparation feels sensual compared to my recent domesticity with Joel. The bath salts, which have been corked for too long, fill my candlelit bathroom with effervescent mist. I spread expensive, silken emollients over my body, and I put on plenty of makeup. Tête-à-tête makeup.

A yellow Medallion chariot whisks me from the curb of my building. This driver must be living right because the traffic down Columbus parts before the grilled snout of his Crown Victoria. He deposits me at the Essex House way too early to play hard to get. What was I thinking when I left the apartment at five thirty? After a couple of minutes of indecision, I head toward the bar to have a drink and rid myself of my schoolgirl jitters.

As I pass the registration desk, a clerk rushes to catch a tall man on his way to the elevators. "Your wife is waiting for you in the restaurant, Mr. Davis," he says.

"Thanks, Dominic," Mr. Davis responds. "She must have plans for me."

They both laugh, and the tall man turns for the restaurant across the lobby. He's middle-aged with sandy hair that has turned loose more than gray. His suit is expensive, well-tailored, but not flashy. He speaks with a twangy drawl that's undeniably Texan, like my dad's. I tail him like a spook, thinking his wife might be the crazy woman who called me looking for a relative.

Kate Davis has morphed into an eccentric Southern socialite in a story I'm crafting, and the chance to put a face on that character is irresistible. I step sideways, craning my neck to try and get a look past the clot of patrons at the entrance to the restaurant. In the process, I bump into Willie's broad chest.

"Whoa! Hey, what's up?" he says, grasping my bare shoulders.

"Willie, it's you. Hi. I was just—I thought I saw someone."

With a firm hand on the small of my back, he sweeps me toward the bar. He has cleaned up in blue jeans, a starched white shirt, and the clean scent of an aftershave I don't recognize. His jeans break perfectly over gray lizard cowboy boots, and my insides flutter as we cross the threshold into the dark lounge packed with suits. Willie speaks to the host, and he seats us at an out-of-the-way table.

"This okay?" Willie asks.

"It's perfect."

A waiter comes around, his apron pulled taut around his narrow waist. "What'll you folks have?" he asks.

"Scotch and water," I say.

"Guinness for me," says Willie.

The waiter leaves, and we stumble around in small talk. In a few hours, we can be lovers, but for now, we're self-conscious and halting, measuring our words and worried about first impressions. Willie tells me what he thinks of New York and the Broadway theater culture. It's all very different for him.

"I grew up in a little old town called Tunica, on the Mississippi River," he says. "Until the casinos came in, it wasn't nothing but bottomland and cotton crops."

"So how'd you get into performing?"

My question draws a hearty laugh that, like his voice, resonates from his chest. "It was a joke. I was a tight end for Mississippi State. My senior year, some of the guys on the team told me I ought to join the drama club because I was always singing in the locker room.

"They were just giving me a hard time, right? But this one guy never knew when to quit. He signed me up for the tryouts for *A Midsummer Night's Dream*. He thought it was a real funny joke. But I thought, why not? So I went to the audition and got Puck. Just like that. Dead cold. Surprised me as much as anybody. Turns out, I can pick up choreography after seeing it once or twice. 'Course I was that way with the plays in football too."

"That's quite a transition."

"Well, I mighta had a shot at the pros. I was a decent player, but ten or fifteen years of getting knocked senseless? Real good money, but the price was too high."

"You're a great dancer, Willie. You have the moves. You know, the Rum Tum Tugger moves." Willie's character is the rock-and-roll cat, all thrusts and grinds, with the female cats screaming.

"Doesn't everybody?" he says.

"No, they don't."

"So how long have you been living here?"

"About three years." The waiter arrives with another round. I can't tell if I'm warming to the scotch or to Willie, but I'm starting to feel relaxed and confident. "I moved here from New Mexico after my first novel sold. I've always loved New York."

"There's a lot going on here."

"Yeah. This city's charged with energy."

He glances around the room. "Lots of people here. Crowds everywhere you go."

"Sometimes too many."

"Too many for this guy." He smiles and his eyes crinkle. He seems amused by New York's hustle and bustle, as if it's all just so much silliness.

"Do you like Chinese food?" I ask.

"Sure, it's okay."

"There's a place around the corner from my apartment. If you're hungry, we could head over that way."

He looks at me a long moment. "Are you gonna show me your place?"

"Sure."

He drains the rest of his stout. "Let's go."

◆ ◆ ◆

Willie follows me up the stairs to the second floor of my building. He stands so close behind me while I'm unlocking the door that I can feel the heat from his body. Anticipation—could it be anxiety?—causes the key to fight me briefly before submitting to the brass slot.

"This is it." I swing the door open. The apartment smells fresh from Estella's scrubbing.

He walks in and looks around. "This is real nice."

"The living room is in there. And the stereo. Pick some music, and I'll get you a beer."

Dusk is coming on, but the apartment still glows with soft light. I open the refrigerator and reach inside for a bottle. In the bright appliance light, I see that my hand is trembling. I draw it into a fist and bring it to my breast. Is fear the rush I feel? It's been a long time since the old days, since Albuquerque, when this was a way of life, and it feels as if there's more at stake now. Have I grown respectable without noticing?

The man in my living room is a stranger. I'm no match for him physically, yet I've given him the promise of my bedroom without a single thought for my safety. Maybe depression has become such a swift current against the underbelly of my life that I don't care if I live or die. I'll have to tell Sylvia about this. She'll have a good time digging around in these emotions.

But I've been here before—it's all coming back to me now—and I know that I won't die tonight, except, hopefully, la petite mort.

Willie turns on the stereo, and music pulses through the apartment. Whatever happens tonight, I'll live, as I've lived plenty of times before. I open the bottle and carry it to my guest. He takes a long pull, emptying half of it. He sings a few measures of the lyrics coming from the speakers.

"I was looking at your books," he says. "No paperbacks."

"I think a book worth keeping deserves a decent cover."

"Hmm." He takes another swill.

"Do you like to read?" I ask.

"Nope. Dyslexic. I can get by, but I don't read much." His foot taps lightly to the beat.

"They can do a lot for that these days."

"It wasn't too important when I was growing up. Now I figure I've made it this far, I'll make it the rest of the way." He looks around for a place to put his empty bottle and then offers to take it to the kitchen.

"Here, I'll take it," I say.

His polite concern about putting a watermark on my wood furniture melts the last traces of my frigid anxiety. I go to the kitchen and set the bottle on the counter. When I turn around, Willie stands in the doorway. He walks to me slowly and with one knuckle pushes my bangs away from my face.

"You're beautiful," he says.

He picks up my hand and holds it. My hand is small within his palm, which is creased and powerful. He has workingman's hands that New York will need a long time to soften. "I noticed your hands all evening," he says. "They're so smooth and fine."

"No housework."

"You're trembling now. Are you scared?"

"No." This is the truth. "No, Willie. I'm not afraid of you."

He leans into me. "I won't hurt you," he whispers.

He nuzzles my face slowly, his freshly shaven cheek against mine. I'm small and fragile next to him, and when he puts his arms around me, the muscles sliding beneath the cotton shirt are no more yielding than polished granite. But unlike stone, his flesh is warm, alive, and moving, and I reach for him eagerly. Our breath mingles, and my stomach plunges like it does on the first big hill of a good roller coaster. In that most intimate of exchanges, we taste one another, and I abandon myself to this pleasure.

We don't talk again until afterward, when he says that he's ready for the Chinese food. I pull myself from the bed and go to the bathroom to freshen up, putting the blow-dryer to my sweat-soaked hair and wiping the smudged makeup from under my eyes. I take my embroidered silk robe from the closet and wrap it around my body, cinching the waist tightly.

When I come out of the bathroom, he's lying on his back in bed, staring at my ceiling, at its punched-tin squares.

"I'll call for the food," I say. "Do you want something to drink?"

"I'll get something in a minute."

After I make the phone call, I get a soda from the fridge and sit on the couch. I stop the cycling repeat of the CD with the remote control and sip my drink in silence. I feel hollow inside, augered out.

The delivery guy knocks at the door, and Willie calls for me to take some money from his wallet. I get up and pay the man from my purse. Willie comes out of the bedroom, wearing only his briefs.

"Smells good," he says. He looks in the refrigerator, gets a beer, and sits down.

I set the table with plates, silverware, and paper napkins and sit across from him. As the food goes into my mouth bite by bite, my mind replays the past hour minute by minute. We should be snuggled together in bed, in the comfort that's supposed to come from physical intimacy. Instead, I feel self-conscious and distant. Willie shovels the food into his mouth heartily. He seems perfectly fine with the silence between us. He finishes quickly and leans back in his chair.

"That was good." He looks around. "You got any toothpicks? Don't get up. Just tell me where."

"In the drawer behind you."

He takes one out and sets the box on the table. He absently works the pick between closed lips as he looks around the kitchen. "I like this place. It's real warm. Some of your stuff reminds me of home."

"I'm glad."

Willie lays the frayed pick on his empty plate, his gaze drifting across the intricate needlework of my robe. He rises slowly and comes around the table to kneel beside me. Easily, as if my weight were nothing, he turns my chair around to face him.

"Are you done eating?" he asks. I nod, and he slowly unties the belt and opens my robe.

He's exhausted me already, but there are still butterflies alive inside, fluttering against my ribs. "Yes. More," they say. I put my hands on his meaty shoulders and run my fingertips over the weave of muscles. I lean forward and we kiss, not groping with our hands, but funneling the tension into our lips. The butterflies beat furiously.

We go to the bedroom, and Willie rakes everything from the bed to make a clean stage for his performance. If he satisfied himself during our first tryst, this time is for me, a sort of thank-you for the evening, I suppose. He coaxes sensations from my body that I didn't know were possible, or at least possible with such intensity. I take everything he gives me, and I would beg for more if I could speak, even though he hurts me. I can't get enough of him. Afterward, I lie flat on my back beside him, too spent to move or even to think. He sighs and sits up on the edge of the bed with a grunt. He reaches to the floor to retrieve his underwear.

"You can stay if you like," I say. I stroke his sinewy forearm with my fingertips.

"Nah, I gotta get on back to my apartment. I need to call home before it gets any later."

"Tunica, you mean."

"Yeah. I always call on Thursday nights and Sundays. They'll be worried if they don't hear from me."

"Your folks."

"Yeah." He stands and stretches his back, twisting first to one side and then to the other. He begins putting on his jeans. "My folks and my girlfriend. She's coming up here to see the city in a few days. It's her first time out of Mississippi."

"Your girlfriend," I repeat woodenly.

He looks down at me, and I finally recognize guileless accommodation the instant before he turns wary. Averting his eyes, he reaches to take his shirt from the doorknob, which gives me a chance to get out of bed. I'm overwhelmed by a sudden need to cover myself, and I grab my terrycloth robe from its hook on the bathroom door. He's buttoning his shirt when I turn back to face him.

"You didn't ask," he says, tucking his shirttail into his jeans. "I figured you were just, you know. . . ."

There's nothing to say. He's right. There were no promises between us.

"It's okay," I say. "It's no problem."

He looks at me doubtfully. "You sure? Are you gonna be all right?"

"Yes, Willie. You were good. I had fun."

He grins, obviously relieved. "Okay, then."

He grabs his belt, kisses me lightly on the cheek, and heads toward the door, scooping his wallet from the table and jamming it in his back pocket on the way. As he puts his hand on the doorknob, I say, "Willie?"

He turns around. "Yeah?"

"I don't think I've heard you say my name all night. Do you remember it?"

He ducks his head, hesitating. "Tammy?" he ventures.

I smile and let him out, locking the door behind him.

"Close enough," I whisper to the empty apartment.

Chapter Nine

T he morning after Willie, my emotions hold me hostage. The hours tick by with me curled on the sofa, drinking cup after cup of strong coffee. I flip through the channels on the muted television, from game show to talk show to documentary, my thoughts darting in circles like excited molecules. Joel thinks I don't have emotions. I wish that were true. I don't know what to call this post-Willie feeling. It's a black hole that folds around me and turns all my reasoning in on itself. Nothing gets out, and nothing gets in.

When I examine the situation in the cold light of day, I see precious little to look forward to as far as relationships go. I'm only twenty-nine years old, but I've pretty much seen and done it all. What are my choices, really? Apparently, the road to happiness must be traveled in vehicles I loathe: Sacrifice. Compromise. Surrender.

Can people only bond after they've hacked off some precious part of themselves? Is life designed so that you can never remain whole and share that wholeness with another? I've resisted the amputation of my dreams at all cost, and I should be happy, but I ache with loneliness.

What are these feelings, except a handful of chemicals coursing through my body? Yet they bully me like armed men. Am I the only person on the planet who feels this way? As singular as I seem to be, I have to believe that I'm not.

I wrote *Double Down Blues* while dealing blackjack at the River Bend Casino in Albuquerque. I told myself that I went to work in the casino to get the experience I needed to develop my protagonist, Jackie. To get firsthand experience of what a dealer's life is like. Now I know I did it to escape the person I was in Phoenix—the mousy, dumpy bookworm I'd always been. My transformation began there, in Albuquerque. Vicariously at first, through the recklessness of my alter ego, Jackie. Then, as I emulated her, through my own recklessness.

A guy I met at a five-dollar table one night took me up in his airplane early the next morning. I remember it clearly, though it seems like a lifetime ago. How long has it been? Maybe four years now?

It was a still and frosty high-desert morning in November. The airplane was parked under a tiny shed out in a field. He pulled the ancient yellow contraption out into the morning sunlight, tied the tail end of it to the shed, and pulled the propeller around and around to start the engine. It sputtered and caught and finally rumbled to life. We got in—me very bravely—and took off from that field.

We climbed out over the valley, alongside the Sandia ridgeline, our cross-shaped shadow gliding across the craggy, cactus-strewn mountainside. As we sailed between the prickly ground and the infinite blue sky, every ordinary thing was transmuted to glorious.

I still remember how I felt, sitting behind him in that narrow, frail contrivance of wood and canvas. Midway Publishing had just accepted my manuscript, and I was drunk on the thrill of it. The freedom of leaving the earth behind, of going wherever we wished under our own power, was a perfect metaphor for my success. At that moment, anything seemed possible.

Then Eddie—his name was Eddie—shouted, "Hang on!" over the roar of the engine.

The plane suddenly heaved backward on its tail, nose skyward, and slowed until we seemed to hang motionless on the whirling propeller. All of the wind and engine sounds faded to silence.

"Autorotation!" Eddie barked.

As if on command, the body of the thing that held us in space shuddered with a death throe and rolled to one side like a breaching whale. The nose fell through the horizon and pointed straight down, toward the pale New Mexican dirt, and the entire machine began to whip around in a tight corkscrew. Fear snatched the breath from my throat, even though I knew it had to be a boyish prank meant to impress me. Then Eddie threw his hands over his head, and the airplane magically began to fly again.

I did not speak to him after that. Ever.

"All I had to do was let go of the controls and it'd fly right out of it," he said.

As if that made any difference.

"Autorotation," I say aloud to the empty apartment.

I now feel that same panic, the whipping, uncontrolled downward spiral. In the windshield the ground spins closer and closer. The eerie silence. If I take my hands from the controls, will everything return to normal as it did on that day? Will my life know how to right itself as that little airplane did?

The River Bend had a pit boss as tough and cold as a drill sergeant. Blackjack dealers turned over as regularly as a four-deck shoe, and each time one left—even someone everyone would miss—the guy's only comment was, "Just like takin' your finger out of water." That's how much of a dent we made in his existence.

I hated that petty, arrogant man. "Big fish in a small pond," I griped behind his back. The day I left the casino, when I knew I would live as a writer, I told him exactly what I thought of him.

"Lemme tell *you* somethin', Lee-ona," he said with a smirk. "You were trash when you walked in that door, and you'll still be trash when you walk out of it."

I'll never forget the cruel precision of his words. I buried Leona Lingo in New Mexico, legally pronounced her dead, and transformed myself into my wildest vision of success. Yet the fulfillment I expected to accompany my metamorphosis remains elusive. I drag my stubborn old self behind me like a corpse tied to my back.

Finally, I put down the remote, pick up the telephone, and punch in my parents' phone number.

"Hello?" The quizzical inflection of my mother's greeting hasn't changed a bit in all these years. She always sounds amazed that the phone has rung, as if it must be a wrong number.

"Hi, Mom."

"Lee, is that you?"

Who else calls her mom? "I called to see how you're doing," I say.

"Your father isn't here right now." My father is never anywhere besides the golf course or home, or en route between the two.

"Well, how are you, Mom? Are you feeling okay?"

She sighs. "Dr. Mason changed my medicine again, but I still feel dizzy when I stand up."

"Have you tried walking? Maybe your circulation would be better if you got some exercise."

"Well, my feet are still swelling, Lee, and your father thinks it's nothing. He's not here now, though."

I don't say, "You already said that, Mom." If I called it every time my mother repeated herself, I wouldn't have time to say anything else. "I was thinking about coming out for a few days. Is it a good time?"

Her voice perks up. "When are you coming?" Then she says, "Your father will like that."

"I'll have to see when I can get a ticket, but maybe tomorrow or the next day. I'll call back and let you know."

"Well, I have canasta on Wednesday, and I go back to the doctor on Thursday."

"Okay, it'll be Monday at the latest. I'll rent a car anyway, so you don't have to worry about picking me up."

"Are you writing another book?"

"The same one, Mom. Remember, I told you about it? It's the one about the woman who works in a bookstore."

"Oh. Well, I knew you were working on one, but I thought you might've finished it. Anyway, I'll tell your father that you're coming, and we'll look for you on Monday."

"I'll call back after I book a flight."

"All right, dear."

I disconnect and lay the phone on the coffee table.

I buy a cheap one-way airline ticket, cancel my next appointment with Dr. Wortham, and write out a note and a check for Estella. It's as easy as that to let go of my life in New York. Nothing to it. Just like taking my finger out of water.

◆ ◆ ◆

Less than thirty-six hours later, I'm standing on my parents' front porch. The night is dark and warm and free of the damp smells I'm used to. Light from a bare yellow bulb bathes the moths and me and the bags at my feet. I pull open the screen door and knock on the bleached wood behind it. Patrick Earl answers in an undershirt, cotton trousers, and leather slippers. This is his around-the-house getup. He looks older—shoulders more rounded, hair a little grayer, a little thinner, skin more translucent and sagging.

"Hi, Dad."

He hugs me quickly, giving me a dry kiss on the cheek. He smells of bourbon and fresh cigar smoke. "How long you stayin'?" he asks.

"I'm not sure. A few days."

"You got business out here?"

"No. I just came to visit."

He grunts the same way he does when one of his cronies lets a story get out of hand. "Well, we're glad to see ya." He reaches past me for my bags and hitches on his bad leg as he carries them to my old bedroom.

My mother's in the kitchen. "You're so thin, Lee," she says when she sees me in the harsh fluorescent light. "Do you want something to eat? There's some Mexican casserole left from dinner."

"No, Mom. I'm not hungry."

Dad brings a bottle of Maker's Mark and a lit cigar from the den and pulls out a chair at the kitchen table. "You want something to drink?"

"Sure. I'll have some of that."

He pushes the bottle across the table. "Help yourself."

I get a glass from the cabinet, sit at the table, and pour myself a few fingers. I'm very tired, but I don't feel sleepy.

"Well, if you two are going to sit up a while, I might as well too," says Mom. She pours herself a glass of Chianti and takes a pack of cigarettes from one of the cartons on top of the fridge. She looks puffy and flaccid in her floral housedress. Her hair, which is cropped short and burned from a permanent, sticks out from her scalp in dry, faded orange tufts. There are dark circles under her eyes.

"Your mother's right," Dad says. "You're too skinny."

"When did you take up cigars again?"

"He spends half his time playing dominoes now," says my mother. "They all smoke cigars down at the domino parlor." Somehow, this bit of information makes me feel ridiculously out of touch, as if they've moved on without me.

Dad taps ashes into an Arizona-shaped ashtray. "Playin' dominoes keeps my mind sharp. Besides, it's air-conditioned down there. I'm gettin' too old to play golf in this heat."

I sip the bourbon and begin to relax. There's no pressure here. No cause for anxiety. My world can begin and end in this kitchen, at this table.

"So how goes it with this boyfriend of yours?" Dad asks.

"Joey," says Mom.

"His name is Joel," I say flatly. The name remains in my mouth, even after I've let it out into the stale air. It fills the space between my tongue and teeth, and I sip the whiskey to burn it away. "I broke it off."

Patrick Earl snorts. "You're better off. What was he? Wasn't he a singer or somethin' like that?"

"He's a costumer," I say. I pour a couple more inches, straight up. No ice. No water. The same as anyone worth her salt. That's how I grew up in this house. You eat your steaks blood rare and your oysters raw, without crackers or sauce. And you drink your whiskey neat. "There's nothing wrong with Joel. He's a good guy."

"Well, why did you break up?" asks Mom. Her tone is tentative from past experience with probing me about personal matters.

"She don't wanna go into all that, Phyllis."

"No, I don't mind. I kinda feel like talking about it."

"You two talk then," Dad growls, shuffling toward the living room. "I'm gonna finish watchin' the news."

In a fit of openness, I tell Mom everything about Joel and me. What I tell her isn't how he made me feel or that I miss him. Instead, I talk about the things we did together. I reminisce lavishly, reliving the shows, the late nights, the Sundays in Central Park. She doesn't interrupt me with questions or advice. She sits quietly, sipping her wine and letting me unload, stream of consciousness. If I jump around in the chronology, digressing or leaping forward on a whim, well, that's okay with her. And if her eyes glaze over from time to time, I don't mind. It doesn't matter how much of it she remembers tomorrow. What matters is the telling.

I end my tale on Ruth's front porch. When I fall silent, Mom nods a few times, as if she's nudging her next words loose. Or trying to keep from falling asleep. "You'll meet someone else," she says.

Patrick Earl comes back to the kitchen with such extraordinary timing that I wonder if he was eavesdropping from the other room. He refills his glass and sits down. He's ready to talk, and soon I'm privy to the business of every family represented at the domino parlor. Then Mom starts in on the canasta club.

I tell them the story of Rachael and Jerome, emphasizing the espionage plot and laying off the metaphors and other writerly devices. Their rapt attention rejuvenates me, lifting me out of my apathy—at least where my manuscript is concerned. We stay up talking until the wee hours, the conversation flowing as freely as our blood alcohol. When we finally go to bed, I toss and turn for a while, then get up again. They're snoring in separate bedrooms when I quietly leave the house.

I greet the morning from the summit of Squaw Peak. I've panted and sweated my way up the trail, the flashlight casting a jiggling beam across the feathery plants, the rocks, and the dry, red dirt. The sky lightens to azure, and the sun rises behind Camelback Mountain, throwing its first rays over the rocky outcrop. My cotton shorts and tee shirt are soaked with eighty proof, but inside, like the morning, I am cleansed.

I pull a quart of water from my backpack and drink it all. Soon people will gather in the parking lot below and cover the trail like ants. For now, I have the view and the silence to myself. Below me, Phoenix spreads past the mountains, its suburbs reaching into the desert like fingers. The air here used to be crystal clear, but now dirty haze hangs over the Valley of the Sun. Like everything else, this place has changed.

At the foot of Squaw Peak, the Arizona Biltmore nestles in manicured lawns. The first time I saw the gray brick and austere lines of the old art deco hotel, I was in the fifth grade, tagging along with my parents to some formal affair Patrick Earl couldn't worm out of. We ate dinner on white tablecloths under chandeliers, their creamy light bouncing off gold-trimmed dishes and crystal vases. The flatware was gold too. I was entirely enchanted by the romanticism of Frank Lloyd Wright's aesthetic.

After that, I began to ride the bus to Twenty-Fourth and Camelback with a succession of best friends. We hiked up Twenty-Fourth Street and down the long, orange tree–lined boulevard to the hotel, where we swam all day in the Catalina pool, pretending our parents were guests. The pool was the nicest one in town, a cool sapphire in an expanse of emerald lawn.

Nowadays, condominiums spring from every nook and cranny of the grounds, and there are at least a dozen swimming pools. But only the beautifully tiled Catalina beckons me.

My gut begins to roll in the rising heat, forcing me back down the trail, past the morning hikers, to the rental car. I drive to a deserted place and pull over. I open the door, lean out, and let my stomach relieve itself.

Chapter Ten

I hold my breath and hang beneath the ladder in the Catalina pool, looking up through a watery lens at a cloudless blue sky. I used to hang below this same ladder when I was a kid, watching boys on the high diving board, their images fragmented by the water's choppy surface. They'd gather their courage, leap, and pierce the water like torpedoes, dragging a flurry of bubbles under with them.

My lungs yell for air, and I shoot to the surface for a few deep breaths before I push off the side and swim to the opposite end.

I'm strung out in every way. Too much drinking and too little food. Way too much smoking and most definitely too much emotion. I've sought my former refuge, the Biltmore, and rented a cabana for the day. The hotel's crawling with guests, whom I see as intruders. My history here gives me the feeling I own the place. I'm no longer a chubby schoolgirl poaching sunshine and water.

I stretch my arms along the tiled lip of the pool, lean my head back, and let my body float weightlessly in the water.

"Would you like another drink, Ms. Taylor?" A tanned waitress stands at the edge of the pool.

"Another Breeze, please."

She walks away to fetch my drink, leaving me to think about my future. Another bestseller to bring more money and more recognition. More novels after that. And more lovers. More loneliness too. Always ever present, the loneliness.

More of the same isn't going to be enough. I can see that now. When I think about it, I realize it isn't strange at all to need new goals after having reached all the old ones. I should've seen this coming. I'm doing okay, professionally, and now I need to concentrate on feeding my soul. Just as soon as I figure out exactly what my soul needs.

The waitress brings my drink. On her tray is a paperback copy of *Blues* and a hand towel. "Ms. Taylor, one of the girls wondered if she could have your autograph, but it's only a paperback. She brought it in today to read on her breaks. Do you mind?"

"Not at all." I dry my hands on the towel and sign my name inside the cover. "I hope she enjoys it."

"She's gonna loan it to me when she's finished. I can't wait to read it."

"Good. Thanks for the drink."

One sip of the Breeze and I'm transported back to my senior prom, which was here at the Biltmore. They served these same Biltmore Breeze concoctions of lemonade, black currant, and tea. I went with Darrell Cassidy, my one and only date in high school. I haven't thought about him in years. I let him kiss me behind the high diving board, which I thought was extremely generous at the time. It was my first kiss.

I can still visualize Darrell clearly. He had fish-belly skin and oily brown hair. He wore baggy trousers and a thin shirt through which his undershirt, a wife beater, could be seen. I was embarrassed to be with him. Darrell was a nerd, and I suddenly realize how much of him is in Jerome. My subconscious never stops surprising me.

It's funny that I recall Darrell so much more clearly than many of the guys I knew later, and more intimately, as if the pleasures I discovered after high school dampened the individuality of the men who brought them. Oh, a few are memorable. Like Joel. Well, that's not right either. Joel was so much more than a roll in the hay.

I accepted Darrell's invitation to the prom because it was the only one I got, and because it saved me the agony of standing around by myself all evening. Of course, I'm sure I would've talked myself out of going solo if he hadn't asked. But I was curious to see what the fuss was all about.

That night, Darrell and I strolled around the Catalina pool under a starry sky. Darrell told me his plans, his hobbies, his favorite subjects in school. He liked to collect Indian artifacts and foreign currencies. He told me people sent him money from countries all over the world, which he listed for my enjoyment. He wanted to enter a field that permitted him to travel, and he had some kind of scholarship to an Ivy League school. None of this impressed me at the time, although now I have to admit he had a bright future.

I climb out of the pool and return to my cabana for a while. The minute I step into the shade, the hot air cools on my wet skin. I lie back on a cushioned lounge and close my eyes.

Why had I seen Darrell as such a loser? He was goofy looking, but he was very nice. He treated me like a queen that night, which only made me think less of him. I was shortsighted, no doubt about it. He probably matured into a great catch.

I vow to look deeper in the future, and to make better choices. I ought to be past the quest for the handsomest man. How about a guy who just wants to share a good time without expecting to tie me down? Surely I can find someone who wants to keep the relationship uncomplicated. To hear some women tell it, that's every man on the planet. How hard can it be?

As I drift midway between consciousness and dreaming, Darrell's moonlit face comes back to me. He says, "You know, people might like you if you gave them half a chance."

✦ ✦ ✦

I pull a box of old yearbooks down from the top shelf of my closet and leaf through the pages, searching for Darrell. I find him right there in the Cs, where he's been all this time. He has a loopy smile and a look of contentment in his eyes. I'm surprised to see a list of activities that would choke a horse under his name: Speech Club. Key Club. Student Advisory Board. And beneath that the most surprising thing of all—he was voted Most Amiable. Could it be that Darrell was the generous one? Why don't I remember any of this?

My own picture looks like someone else. My face was round with adolescent fat, and my dull brown hair lay flat to my head, accentuating the fullness of my cheeks and neck. I wore no makeup at all. I recognize my eyes, though. They were filled with the same combative skepticism that looks back at me from the mirror every day.

I flip through the pages and find a few surprises. Many of my classmates' pictures are embellished with nastigrams like "snob" and "slut" and worse. The handwriting is definitely mine, but I can't remember scrawling such offensive things in my yearbooks. I gather all of them in my arms and make my way to the backyard, passing my mother's open bedroom door. She's lying on the thin bedspread, but she doesn't stir. Her forearm is bent over her eyes to shut out the afternoon light, and the crepey skin drapes across her nose like a curtain.

I drag my father's propane grill off the patio, out from under the awning, and into the middle of the ragged cactus garden. After I dump the books on the ground and remove the grill and ceramic briquettes from the drum, I return to the house for matches, cigarettes, a soda, and Dad's hacksaw.

In the scorching desert afternoon, I turn on the gas and light it. When the air around my makeshift incinerator is fluid with heat, I carve my yearbooks into chunks and toss my history, piece by piece, onto the blue flames. The memories burn in astonishing colors. The heavy paper of the elementary school jackets shrivels within flashes of green and orange. The glossy high school hardbacks hiss as their shiny coating evaporates, then char like old wood. I light a cigarette, open my drink, and watch the evidence of my own lack of amiability vaporize.

"Lee, what are you doing?" Mom's voice is urgent, frightened.

"Just burning some old books," I say without turning around.

"What *is* that?" She steps closer, peering into the flames. "Are those your school books?" She looks at me as if I'm disposing of a body. "Why would you burn them? I wanted to keep them."

I toss the cigarette butt into the fire. "They weren't yours to keep, Mom." I turn and go inside.

She comes through the patio door right behind me. "Well, your father's going to have a fit when he sees that mess in his grill."

I sit down and sip my soda. "I'll clean it up."

She hovers near the kitchen table, nervous and exasperated. "Why would you do something like that?"

"I just wanted to, Mom. Looking at them made me feel, I don't know, gross."

"Well, that's just silly. Someday you'll wish you had them back. You'll want to give them to your kids."

I laugh harshly. "Not that old stuff. Trust me, Mom." I point toward the backyard. "*That* was for the best."

"Well, I don't know. . . ." Her hand flutters to her face.

"There's nothing to know. It's done. Forget it. Do you want me to get you a soda?"

"No, no." She slumps in a chair and takes a cigarette from the pack on the table. "Want one?" The ultralight bobs between her dry lips.

"Not right now."

"I thought you might come to canasta club with me this week. The girls would love to see you."

"I don't know, Mom."

"I want to show you off, Lee. I told them you're in town."

I pull a cigarette from the pack. "I don't even know how to play canasta. Besides, I need to finish my manuscript while I have some momentum."

"It's only for a few hours."

"I'll think about it."

She brightens. "I got steaks for dinner tonight. We'll have salad and baked potatoes. Of course, now . . ." She looks sideways out the patio door.

I get up from the table. "I'll clean it up, Mom. It'll be like it never happened."

◆ ◆ ◆

After dinner, while the folks settle into the den for their nightly television lineup, I retreat to my room and plug the laptop into the phone jack to download email. I should be writing but can't make myself go back to the manuscript yet. What if it's no good?

There are forty-three emails, but they're all advertisements. Nothing sent to *me*. Against my better judgment, I call my answering machine. There's no excuse for this, except that I'm a glutton for punishment. The great thing about all this technology—cell phones that work everywhere and computers the size of composition books—is it lets you know in seconds just how disconnected you are. When the answering machine picks up, I punch in the access code and let it cycle through the recorded calls. Mostly they're hang-ups, but one surprises me. It was left this evening by the inspiration for my intriguing Southern protagonist.

"Hello, this is Kate Davis," she says. "I called you a few months ago, and well, you've been on my mind since then. I felt so bad for catching you off guard and giving you a scare, but I found you and your parents on a genealogy chart done by someone in the family and—"

The machine cuts her off. I bet with myself that she'll call back to finish the message, and sure enough, I win.

"I'll finish fast. I'd like to take you to lunch this week if you're free. If you're busy during the day, maybe Tom and I could take you to dinner. Please call me back when you can."

She leaves the room number at the Essex House. Oh yes, Kate Davis, I'll have lunch with you. You're just the thing to grease my creative skids.

It's too late to call her tonight, but I make up my mind to get back to New York before the week is out.

A cirrus cloud of smoke hangs near the ceiling in the living room, its center swirling in a lethargic cyclone around the blades of the ceiling fan. The folks are watching a rerun of *The Rockford Files*. When the program goes to a commercial, Patrick Earl flips to a baseball game, and Mom sticks her nose into a mystery novel. I plop down on the couch and light a cigarette from one of the packs lying around. "I got a call from one of your relatives, Dad."

He doesn't move his eyes from the ball game. "Oh yeah? Who's that?"

"Her name's Kate Davis. I don't know the relation, but she said she saw us on a genealogy chart."

"She here in Phoenix?"

"No. Down South somewhere. Texas, I think. But she's in New York with her husband. Business or something. She wants to have lunch."

He grunts.

"I got a chart of the Lingos in the mail," Mom says. "Did I show it to you, Pat?" She lays the paperback in her lap. "I wonder what I did with it."

My father grunts again and asks who gives a rat's ass.

Mom gets up to go look for the chart, and I snuff out my smoke and follow her. She rummages through the papers and opened mail piled on the built-in desk in the corner of the kitchen. Finally, she pulls out a dog-eared manila envelope. "Here it is. It's from Ronald Lingo in Fort Worth."

She hands me the envelope. Inside are papers and photocopies of newspaper articles, which I set aside unread. There's a chart, a computer-generated graphic of a tree with surnames hanging off the branches. Each name has a reference number that points to lists of names and dates and cities of residence in the enclosed papers. I find us squeezed onto a branch with other names, giving the illusion we're nestled in among the rest of the clan. The chart is obviously not to scale, but the information is accurate.

Patrick Earl Lingo
b. 3/3/27 (Fort Worth, TX)
m. 7/4/55
Phyllis Elaine Sanders
b. 10/16/33 (Rockford, IL)
res. Phoenix, AZ
daughters (1); sons (0)
Leona Camille Lingo
b. 9/15/68 (Phoenix, AZ)
res. New York, NY

Ronald hasn't discovered my alias. I scan the chart until I find the Davis family.

Kathryn Anne Lingo
b. 12/14/51 (Fort Worth, TX)
m. 12/2/72
James Thomas Davis
b. 4/20/51 (Dallas, TX)
res. Dallas, TX
daughters (1); sons (1)
Elizabeth Anne Davis
b. 7/23/74 (Dallas, TX)
m. 5/1/96
Joseph Alexander Gibbs
b. 10/19/72
res. Roja, Latvia
Jake Thomas Davis
b. 5/19/79 (Dallas, TX)
res. Austin, TX

I look at the chart again. Kate's family lies on the other side of the tree from us with a tangle of branches in between. "That's her," I say, pointing.

"Hmm," says Mom as she reads the names through her half glasses. "Well, they seem nice enough." She turns and goes back to the den to return to the more interesting worlds of Jim Rockford and her mystery novel.

Chapter Eleven

I have a favorite spot at the Biltmore Fashion Center, where I can while away time drinking iced coffee and smoking cigarettes. Today the temperature soars over a hundred before nine o'clock, but I'm cool and comfortable in the shade of the mall's covered promenade. Wispy fog from a web of pipes overhead swirls above me, cooling the parched air. My habit is to buy a book at the store around the corner and alternate between browsing its pages and watching the passersby. Today's selection is research more than pleasure reading—an anthology of the year's best short stories. Studying my peers' work sharpens my own saw.

Phoenix has helped my frame of mind. Maybe it's the distance from New York, or maybe it's the sunshine, or maybe it's the rest I've gotten the past couple of days. Maybe it's just taking a holiday from my life. Out here it's easy to fool myself into believing everything will go my way. Nevertheless, I'm anxious about the book, and I need to work through the feeling that my characters and their escapades aren't as exciting as I first believed.

Up until a few months ago, my feelings held absolutely no power over me. Now, thanks to Joel and Dr. Wortham, I have a legion of new taskmasters. But I've fought off the blues before. The only trouble this time is I've let my self-doubt get too good a foothold. I'm equal to this. I'm at least equal to this.

In fact, these past couple of days spent lying by the pool and resting my mind have renewed my will to shove all this negativity aside. Everything I've been dealing with is internal, as far as I can see. It isn't as if some giant crisis is bearing down on me, some financial catastrophe, or an illness. What's going on here is too much introspection, pure and simple. Too much worrying about my shortcomings and feeling lousy about myself instead of charting a new course and getting some momentum going. Powering out of this rut should be as simple as turning my thoughts outward, toward a worthy goal.

And as far as the new book is concerned, I'm in the homestretch, ready to write the last few scenes. All I need is a burst of creative confidence to cross the finish line in a blaze of glory. The minute I have that edge back, I'll finish the manuscript in a few white-hot days.

Phoenix declares an unofficial ban on men's neckties in the summertime because of the heat, so I notice when a guy who's about my age strides toward me in dark slacks, a white shirt, and a tie. Well, I would've noticed this one anyway. He's built like an athlete. Not bulked up, but cut. His thick chestnut hair is combed back neatly from his face, and his wire-rimmed glasses give him a professorial air. His brisk gait slows as he approaches, and then he stops and scans the area. I take a pull on my cigarette and exhale slowly.

His name is Guy Whittaker, and he was a star tennis player at our high school. He checks his watch and looks around again. I catch his eye and he nods a courteous, noncommittal greeting. "You look like you're in a hurry," I say, snuffing out the cigarette.

He smiles. "My wife says I'm always in a hurry, even when I'm not. I'm afraid there's some truth in that."

"Are you meeting her here?"

"Supposed to be. She must've gotten tied up." He glances down at the table. "Is it good?"

"The book? Yes, as a matter of fact, it is."

He comes closer. "May I?"

"Sure."

He picks it up and thumbs through it. "Yeah, I know a few of these authors," he says. He remarks that I've picked a good place to relax, and then he looks around some more for his tardy wife. I can see he doesn't want to be tied up talking with me when she arrives.

Guy was smart in high school too. I remember admiring him from a distance, watching him play tennis. We were in World History together, where he joked with the other students one minute and explained the salient issues of the Stalin years the next. He never noticed me, and there's certainly no hint of recognition now. I never bump into anyone from school when I come home—my visits are infrequent and brief—so it seems a strange coincidence that I came across two old classmates this time. Until I remember Darrell was only in my thoughts.

Guy's wife still hasn't shown. It probably isn't wise to keep him waiting today. He drifts around the fountain, fidgeting with the change in his pocket. I pick up the book and pretend to read. He checks his watch again. "This is probably silly," I say, "but did you by any chance go to Barrett High?"

"I did. You?"

"Class of eighty-seven."

"Me too. How about that? What's your name?"

"Cami Taylor. I believe you were in my World History class. Second period. Let's see, Mr. . . ."

"Stelrick. Jim Stelrick," Guy says enthusiastically. He comes back to the table and shakes my hand. "Guy Whittaker. Forgive me, Cami, but your name doesn't ring a bell. What's your maiden name?"

"Taylor is my maiden name."

"World History, huh. Imagine that. I'm trying to picture the people in the class, but I'm drawing a complete blank."

"Well, it's been ten, no, eleven years. That's a long time."

"Did we have any other classes together?"

"Not that I remember."

"I'm surprised that, well, I'm repeating myself." He gives me a charming, self-effacing smile. "You didn't turn me down for a date, did you? Maybe I blocked out the memory."

I laugh. "No. I don't think that's it. I can't imagine I would've turned you down."

"So, do you live in Phoenix?"

"No. New York. Actually, you're the first person from school I've run into on any of my visits home."

"You don't keep up with anyone?"

"I'm afraid not. Things change. You move on."

"Yeah, I know what you mean. I lost touch with guys I thought would be friends for life. You drift apart over the years. I caught up with a lot of them at the reunion last summer. Were you there?"

"No. Book tour," I lie. "My publisher doesn't give me much latitude when it comes to the promotion they're paying for."

"You're a writer? What do you write?"

"Fiction. I'm still new at it. I've only been published for a few years."

"So if I go around the corner and buy one of your books, will you autograph it?"

"You bet. I'll even include my phone number in case you're ever in New York."

"My wife and I might just take you up on that. We've never been to New York."

"Well, I'd be happy to show you around," I say. I get up and gather my things to go. If Guy married his high school sweetheart, Marilyn, I'm not interested in playing host to her. She's one of the ones who earned a caption in my yearbook. At that moment, Marilyn walks up behind him with an air of proprietorship, sizing me up with critical blue eyes. She's stunning in a well-tailored suit, and her dark hair and fair skin remind me of Joel.

"Sorry to keep you waiting, sweetheart," she says to Guy.

He slips his arm around her. "This is Cami Taylor, honey. She graduated with us. Cami, this is my wife, Marilyn."

"Hello," she says coolly.

"Hi."

"I'm sorry, but I don't remember you, Cami."

"I don't remember you either, Marilyn. Different circles, I suppose. That's the thing about high school—everyone's circles were so small. Who knows what kind of interesting opportunities we missed because we couldn't see past our noses."

"What an unusual thought. Don't you think so, dear?"

"Cami's a writer," Guy blurts. Then he quickly adds, "Yes, it is unusual. Well, Cami, it was nice to meet you, uh, to see you again."

"You too, Guy."

They say good-bye and leave, and I take a lot of satisfaction from the look in Marilyn's eyes. "Stay away from my husband" came through loud and clear. Sometimes just being a threat is enough.

On the drive to canasta club, I call the apartment to check my answering machine. I left Kate a voice mail yesterday, telling her I can have lunch on Friday. She left a message in response saying she'll meet me in the hotel lobby at noon. There's also a message from Christopher, my editor. During my post-Joel writing blitz, I promised him a manuscript by August. This "how goes it" call is his way of reminding me my deadline's approaching.

I pull into the community center where Mom and her friends meet each Wednesday to gossip and play cards. By the time I get out of the car, my dread has blossomed into a full-blown desire to be anywhere but here. I know these women—they've been around all my life. They'll be on me like vultures on roadkill. "So how's your love life, Lee?" and, "How much do they pay for a novel, anyway?" and my personal favorite, "Why hasn't a pretty girl like you found Mr. Right?" No topic is off limits. Mom will keep quiet, looking sideways with pursed lips and pretending not to be interested, all the while hoping she'll pick up a few crumbs she can't wrangle out of me herself.

Inside the dingy beige building, the cinderblock walls echo the scrape of metal chairs across dull linoleum. The first thing that hits me in the face is the stale air, fetid with decades of cigarettes and cheap perfume. Even the coffee from the perpetually flowing Bunn smells as if it's cooked for days.

My mom belongs to a tenured group that lays claim to the best table, halfway between the coffeepot and the ladies' room. She beckons enthusiastically the second I come through the door. "I was about to give up on you," she chides when I reach the table.

"I ran into an old friend from school."

"Well, you're here now. Pull up a chair and visit with us. You know Betty and Doris, but have you met Jenny?" Mom waves her cards at her companions, uncharacteristically animated and loud.

Jenny lifts a heavily jeweled hand. I'm guessing cubic zirconia. Her fake fingernails are two inches long and painted a pearled ivory that matches her bleached hair and glows in startling contrast to her skin, which is the color of old pennies. Both sides of Jenny's throat have purple hickeys, yellow around the edges. She's about ten years younger than the other women, if you don't allow for mileage.

"Nice to meet you," I say.

"Phyllis told us so much about you that I feel like I know you already." Her breath scrapes across her vocal cords like wind on dried reeds.

"That's a mom for you." I look around for an empty chair.

"Sit here, Lee," says Betty. "I promised Bill I'd be home early to help him get the motor home ready."

"Betty and Bill are leaving for Colorado in the morning," explains Mom. "I wish I could get Pat to make a trip. Let's just finish this hand."

"I really don't know how to play," I protest.

"Oh, there's nothing to it," says Betty. "You'll catch on in no time."

"I think I'll get some coffee," I say.

"Come around here behind me, honey," says Betty. "Watch me play out this hand, and you'll get the hang of it."

I stand behind her and watch, exasperated and bored. The truth is I know all about canasta. We played it in the break room at the casino until I was sick of it.

Mom studies her cards as if they hold the keys to life, alternately pressing her lips or raising her eyebrows, depending on how things are going. I notice Betty is holding cards she could play, so I start watching Jenny, Betty's partner, whose furtive glances let me know she's in on it. Jenny draws from the deck, slowly and dramatically. She winks at Betty and lays down all but two of her cards.

"Uh-oh," Mom says, but it's pretty clear she has no idea what's about to happen.

Betty draws a deuce, lays down about a thousand points, and goes out. She laughs and says, "See, there's nothing to it."

"Yes, I see that."

I'm overwhelmed with defensiveness for my mother. She may be goofy, but she's my goof and I don't like anyone else taking advantage. Betty gets up, and I take her chair across from Jenny. "Hope you don't mind playing with a rookie for a partner," I say.

"Not at all, sweetie. It's always fun to teach a kid a few new tricks."

The women wave good-bye to their good friend Betty before they give me a quick rundown on the rules of the game.

"It's your deal, Lee," Mom says. "Remember, eleven cards each."

"Yes, I think I've got that." I take the deck and beat it to pieces with a few shuffling tricks I learned at the River Bend.

"Well," says Jenny. "Your daughter seems to know her way around a deck of cards, Phyllis."

Mom says, "Oh, I didn't think to mention—"

"That we played all the time in college," I interrupt, and Jenny folds her arms under the leathery cleavage bunched in the V of her polyester blouse.

"My daughter read your book, Lee," says Doris in her timid voice. Her gray hair curls under her chin in a Dutch Boy bob, and her enormous glasses make her eyes leap out at me. "I wanted to, but I fall asleep every time I try to read anything. Not that I'm bored. I've just got that, what did you call it, Phyllis?"

"Narcolepsy," says Mom. Mom is the local medical expert, advising and diagnosing from the library of reference books she's accumulated during her tenure as a professional patient.

"Yes, narcolepsy. But Debbie—she's my daughter—Debbie read it, and she said it was very interesting."

"Thank you, Doris."

"Why didn't you use your real name?" she asks.

"Cami Taylor is my real name."

Jenny lights a menthol cigarette about as long and thin as a soda straw. "You know, I lived in New York," she says.

I take the Marlboro Lights from my purse and lay the pack on the table so Mom can help herself.

"That's nice, Jenny," Mom says. "Did you like it?"

"It was a hoot for a while. But after that New York was just another big city, dirty and overcrowded." We all make our melds, and Jenny continues, "I didn't think it was all it was cracked up to be." She pulls an ace from her hand and lays it on her run. Then she adds a six to mine. "Don't you think New York is crowded and dirty, Lee?" she asks, smiling sweetly. "Or should I call you Cami?"

"I don't think it matters what you call me, Jenny, since I'll probably never see you again. As far as New York is concerned, sure, there are plenty of rough neighborhoods. But the Upper West Side, where I live, is lovely. It's quaint actually, and I just love it."

I draw an eight and chew my thumb, feigning concentration. I look over Jenny's runs of aces, queens, and tens. Then I wipe my wet thumb across the face of the queen in my hand, stick it to the back of the eight and discard both of them.

Jenny has enough sense to drop the subject of New York before things really get ugly. We take our turns with me throwing off good cards tucked behind trash and picking up extras to cover my tracks. I make a couple of low-grade melds so my torpedoes won't leave too much of a wake. Mom and Doris go out with about twenty-five hundred points, and Jenny stares at me with daggers in her eyes. I pretty much ruin the game for her the rest of the afternoon. She hardly says good-bye when we leave the community center. She squeals out of the parking lot in her scarred black Grand Am.

"That was fun, honey," Mom says. "I'm glad you played, but I'm sorry we beat you so bad." She nudges Doris and giggles like a schoolgirl.

"I'll have to brush up before I come back next time," I say. Tossing a little self-esteem Mom's way makes me feel better about myself than all of my therapy sessions put together.

Chapter Twelve

I arrive at Newark after ten on Thursday night, and the cab ride into the city takes another two hours because of a wreck on the Jersey side of the tunnel. A Fiat and a small truck are twisted together and shoved onto the median. The flashing red and white lights of the emergency vehicles infuse the scene with urgency and movement, as if the wreck is happening over and over again. The vehicles are such a gnarled mess that I doubt anyone survived. It's a disagreeable note on which to return home.

The apartment should be musty from being closed up, but it isn't, thanks to Estella. All I smell when I walk through the door is the fresh scent of clean. I toss my purse and keys onto the table and drop my luggage in the bedroom. The empty silence and the threat of a sleepless night try to shoulder me back into the corner of despair, but I refuse to brood. I open a bottle of Joel's cab and pour a generous nightcap.

In a fit of brazen courage, I sit down at the computer and open the window on Rachael and Jerome.

"Yes, you are a pair," I say.

I open a blank document and begin to type. This is new composition, and I can afford to take chances. Without regard for form, I write the last scenes that have been in my head, telling the end of their story, as I told it to my folks the other night at the table. When I finish and shut off the monitor, the wine bottle is empty and it's five thirty in the morning. I love the freedom of a writer's life! I don't have to worry about going to the office. I can fall into bed and sleep as long as I wish.

I wake up around eleven, groggy, but rested. Then I remember my lunch date with Kate Davis. I consider calling to say I'll be late and then decide I can make it if I hurry and don't wash my hair. In no time at all, I'm in a taxi headed for Central Park South.

I scan the lobby for the flamboyant, eccentric character I've concocted, but she's nowhere to be found. What I see instead is a very ordinary-looking woman sitting in one of the lobby chairs, reading a *Martha Stewart Living* magazine. She looks up and smiles, stands, and walks toward me. I'm disappointed, and I even wish I'd canceled the lunch and slept in. No big Texas hair. No clunky costume jewelry. No flowing scarves in outrageous colors. No new inspiration for my story.

"Cami?" she asks.

Good memory. That's how I introduced myself on the voice mail I left for her.

"It's nice to meet you, Kate."

"Tom, my husband, thought I was crazy for calling you, but it was just one of those things. And now, here we are." She smiles warmly.

I'm with Tom. This woman may look as banal as Junior League, but she must be a little crazy to have called me out of the blue. "It was kind of unusual," I say.

"Well, I can't deny that."

When it comes to looking wealthy, God is in the details. It's the cut of the clothes and the brand of the handbag, the choice of colors—taupe and cream—and the carriage of the wearer. People who have it all don't feel the need to broadcast their affluence. If anything, they downplay it. Kate wears that look from the crown of her perfectly cut gray hair to the toes of her Cole Haans. Whereas I'm an impostor, she's a bona fide member of the club, and I feel underdressed in my jeans, cotton blouse, and sandals.

"So, do you have a favorite lunch spot to take me to?" she asks. "I hoped you would."

"Have you been to Serendipity?"

"No, but the name sounds perfect for our first lunch together."

First and last, but okay. We walk outside into the muggy heat, and the doorman tips his hat.

"Can I get you a cab, Mrs. Davis?"

"Yes. Thank you, Philip."

Philip smiles as if hailing a taxi for us will just make his day. He walks toward one of the waiting cabs, but the driver seems to have remembered urgent business elsewhere and tries to nose the vehicle away from the curb into the bumper-to-bumper traffic. This is the time of day when all the cabbies want airport fares instead of short hauls around Midtown. But Philip is too quick for this one, and before the guy can pull away, he opens the front door and dresses him down.

"This is a never-ending battle," Kate says wearily. She gives the doorman a folded bill, and we get in the cab for our ride a few blocks up the street. On the way, I take the genealogy chart out of my purse and ask if it's the same one she has.

"Oh, you have it! Yes, this is the one."

"Looks like we're distant cousins, at best."

"Let's see." She takes it and looks it over. "I'm no expert at this, but I think your father and I are fifth cousins."

"Not quite six degrees of separation, but close," I say.

"What? Oh yes, well, I guess that's true."

I lean toward the lilt of that Southern accent, just as I did with Willie, and keep the conversation going to give my ear a chance to memorize the soft consonants and lazy vowels. I've already decided that my next novel will be set in the Deep South so I can immerse myself in the rich flavors of that region.

The cab pulls to the curb, and we get out. Kate insists on paying the driver, and I notice she gives him a twenty. No change.

"What a fun place!" she says when we walk into Serendipity.

The head waiter, Bernie, greets me enthusiastically. "Ms. Taylor! Good to see you!"

"Hi, Bernie. Is there much of a wait?"

"For you and your friend, I'll make room." He hurries away to find us a table.

Kate browses the shelves of bric-a-brac while Bernie finds a place for us. Bernie is older than the rest of the staff. I first met him when he was maître d' at a book launch party Christopher threw for *Double Down Blues*. He's a short, sinewy man and a fantastic character actor, but his looks limit him to an unfortunately small number of roles. Serendipity pays the rent when Broadway won't, which is most of the time. Joel was good about pushing Bernie to his network, and he's always treated me like a queen because of it. But his presence here tells me the work has dried up. I'm sure he's dying to ask about Joel, but he's smart enough not to. I doubt Joel's been in. Serendipity was always my idea.

Finally, Bernie returns and escorts us to the back of the tiny café, which is crammed with Tiffany lamps and funky art. The waiters, young and energetic, weave their way through crowded tables, toting trays laden with sandwiches, salads, and goblets of towering ice cream bathed in decadent sauces.

When we're seated, Kate says, "I noticed the host called you Ms. Taylor. Did you marry recently?"

"No, I changed my name when I sold my first novel. The phone book listing is for emergencies, in case my parents' friends or family are looking for me."

"Your first novel. How exciting!"

"Probably not as much as you think. I spend a lot of time pounding away at a keyboard."

We order sandwiches and iced tea. "It's none of my business," she says, "but I'm curious. Why did you change your name? Please say if I'm being too nosy."

"I couldn't quite imagine Leona Camille Lingo on a book jacket, so I changed it," I lie.

"Cami from Camille."

"That's right."

"Where'd you get Taylor?"

"There's a bookstore chain called Taylor's. At least, there used to be."

"I love it!"

I give her a genuine smile.

"So tell me about the book."

"Well, it's a bestseller."

"Oh, Cami. I'm so impressed. Really, really impressed."

"Thanks. It was a surprise. I was just hoping to see the work in print, you know? I have to say, since then, pretty much anything seems possible."

"So what's next?"

"I'm writing a second book."

"And besides that?"

"Actually, I'm trying to figure that out."

Our food arrives, and she makes a fuss over how good the sandwiches are. She offers me some of hers and wants to try mine. Her lack of pretension is appealing. I suspect she's a socialite, but her demeanor doesn't fit the stereotype.

"What brings you and Tom to New York?" I ask.

"Advertising. Tom, that is. I'm just along for the ride. I hope he can meet you before we leave. I wish you could've met my son, Jake. He was up over the weekend, but he went back home." She winks. "Too much togetherness with Mom and Dad."

"You must enjoy the city, to spend so much time here."

"Oh, of course. Who doesn't love New York? Tom has to be up here so much that I try to come with him as much as I can. He gets tired of traveling alone."

"Do you work in Dallas?"

"Volunteer work, but they can make do without me for a week or two."

After lunch, Kate asks if I have time to stroll. "It's so much more fun to window-shop with a friend," she says.

"Sure."

Out on the street, we come to a small bookstore.

"Do you think they have your novel?" she asks.

"I imagine so."

"Lead the way."

I take her to the literature section, which I'm proud to see has half a dozen copies of *Blues*, front side out. I pull one from the shelf and hand it to her. "Here you go."

She examines the cover, which is very simple: a partial shot of a jack and an ace on the green background of a gaming table. The title and my name appear in plain white letters to the right of the cards. Kate opens the flap to the author blurb. "'Ms. Taylor lives and works in New York City,'" she reads. "Not much information there. What does double down mean?"

"It's a blackjack term. If your cards total ten or eleven, you might want to double your bet. But you only get one more card, so you'd better be willing to lose it all."

"Sounds like you know a lot about the game."

"I dealt blackjack in a casino while I wrote it."

"I see. Well, I can't wait to see what the story is about, besides cards."

She takes an expensive-looking fountain pen from her purse, and I sign my name on the title page. Some people are pissed that I don't write personalized notes, as if we're besties, but Kate seems okay with it. She takes the book to the checkout, and the clerk tries to charge extra because it's a signed copy.

"That's more than the price on the sticker," I say.

"Listen, lady," says the clerk, "signed copies cost more. Take it or leave it."

I feel my blood pressure shoot up like Old Faithful, and I say, not quite yelling, but almost, "You listen to me, asshole. She's not paying extra, and she's not leaving the book. Ring it up at the price that's marked."

"Nice," he says. He looks past us. "Who's next?"

"It's okay," Kate says. "Let's just put this one back and get another copy."

"No way! I'm not *giving* them a free autograph. Forget it. Get the manager!" I bark at the kid.

He completely ignores me.

"Really, Cami," Kate says. "It isn't worth it. It's just a misunderstanding."

"This is New York, Kate. People here will walk all over you if you let them."

The manager must've heard the commotion because he appears out of nowhere and ushers us to the side, away from the other customers. "What's the problem?" he asks.

"This is *my* book." I wave the hardback in his face. "I signed it just now, and when my friend tried to pay for it, that idiot running the register jacked up the price."

He takes the book from me. "You're Cami Taylor?"

"That's right."

The manager hands the book to Kate. "No charge," he says.

"Please, I'm happy to pay."

"No, ma'am. I'm sorry for the misunderstanding. It's on the house."

Kate hesitates.

"I insist," he says.

"Thank you," says Kate.

She gets quiet after we leave the store. No doubt my fit over the book offended her. Well, too bad. That's the way things work around here. If she plans to spend time in New York, she might as well wise up and get used to it.

We walk a few blocks in silence. Finally, without much enthusiasm, she says, "Tom wanted to meet you. We were thinking about going to a show tonight. Maybe you could join us if there's something playing that you haven't seen."

"Isn't this your last night in New York? Don't you want to be alone?"

"We get plenty of time alone these days, especially with the kids out of the house. Besides, Tom's worn-out. It'd do him good to get his mind off work for a while."

"Well, there's a good comedy at the Promenade. The Prom's off the beaten path, but they always put on good productions."

"When we get back to the hotel, we'll check with the concierge." She brightens. "Oh, look, there's Bloomingdale's. Do you mind if I run in while we're here? I saw a jewelry box I want to pick up for Anne. Maybe I can get your opinion on it. Anne's a few years younger than you, but I think you have similar taste. She'd like what you're wearing today."

"She's in Latvia? I saw it on the genealogy chart."

"She and Joe are teaching there. And translating."

We cross the street to Bloomingdale's and push through the old revolving doors.

"Listen, Kate, I probably shouldn't have made such a scene back there at the bookstore, but I couldn't stand watching that kid get away with that attitude. It just wasn't right."

"The manager made up for it, though, don't you think? He was very kind to give me the book."

"Sure. Of course. The guy was a sweetheart."

Kate stops and browses the sunglasses. She tries on a pair and looks at me through the mirror. "I'm not upset, Cami," she says. "The boy made an honest mistake, but his attitude could've been a lot better. What do you think of these?"

"They're cute."

"I think I'll get them." She takes out her pocketbook.

"That attitude, that's what I'm talking about," I go on, justifying myself. "New York people are different from people down South, especially the ones who have to hustle to get by, like that cabbie who took us to Serendipity. It was nice of you to give him a big tip, but I'm not really sure he deserved it. Or even appreciated it. He was just gonna take off and leave us standing at the curb."

She nods and smiles. "He was indeed."

"Well, so, that's the thing."

The associate finally makes her way around to us, and Kate hands her a credit card. When the girl moves to the register, Kate says, "I'm sorry, what are you saying?"

"Maybe it's better to save the big tip for the guy who deserves it," I say, stupidly. Why have I gone into all this?

She smiles, as if she's indulging a child, and I feel like an idiot.

"I appreciate your counsel, Cami, but what makes you think that was a big tip?"

Huh? It was a six-dollar fare. "Look, never mind," I say. "I don't even know why I brought it up."

"You know what I think?"

"No, Kate, what do you think?"

"I think people are the same no matter where you go. And, frankly, a little undeserved kindness goes a long way toward softening up the hard ones."

"I don't know about that. I'm pretty sure they'll take advantage of you every chance they get."

"That's the price you have to pay," Kate says. "You know, you should come to Dallas. Let me return the favor and show you around town. You can stay with Tom and me. Now that the kids are gone, we have all kinds of room."

"That's very nice of you."

She looks at me expectantly. "I'm serious. We'd love to have you."

"That's so nice," I repeat. "I'm kinda in the middle of working with my editor on the manuscript right now, but maybe I can take a rain check?"

"Consider it an open invitation. Now, I've managed to get turned around. Which way to the jewelry?"

"This way," I say, pointing. "Come on, I'll take you there."

Chapter Thirteen

Victoria.

Victoria is the name of the white feline in the cast of *Cats* whose sensual ballet opens the show. Victoria, sans costume, sits next to Joel on the third row. I can't remember the dancer's name, but I recognize her from rehearsals. Her name is beside the point anyway. My own tête-à-tête with Willie does absolutely nothing to mollify the feeling that I'm being betrayed. I wish I'd remembered that the Promenade is Joel's favorite theater before I let my subconscious drag us here.

I stand in the aisle with Kate and Tom, waiting for a plug of people ahead of us to loosen and disperse to their seats. I can't take my eyes off Joel. He leans over and whispers in Victoria's ear, his mouth brushing her cheek. I remember sitting where she sits. I remember our closeness, our rising desire, our eagerness to get back to my apartment. I remember after that too.

"Cami, this is us. Cami?"

I pull my gaze from Joel and look at Tom, who stands in front of me with his arm extended toward a row of seats. Bespectacled and balding, tall, lanky Tom, whom I saw the night I met Willie in the lobby of the Essex House. He's hardly said a word tonight and seems tired and distracted.

"Are you okay?" he asks.

I nod and sidle into the row to take my seat, which is perfectly situated to afford an unobstructed view of Joel. I slouch down to brood, while Tom and Kate pore over their programs. The only razor-thin silver lining is that Joel hasn't seen me.

The house lights dim, and the actors step onstage to a round of applause. I spend the first act planning my escape at intermission. I lean over and tell Tom I have to make a phone call. Then, when the curtain closes, I practically dive over them into the aisle to get out of there before the house lights come up.

Outside, I stand at the side of the theater entrance in the sultry night air and light a cigarette. A young guy emerges from the shadows and ambles toward me. "Got a spare smoke, sister?"

From the sight of him, he's about college age and living on the streets. His pants and tee shirt are soiled to the same dull gray as the asphalt, and his hair, which is twisted into dreadlocks, looks dry and dusty. An immature beard clings to his cheeks and chin. I knock a cigarette out of the pack and hand him the box of matches.

"How 'bout one for the lady?" he asks. He hooks one arm, and a girl even filthier than he steps out of the darkness, shuffling toward us along the wall. Stringy black hair obscures her down-turned face. When she steps into the light from the bright marquee and reaches for the cigarette, I see needle wounds on the inside of her wrist. She takes it without looking up at me. She smells as pungent as vinegar.

We smoke together in silence, producing a cloud that hangs in the still air. The sidewalk in front of the Promenade's entrance fills with people holding drinks in plastic cups, talking and laughing and smoking. Some are formal, as I am in my fitted black dress. Others less so. A few tourists wear blue jeans and white athletic shoes, as if they're attending a dollar movie back home instead of a live Broadway performance.

"How's the show?" the young guy asks.

"All right, I guess. If you want to know the truth, I haven't paid that much attention."

"Why's that?" He meets my eye, alert and interested.

"My ex is in there with a date. We broke it off, but still . . ."

". . . it's still a drag," he finishes.

"Yeah." I glance at his girlfriend, who blows thick jets of smoke at the sidewalk through that oily black curtain.

"Junkie," he says, watching me.

"So I see. What are you doing?"

"Just hanging out." He flicks his ashes away.

"You been in the city long?"

He nods, drawing deeply on the last inch of tobacco.

"Have you been on the street long?" I ask.

"A while. I was screwing around at NYU and my folks cut me off." He waves his hand dismissively. "I can't really blame 'em, but I didn't wanna go back home either. So"—he shrugs—"here I am."

"What was your major?"

"History. Man, I love history. I wanna teach it, you know?" He starts to take another drag but sees it's burned down to the filter. He drops it and grinds it under the heel of his Converse.

"Another?" I offer the pack. He takes two and hands one to the girl. The theater lights dim and flare, flashing the five-minute warning. I'm a strict disciple of the "never give money to the homeless" rule, but this guy tugs at me. I want to help him. "Could you use some cash?" I ask.

"I wouldn't turn it down."

I fish two twenties from my purse and hand them to him. The junkie takes a step forward, interested.

The tail of the crowd withdraws into the building. "I better get back," I say. "Good luck."

"Thanks again for the money. And the cigs."

I leave them and walk toward the door.

"Hey!" he calls.

"Yes?" I answer, turning.

"That guy's an idiot!"

I almost ask what guy before I realize he's talking about Joel.

◆ ◆ ◆

Kate and Tom stand to let me in the row. "Is everything all right?" she asks.

"Sure. I just grabbed a cigarette before coming back in."

I decide it's no big thing if Joel sees me. I'm making too much of it anyway. I focus my attention on the show, but now I'm hopelessly behind in the story and can only appreciate the one-liners. So instead of watching, I spend the time mulling over my book.

When the curtain falls, Tom turns to me. "Well done. I enjoyed that."

"Yes," I agree. "It was great."

People pack the aisle, blocking our exit. I glance toward the front, and Joel immediately makes eye contact. He smiles weakly, and I put on my best game face. He and Victoria manage to make it almost to our row before we're out in the aisle, thanks to an old lady who's glued to the floor.

"Hi," I say, as we step out in front of them.

"Hi."

We get to the lobby and the crowd thins. It would be too weird to leave without saying something, so I stop and introduce Kate and Tom, my cousins from Texas. Joel introduces himself and Victoria, whose real name is Linda Harris.

"You never mentioned having family in Texas," Joel says to me, a little accusingly.

"I didn't know."

"I stumbled across Cami by accident," says Kate. "It was just a fluke, really."

"Must've been," Joel says, still looking at me. "Did you get that tan in Texas?"

"No. I went out to Arizona for a few days, to visit my parents."

"Oh."

We stand there in silence that threatens to become awkward, with Joel looking betrayed, and like he's trying to figure out what's going on with me.

"So how's the show?" I ask. "Your show, I mean."

"It's fine," he says.

"You caught us playing hooky tonight," Linda says.

I remember playing hooky, long before you, sweetheart. I glance at Joel, and he looks away. I turn to Kate and Tom. "Have you seen *Cats*?"

"We have," says Kate, "and we loved it."

"Linda's in the cast," I say. "White costume. She has a solo in the first act."

"Oh, yes. Beautiful performance," Kate says, as if she just saw the show yesterday and Linda's performance was the highlight. I wonder if this is one of her kindnesses.

"Thank you," says Linda.

We exchange a few more pleasantries and take our leave. Joel and Linda disappear into the night as soon as we reach the sidewalk.

"Why don't we walk a while?" says Tom, looking at all the people waiting for cabs. "I could use the exercise." I'm glad for a chance to shed some tension and readily agree. Kate says she can make it a few blocks in her heels.

My intermission buddy calls to me from the shadow of the building, "Hey, sister! How 'bout one more smoke before you go?" His girlfriend sits with her back against the brick wall and her head between her knees, but she rouses herself and stands when I start toward them.

I give him the pack. "Keep it," I say.

When I join Kate and Tom again, she asks, "Is that someone you know?"

"No. Just a dropout having a rough go of it."

They nod with solemn faces, and I remember their son is about this guy's age. No doubt the sight of him would make any decent parent sad. After we make it half a block, Kate stops abruptly. "Wait. Wait here just a minute," she says. She turns and walks back to the theater so quickly that she's practically trotting.

"What's this?" I say, to no one in particular.

Kate goes directly to the homeless guy and starts talking to him ninety to nothing. I move toward them, trying to get within earshot. Suddenly the junkie hisses and swipes at Kate like an animal. Her greasy hair swings back, and I'm startled by the anger in her black eyes.

"No!" Kate says so sharply that the rebuke echoes off the wall like a rifle report. A few theater goers waiting for cabs stop chatting and look around. The junkie slinks back to the shadowy wall to sulk. Then Kate takes the guy's hands in hers. She keeps talking, and he listens intently, his gaze never straying from her face. Soon tears stream down his cheeks.

I turn to Tom, who's watching with focused concentration, his lips drawn into tight little crescents. I start to move closer still, but he grasps my arm. "Not now," he says.

The boy lowers his face, and his shoulders heave. His knees bend, and for a minute I think he's going to collapse. But Kate wraps her arms around him, supporting him as if he were a child, lice and all. It's a stunning image: A middle-aged woman in evening wear, cradling a derelict, her face hidden by dreadlocks as she speaks into his ear. Definitely something you don't see every day, even in New York. I close my mouth, which at some point has fallen open.

Kate steps back and holds him at arm's length, grasping his shoulders. Then she lets him go and pulls a small card from her purse. She hands it to him. I see his mouth form the words, Thank you. She hugs him one more time and sends him on his way, as if he were her own freshly scrubbed offspring going out into the world.

"What was that?" I ask when she comes back to us. She dabs at her wet eyes with a tissue and walks past us, letting my question fall to the sidewalk, unanswered. I glance back at the guy, who's slumped against the wall, staring at the card in his hand. We hail a cab two blocks down.

"We can get a bite to eat if you want," Tom offers.

"I'm fine," I say. "It's up to you."

"It's a little late for me," says Kate, "but maybe we could come inside for a few minutes when we drop you off at your apartment, if you don't mind."

"Sure, of course," I say.

The cab drops us at my building, and after we trudge up the stairs, I usher them inside. "Would you like something to drink?" I ask. "A glass of wine?"

"Cami, you're a godsend," says Tom.

"Just water for me," says Kate.

I direct Tom to the sofa and give him the remote control. He takes off his jacket and loosens his tie before settling into the deep cushions and turning on the news. "I'm getting too old for these early mornings and late nights," he says.

Kate goes behind him and bends down to kiss him on the cheek. "It's been a long week, honey. Relax for a few minutes."

"Is Pellegrino okay?" I ask, taking a bottle from the fridge.

"Perfect," she says. "From the bottle's fine." She sits at the kitchen table and slips off her shoes. "I have to get out of these pumps for a minute."

"Make yourself at home." I open a bottle of cab and take a generous glass to Tom before pouring another for myself.

"You've done a lot with this space, Cami."

"Thanks. Will it bother you if I smoke?"

She barely hesitates before saying, "No, go ahead." After all, it is my house.

I light up. "So what was the deal with the guy at the theater?"

"I was going to ask you the same thing."

"What did you say to him?"

"I just let him know he isn't as alone as he feels."

"That was nice, Kate."

"He broke my heart," she says.

"It makes me want to slap his parents for cutting him off."

"Yes," she says. "That's heartbreaking too. I agree that parents' love needs to be bigger than that. Hey, speaking of family, I have an idea. The Lingo reunion is in a few weeks, and I was thinking about how much everyone would love to meet you. Think you might like to come? You could stay with us."

A family reunion sounds like a great crucible to heat up a big, sprawling Southern novel, and I can't think of one good reason not to go.

"Maybe," I say, taking a last drag on my cigarette. "Yes, I think that'll work."

"Here." She takes a card from her purse, ivory linen, with her name and a phone number embossed in black. "If you come a few days early, we'll show you around town. But anytime is okay. We'll be happy to pick you up at the airport. And don't worry about putting us out. We have plenty of room."

"Thanks, Kate."

"It's our pleasure."

She smiles, and I wonder why she looks so satisfied.

Chapter Fourteen

I 'm about to be late for my appointment with Dr. Wortham because I can't get off the phone with Christopher.

"I could've used that manuscript two weeks ago," he says emphatically.

"But my deadline's still a week away. What promises did you make to your people?"

"That you'd deliver. On time." His voice has an edge that says I have to back off. I know from experience that his face is growing crimson.

"I always deliver, Chris. I have a complete manuscript, but it still needs work."

"I want to see it now, Cami. There isn't another editor in town who doesn't at least get a peek at a work in progress. I'm completely in the dark here, and I look like a fool."

It's premature to let the novel see the light of day. I know this, but my back's against the wall. "You know you're asking me to serve up a half-baked cake."

"Half-baked?"

"Well, not quite done then. I just need this final week of revision. One last round."

"It's time you started trusting me, Cami. Do you really think I'll ever lose confidence in you?"

That's exactly what I think, but I don't tell him that.

"Don't you have more faith in me than that?" he says.

"Look, okay. I'll give it to you."

"I'll send a courier this afternoon."

"I'll be out until three. So make it after that."

"You got it. Thanks, kiddo."

I don't like it, but it's done. It'll take too long to walk to Dr. Wortham's, so I go around the corner to Broadway and hail a cab.

The doctor got a perm while I was flying solo. Her new coif is a textured style that's a lot wilder than she is. Now she needs new frames to complete the look.

"How've you been?" she asks as we sit down.

"Good. Well, better lately. I went to visit my parents in Phoenix."

"How'd that go?"

"As expected. They haven't changed much. My dad's taken up dominoes, so that's new. Everything else is pretty much the same."

"What's been happening?" she asks, turning on the recorder and picking up her pen and notepad.

"Right now I'm under the gun on my manuscript, but I'll get it done."

"Good. Your attitude seems to be great."

"Yes, well, I'm working on it."

"Is there anything in particular you'd like to talk about today?"

"I had a one-night stand."

"Okay."

What was I going to tell her? All the emotions I felt after Willie seem far away now, and I'm not too interested in dredging them up again. I'm past him. Way past.

"Was it your first time having sex with a stranger?" Dr. Wortham asks.

I'm a little shocked. I hadn't quite thought of Willie as a stranger, though of course he was. Is. And I'm not too keen to lead today's discussion with the long list of nobodies who preceded him. "Well, you know, when I was in New Mexico, I was—"

"Promiscuous?"

This is different. Dr. Wortham never butts in, but her tone is inoffensive, as if she were asking my preference in salad dressing.

"I got around a bit."

"I'm not judging you, Cami. I'm only interested in how you feel about it."

"The other night I felt like offing myself. But I got past it, and I really don't want to relive those feelings today."

"No. I don't want you to either. It was intense, though? The aftermath?"

"A little."

"How does that compare with your feelings when you were in New Mexico, working at the casino? How did you feel after sex back then?"

"It was a long time ago, and I don't really remember." The truth is I only remember how Jackie felt. I took a break from myself while I was writing her.

"I see. How do your expectations now compare with your expectations then? In New Mexico?"

"What do you mean?"

"What do you expect from a man you've had sex with? Or are having sex with?"

"Nothing."

This is a lie, of course. I'd worked up a whole fantasy with Willie, imagining us on the street together, going to dinners and shows. Walking the city. Turning heads. I'd imagined being Rum Tum Tugger's squeeze. I never would've expected, or even wanted, anything close to that with the guys who blew through the casino.

"Maybe we should talk about what you're looking for in a relationship," she says, "if you're looking for a relationship at all."

"Well, of course I want a relationship. I don't want to spend the rest of my life alone."

"I see. And what does that mean? To have a relationship?"

"The usual stuff."

"What stuff?"

"I don't know. The *usual*. Spending time together. Doing all the things couples do."

"What things?"

"Going out. Hanging out. Staying in. Everything."

"What about making each other happy?"

"That's the whole point."

"What about taking care of each other when one of you is sick or upset?"

"Sure. Of course. That too."

"What about helping each other reach goals? Achieve dreams?"

Oh, I see where she's headed. Even so, I nod.

"Even if it's inconvenient?"

"Well, as long as it isn't *too* inconvenient," I say with a laugh because I'm so droll.

"Relationships, deeply committed relationships, are they a joke to you, Cami?"

"What happens between two people is never a joke," I say, "but maybe codependent relationships just aren't really my thing."

"I read your novel again last weekend. I was thinking about Jackie. Your character."

"What about her?"

"Jackie and her double down blues."

I don't care for the doctor's tone. Not one bit.

Dr. Wortham continues, "Jackie wasn't just a dealer. She was a gambler too. Always laying it all on the line, hoping for the big payoff."

"Jackie didn't believe in the big payoff."

"It's a good thing, because there wasn't any payoff at all, was there? Hence, the blues."

I look at her through narrowed eyes.

"Jackie never gave out of love," Dr. Wortham says. "She never gave for the pure joy that giving brings. Why would she? The men she met in the casino certainly didn't deserve her devotion. But that friend of hers, the other dealer . . ."

"Hank," I say.

"Yes, Hank. The first time I read the book, I thought that relationship might go somewhere. Jackie seemed to care for Hank, and he was in love with her."

"He was."

"Everyone fell in love with Jackie, didn't they?"

"That's the way I wrote her."

"But Jackie didn't fall for anyone. She was only out for herself, which was odd because she didn't seem to like herself very much. Not very much at all." Dr. Wortham takes off her glasses and regards me as if I'm a magician who's just been uncloaked. "Perhaps you didn't characterize her entirely as you intended."

I frown at her attempt to reduce my highly original novel to an admission of my own selfishness and self-loathing. "I'm not Jackie," I say.

"There's a book," she continues, as if I've said nothing. "It was published years ago, but you can find it in any bookstore. It's a children's story with a very grown-up message. *The Giving Tree* by Shel Silverstein. I want you to buy a copy and read it. I think it will clarify what I'm talking about."

"I'm not Jackie," I repeat. "You're acting as if I never give anything to anyone, and that simply isn't true. I gave forty dollars to a homeless guy just the other night." My forty bucks paled in comparison to what Kate gave him with a hug and a few words. What did she say to that guy?

"Why did you give him the money?"

"He needed it, and I had it. It's that simple."

"Every homeless person on the streets of New York needs money. Why him?"

"He was young. He wasn't all strung out from the life. He looked like he still had a chance."

"A chance for what?"

"You know, to get back in the mainstream. Back on his feet."

She scribbles on her notepad. "So your money might not have been wasted?"

What is this? She's never this combative. It's as if she's affecting a new psyche style to go with her new do. "Well, I didn't think he was going to blow it getting high, if that's what you mean. What are you getting at?"

She looks up. "Why are you so defensive?"

"Because you're attacking me. You're projecting all this selfish crap onto me, and you don't know what you're talking about." I force my fingers to release the arms of the chair.

"Okay. I don't know what I'm talking about. I think we've had enough for today." She clicks off the recorder.

"That's it?"

"Yes. I believe so."

"Well, thanks for the crucifixion. Once again, I feel so much better."

"Enlightenment doesn't always bring warm, fuzzy feelings at first," she says. "There's something we need to take care of, and I've been remiss not to insist before now."

"What's that?"

"Your last physical was cursory at best. There was no blood work at all. We need a baseline, a complete profile, in case we get into the area of medication."

"We haven't discussed medication. Why are you bringing it up now?"

"This is routine with all my patients. I wouldn't feel comfortable issuing you a prescription if you needed it. Wouldn't you like to rule out any physical issues?"

She has a point, I decide, even though I'm still irritated about our session.

"Virginia has a packet of forms. See her on your way out."

♦ ♦ ♦

The next morning, while I'm brushing my teeth, I vomit into the sink.

"What's this about?" I ask my reflection.

The phone rings, and I rinse my mouth quickly and answer it. "Yes?"

"Good morning, Ms. Second Bestseller!" Christopher pipes enthusiastically.

"You liked it, then? I told you it's still rough."

"I love it. I didn't get any sleep last night because of it. Oh, you have some work to do, but actually I thought it was in pretty good shape. Don't wreck the pace during the revision. Go easy."

I bask in the glow of his praise. It's the crème de la crème of the writing life to hear someone you respect say, "Oh, I just love your work!" or, "Your prose is beautiful!" and most especially, "Your story moved me." I shamelessly beg for more. "Well, what did you think of the story arc?"

"It's original, and your readers are going to love it. Look at my suggestions, and we'll go for it as soon as you send the final draft. We can have it on the bookstands for the holidays."

"That soon?"

"I told you timing's everything. There's a gap we can slide you into that'll make a tremendous difference in first-run sales. I'll send the edits this afternoon. Will you be home?"

"Sounds like I'll have to be."

"That's my girl. We're going to make a lot of money on this book. I think you're going to be pleasantly surprised at the advance when we sit down with a contract, which by the way, should be sometime next week."

"I'll wait for your call."

My mood soars. I throw on some shorts and a tee shirt and hit the street for a run, taking a route up Broadway where I can relish my West Side neighborhood. I run for many blocks, past all kinds of people. My neighborhood is as diverse as any on the planet, and here I am in the middle of it, in the middle of everything I've ever wanted.

I push my body hard to get an extra dose of endorphins, and then I walk a long cooldown to a park north of Ninety-Third, where I buy two bottles of water from a sidewalk vendor. I like the feel of my body after a run—I'm as light and agile as a gazelle. My cotton shorts cling to my hips, and my sleeveless top blouses over them, letting the heat dissipate. Too tight clothes are a thing of the past. Now, unbelievably, I'm lean and cut.

On the walk home, when I've dried out, I step into a bookshop and ask about *The Giving Tree*.

"Oh yes, Shel Silverstein," the elderly clerk says.

"That's it."

"I'm sure we have a copy back here. Have you read it before?"

"No. It was recommended to me."

"Well, it's a beautiful parable."

She finds the slim hardback, and a few minutes later, I'm reading it on a sidewalk bench. The story is a simple one: The tree gives, and the boy takes. In the end, the boy, now a man, comes back to her, but I can't get past the way he used her. Who in her right mind would want to be like the tree, unrequited and unappreciated? I close the book and toss it into the wastebasket.

Over the next week, I arrange my days into a routine that not only feeds my creativity but is cheerier than the exhausting stretch of writing I did after the breakup. I begin each morning with yoga to get the juices flowing, and then I run. After a cooldown and plenty of water, I get a strong coffee, a muffin, and a newspaper from the café on my block and relax in a pleasant sidewalk sitting area. We regulars nod to one another with the reserved civility of veteran New Yorkers. Then I return to the apartment and work the rest of the morning.

I take naps and wake up refreshed enough to get in four or five hours of steady work in the late afternoons. I cook all my favorite foods—comfort foods like chicken with rice, green chili enchiladas, and tortilla soup, and I watch late night television and eat the leftovers.

I look forward to visiting the Davis family in Dallas and going to their reunion, sure the trip will open a wellspring of ideas and images for my next novel. I'm excited, even though I don't like staying in other people's homes. I much prefer hotel rooms, where I can lounge around in threadbare sweats and pay people to wait on me. But for the sake of satisfying my creative curiosity, I'll make an exception.

I cancel my next few appointments with Dr. Wortham. Who needs the aggravation? I would blow off the appointment with Dr. Kuri too, except on several mornings I'm as nauseous as a rookie sailor. There are a couple of other things that bother me too. When I take a break from my birth control pills, I hardly spot, and on some mornings, after my run, I have to rest a long time to get my energy back. Besides that, my body *feels* different in a way I can't quite put my finger on.

I was so bummed after Joel that I screwed up the Tri-Cyclen schedule, and I wonder if that carelessness is coming back to bite me. It would be easy to run down to the drugstore and get a pregnancy test, but the last thing I need is juggling a significant emotional event with a publishing deadline. I make my appointment with Dr. Kuri for the day before I leave for Texas. I'll have the manuscript to Chris by then, and I'll be in a better frame of mind to handle any bad news that's headed my way.

Chapter Fifteen

My gyno, Dr. Kuri, has an accent that's as English as high tea, and I enjoy listening to him talk, even when I'm in the stirrups.

"I see no evidence of enlargement of the uterus," he says. "You thought you might be a couple of months along?"

"Not quite."

"I see. Well, we'll know for certain very shortly."

"I'm not prepared to have a baby, Dr. Kuri."

"You may sit up now, Ms. Taylor. There could be many reasons for the symptoms you describe." He pulls off his latex gloves and picks up my file. "I'm concerned about this weight loss. Eight pounds since your last visit. Prior to that you were consistent within a pound or two. It isn't a great deal of weight, but you aren't a large woman to begin with."

"I've had some issues lately."

"Oh."

He doesn't ask about my issues, and he seems to be avoiding eye contact. Dr. Wortham probably called and gave him the lowdown on me—her version of it anyway. Would she have done that?

"You could be anemic," he says, "or it could be stress." He gently probes my neck and throat and then massages the hollows of my armpits and down my arms.

"What are you doing?"

"Checking your lymph glands."

"I don't remember you ever doing that before."

"We're going deeper this time."

He feels me up one side and down the other, while I sit with the Big A looming large. I have enough of my parents' values to feel crappy about snuffing out a life growing inside me. Still, I'm not about to have a baby.

"If it comes to it, Dr. Kuri, can you help me terminate the pregnancy?"

He glances up. "Let's wait and see what the test says."

For an instant I imagine I see disapproval in his eyes, as if I'm one more sorry case in a long line of sorry cases. But it's just a flash, and then he's 100 percent dispassionate professional again.

He checks my ears and my eyes. He asks me to open my mouth and spends a long time poking around my gums and under my tongue. I've never enjoyed so much of my physician's time.

"Have you had any soreness in your mouth?" he asks.

"No."

"Any ulcers? Any bleeding when you brush your teeth?"

"No. Why do you ask?"

"Sharon, would you see if they've done that test? Get them on it if they haven't."

"Are you looking for something in particular?"

He smiles. "Just trying to turn over every stone. You can get dressed now."

He leaves the room, and I put on my clothes and pace in a jitter of nervous energy. I don't think the doctor believes I'm pregnant, which I find both encouraging and discomforting. Something's going on, and I don't like not knowing what. To pass the time, I read and reread the charts and pamphlets about everything from childbirth to syphilis. I might as well be trying to read the lines in the wallpaper.

Finally, Dr. Kuri opens the door. "Negative," he says brightly.

I blow out a long breath. "So what's going on with me?"

"It could be any number of things. We'll know more when we get the blood work back. Until then, spend some time relaxing, doing things you enjoy. Try to keep your stress to a minimum and see if that helps."

"All right."

"The lab work should come back early next week. I'll call you."

Chapter Sixteen

*I*t's well after dark when the plane touches down in Dallas, and I expect to spend another hour waiting for my bag, then schlepping it to the rental car lot. Before I left New York, I printed an airport layout map from the internet. From the looks of it, DFW Airport is spread over Hell's Half Acre.

I'm surprised to recognize Kate and Tom among the crowd of people meeting friends and family at the gate.

"I hope you don't mind, but we thought you might have trouble finding our street in the dark," Kate says. "So here we are."

"Of course I don't mind. Thanks."

Tom hugs me and then reaches for my carry-on. He seems much more rested than the last time I saw him. "How are you, Cami?" he asks.

"I'm good. You?"

"Can't complain. You sure you're ready for this shindig tomorrow?"

Kate elbows him. "You hush, bub. Don't let him fool you, Cami. He'll be the first one out of bed in the morning." She hooks her arm in mine as we walk to baggage claim. "We can drive you to the rental cars, but you're welcome to use one of ours."

"Thanks, but I'll get a car."

"When do you have to be back in New York?"

"Tuesday. I have to meet with my editor on Wednesday." We stand beside the polished steel baggage carousel with the other people from my flight.

"About your new book?" Tom asks.

"To sign the contract."

"That's a big deal!" Kate says. "We need to celebrate."

"What's the title, Cami?" asks Tom.

"You know, we haven't decided. With *Blues* I knew all along what I'd call it, but this time nothing seems right."

The red light flashes, the buzzer sounds, and the machine pushes out luggage in heaps and dribbles. A woman standing nearby glances at us repeatedly. Then she whispers to the man next to her. Finally, she says, "Excuse me, but are you Cami Taylor?"

"That's right."

"You wrote *Double Down Blues*?"

"Yes."

She gives me a wide smile. "I *loved* that book. I read it twice. Didn't I, honey?"

"She certainly did," says the man. He looks pained, embarrassed even.

"I can't believe I ran into you. I just wish I had my copy for you to sign. I heard you say you have a new book coming out. When is that?"

I return her smile with genuine warmth. "Hopefully before Christmas."

This recognition—you could even call it celebrity—is as sweet as honey as far as I'm concerned. You can't live on it every day, but it sure is yummy when it comes around.

"Well, I hope you make it to Dallas for a signing."

"I'm sure I will this time. Thank you for reading my work."

I spot my bag, and Tom grabs it off the conveyor for me. When we're out of earshot of my fan, Kate nudges me with her elbow and says, "Ooh! I'm impressed."

"Maybe you two commoners should walk a couple of paces behind me. Just hang back there and bask in the glow of my, you know, aura."

"Your aura, yes," says Kate. "Well, honey, I'm glad you ran into a fan tonight so you won't feel quite so humbled by your roots tomorrow."

Roots. It doesn't quite seem possible. "I keep forgetting these people are my family too."

We reach at the car, a silver Lexus sedan. Kate squeezes me. "They are indeed. This is going to be fun."

◆ ◆ ◆

The Davis place is a two-story white frame house with a carriage drive on one side. The headlights sweep the yard as I pull in behind Tom, illuminating a waxy-leafed magnolia tree covered with white blossoms the size of cantaloupes. Tom pulls through to the back. Kate, who has ridden from the airport with me, says to stop under the arch next to a side door. We enter through the utility room into the kitchen. A large red and white ice chest sits beside the refrigerator.

"I'll take your things upstairs," says Tom.

I follow the two of them through the house, which smells of summery potpourri. Kate's taste is not so different from mine, but she's had much, much more to work with: Big rooms with wide plank floors and curved archways, high ceilings with crown molding, and lots of light from lamps everywhere. Judging from all the tall windows, I imagine the sunlight pours in during the day. The whole effect is inviting and informally elegant.

Tom and Kate lead me upstairs to a guest bedroom that holds a double bed with a tall wooden headboard, a matching dresser and chest of drawers, a writing table and chair, and a settee. In one corner is a beautiful, full-length mirror on legs. Very old. There is a rag rug on the floor and a lattice-style quilt on the bed. The windows are without dressing to show off the wood trim and leaded glass.

"This is a beautiful quilt," I say as I run my hand across the stitching. "Is it an heirloom?"

"No, I made that," says Kate. "I used to quilt all the time."

"It's good work. Your stitching's even, and so small."

I sit on the edge of the bed to check out the mattress, which is firm enough for me to look forward to a decent night's sleep. Tom has wandered out of the room.

"The bathroom's in there." Kate points to a door on the same wall as the closet. "Are you hungry? Would you like to freshen up and have a bite?"

"I'm really not hungry."

"How about a cup of tea?"

"Sure."

When I come downstairs, Kate's son, Jake, is scrubbing his hands at the kitchen sink. He's lanky and tall, like his dad, with very blond hair. He's wearing faded Levi's and a white V-neck tee shirt, and his face and arms are tanned, as if he's spent the summer outdoors. He dries his hands hastily when Kate introduces us.

"Hi, Jake." I shake his still wet palm.

"Uh, sorry." He finishes drying his hands. "Been working on my bike."

Jake has his mother's pale eyes, and he's charmingly shy. And young. Barely nineteen, if I remember the genealogy chart.

"Motorcycle?" I ask.

"Yeah. Wanna see?"

"Sure."

He leads the way through the French doors, past a covered flagstone patio that's furnished with a table and chairs, and a few Adirondacks. We cross the backyard to the detached garage. The yard is quiet, sheltered within a high privacy fence bordered by crepe myrtles in full bloom. The swimming pool throws waves of blue light on the white wall of the garage. As I follow Jake across the thick St. Augustine, my eyes rest on his narrow hips, on the perfect swell of his butt in those Levi's. My goodness, it's sweet. I look away and scold myself for going there at all.

Jake's bike, a midnight blue Harley Davidson, gleams under the overhead lights in the garage. Our reflections slide across its curved chrome pipes.

"It's a sixty-two police cruiser," Jake says. "My dad found it in Houston. Rebuilt it myself."

I run my hand along the black leather of the tandem saddles.

"I added those," he says. "Originally, it wouldn't take a passenger."

"I don't guess the Houston police needed to take girls out."

"Wanna go for a ride?"

"Sure, why not?"

He unfastens the spare helmet and hands it to me, then gets on the bike and kick starts it. The thing comes to life with a throaty rumble that fills the garage. He revs the engine and shouts, "This is one reason there's no other bike like a Harley. Get on." I climb onto the back saddle and rest my hands on his waist. He's slim, not yet having filled out into the man he'll become. He's also as tight as a drum.

The huge bike vibrates under us, its big, sexy engine reverberating off the garage's wooden walls, as if it can't wait to show me what it's got.

Jake glances over his shoulder. "Ready?"

The minute I say yes, we shoot out of the garage and through the carriage drive, slipping between the rental car and the house at a speed he seems far more comfortable with than I am. I catch my breath and grab two handfuls of tee shirt as he slings us onto the street. Soon we're gliding over the asphalt like water through a pipe—the ride is just that smooth. He leans deeply into the curves. I lean too, expecting the footrests to spark on the pavement with each turn. Miraculously, they don't.

When we reach the freeway, he opens it up, and I clasp my hands together over his flat belly. I'm exhilarated by the power of the bike, our speed, and our raw vulnerability to the rushing asphalt and the cars we fly past. We're a jerk of the handlebars away from catastrophe. A pothole away from death. Bare against the wind. Impulsively, I press my knees against the broad machine, throw my hands into the air, and close my eyes in pure and absolute abandon. I am invincible! Nothing can touch me now.

"Whooeee!" Jake yells.

When we slow to take an exit, I open my eyes and rest my hands on my own knees. We turn left under the freeway and speed down a deserted street between vacant, run-down buildings. One more corner and we've crossed an invisible boundary, beyond which are lights and people and capitalism. "Deep Ellum," he says over his shoulder.

"I've heard of it."

We cruise up and down the streets of the reclaimed district, passing galleries and bars and all kinds of people, just as in New York.

"Do you hang out here?" I ask.

"Nah, not much."

He makes a U-turn and speeds back toward downtown, crossing under the freeway again. "Our theater district," he yells, pointing to an old playhouse, the Majestic, with a lighted entrance like the ones on Broadway. We turn right and then left, weaving our way between the towering downtown buildings. Jake ignores the traffic lights at the deserted intersections. Only the vagrants are about.

Farther on, we pass a rough-hewn red granite building. We glide through the intersection in front of it and down a gentle slope that I've seen on television. Jake slows and pulls to the curb.

"Do you recognize this?" he asks.

I look around. "The grassy knoll? The book depository? There?"

We both look up at the sixth floor.

"The shots came from the window on the corner, supposedly," Jake says.

"You don't believe it?"

"I dunno. Where they came from is beside the point."

"True," I say.

"Well, Miss Taylor, that concludes your Circle Line tour of Big D. Don't forget to tip the driver." He puts the bike in gear and gives it the gas.

It's well past midnight when we get back to the house. Considerate of the neighbors at this late hour, Jake keeps the motorcycle to a low growl. We ease into the garage, and he cuts the engine. I get off the bike, feeling as if I've been on horseback. I pull off the helmet and fluff my damp hair. "That was fun, Jake. I can see a future for you in the tour business. Your own bus. Maybe a couple of drivers. It could be big."

"Well, you know, Southern hospitality and all of that. We've got an image to keep up." He takes my helmet. "I'm gonna do a few things out here. The back door's unlocked."

"All right. See you later." I leave the garage and make my way back across the yard, stopping at the pool to dip my hand in the warm water. It's a perfect night for a swim. Maybe later, I think, when everyone has gone to bed.

I shake the water from my hand and enter the kitchen through the back door. Kate is scooping potato salad into a Tupperware container.

"What did you think of Jake's baby?"

"He rides like it's part of him."

Kate rolls her eyes. "I just have to bite my tongue and trust he won't get too crazy. I hope he didn't scare you."

"Not at all. It was fun. Can I help you with anything here?"

"No, this is the end of it." She slides the bowl into the refrigerator. "It'll be country fare tomorrow. Fried chicken and potato salad, things like that. Do you like that kind of food?"

"Who doesn't love comfort food?"

"I guess the apple didn't fall too far from the tree."

"Oh, yes, it did. Plenty far. Until I saw that genealogy chart, I thought Patrick Earl dropped out of the sky in a staff sergeant's uniform. As far as he's concerned, he has no family outside of his old Air Force buddies. Do you mind if I get a glass of water?"

"Help yourself. The glasses are in the cabinet, there. Makes you wonder what happened between your dad and his family, doesn't it?"

I get a glass and fill it with ice and water from dispensers on the refrigerator door. "Not really. Not if you met him. It's no big mystery." I sip the cold, sweet water. "Your pool looks inviting."

"The water's warm, too warm really. It's been stiflingly hot here. But you're welcome to have a swim."

"Hey, I brought you something."

I leave the kitchen and run up the stairs to get the package I brought in my carry-on. I also grab my cigarettes and matches. I return and set the parcel on the table.

"You didn't have to do this," Kate says as she pulls away the brown paper the shop owner wrapped around the gift. She smiles when she sees the apricot carnival glass bowl. "It's gorgeous."

It ought to be. I paid a small fortune for it at a tiny shop in Greenwich Village, but I wasn't about to come to Texas empty-handed. When I saw Kate's house, I knew she'd like it.

When she holds it up and turns it under the light, tiny rainbows move across the curved, iridescent surfaces.

"I love carnival glass, Cami," she says. "You made a perfect choice. Thank you, honey."

She hugs me and busses my cheek. Kate is quick to embrace, but her touch doesn't feel clingy or make me want to push her away. In fact, she makes me feel the same warmth that college dropout in New York must've felt, a human connection that says "I'm here. Lean on me if you need to." I'm drawn to Kate in an unfamiliar way. It isn't sexual, but it's still a strong attraction.

She sets the bowl in the middle of the table. "I'll find a place for it tomorrow."

"I think I'll have a cigarette on the patio."

"There's a fan out there. Here, let me turn it on and maybe it won't be quite so muggy."

I follow her outside.

"Is it too warm out here for tea?" she asks.

"I'm okay with it. It's cooler than Arizona."

"I guess it is," she says. "I'll fix it and join you."

I settle in a chair at the patio table and light up. Jake's white tee shirt floats out of the shadows near the garage and moves toward me. "You know those things'll kill you," he says when he reaches the patio.

"I'll likely get killed on a motorcycle or something like that first, don't you think?"

"Nah. Not a chance. Well, 'night. See you in the morning."

"Goodnight, Jake. Thanks again for the ride."

He opens the door and Kate comes through it with two cups and saucers. He kisses her cheek. "'Night, Mom."

"Goodnight, honey. I'll get you up around eight."

When she sits down, I say, "You must be proud of him."

"Very proud. Jake and Anne are the best part of Tom and me." She sips her tea. "For a woman like me, my kids are everything."

"That's probably why that guy in New York got to you."

"Maybe. Probably. I thought he was at a crossroads. I just wanted to give him a push in the right direction."

"That's what I told my shrink, that I thought he still had a chance."

Kate sets her cup down. "Why do you see a psychiatrist, Cami?"

I have no answer for this. It hasn't done much good. Any good that I can tell.

"I haven't been in several weeks. I went when I was having trouble with my, well, with Joel. You met him at the Promenade."

"Yes, I remember Joel."

"Joel and I were—I don't know—I thought we were doing fine. Then he up and decided to take it to the next level, only there really wasn't any next level to go to. I liked spending time with him, though, and I miss him a lot. He's fun to be with, and he's so good in—what I mean is we were a good fit."

"That must've been painful for you then, the other night." She looks at me steadily.

I snort a short, hard laugh. "I was kicking myself for suggesting that theater, I can tell you that. But I suppose I'm getting over it. At least I'm not feeling all the ways I felt before." I drain the rest of my tea and take a last drag. Then I stamp out the butt in the saucer.

Kate glances at the saucer about the time I realize she might not appreciate me putting out a cigarette in it.

"Sorry," I say.

"Oh. No, it's . . . it's fine. How long were you and Joel together?"

"About a year and a half. A long time."

We fall silent for a while, and I light another cigarette. I've gone from not smoking at all to a pack and a half of Marlboro Lights a day. I can tell the difference in my morning runs, and I make myself a silent vow to cut back.

"It's getting late," I say.

"Yes, and tomorrow will be a long day." She looks at her watch. "Today, that is, will be a long day. It's after one." She stands and pushes her chair under the table. "Will you lock the back door when you come in from your swim?"

"Forget the swim. I'm tired too. Maybe I'll catch a run in the morning. I'll be sure to lock up."

"All right. Goodnight, Cami."

"'Night, Kate."

After she leaves, I sit alone for a long time enjoying the peace. There are no city sounds, only the singsong trill of cicadas. Wisteria vines hang from a trellis along one side of the patio, perfuming the air with their heavy sweetness. Not a breath stirs except for the lazy breeze from the overhead fan.

Chapter Seventeen

When I come downstairs at six thirty the next morning in my tee shirt and shorts, Tom is the only one in the kitchen.

"So you are the first one up," I tease.

"Guilty as charged," he says, not moving his gaze from the newspaper. "Too many early mornings at the office. Now I can't sleep in, even when I want to." He looks at me over his reading glasses. "I hope you're not thinking of running off. Kate will be disappointed."

"I wasn't, but the way you made this outing today sound, maybe I should."

"There's nothing to fear but fear itself, my dear."

"In that case, save some coffee for me."

"I'll keep the home fires burning," he says, and he turns his attention back to the business section.

The morning is warm and muggy. I stretch, using the railing on the front porch, and then begin an easy lope up the street. A few neighbors are out for a morning run, and we nod to one another when we pass. The neighborhood is quiet, and it feels safe, as if I've traveled across time

126

as well as distance to a place that knows nothing of poverty or drugs or gangs. In New York, the rich and poor live much closer to one another. Here in Dallas, the less fortunate are nowhere in sight.

I run on the sidewalk, which is buckled in many places from the roots of the ancient trees that shade the front yards and the street. I pass house after house like the Davis place: well-kept brick or stone or frame structures set in carefully groomed yards. I watch their cozy rooms waking up through windows that are as open as shop fronts.

The humidity and cigarettes are taking a toll, and I'm exhausted in no time. It'll be a long day, and there's no sense in wearing myself out, so I turn back toward the house. I let myself into the backyard through the unlocked gate and walk around to the patio to cool down. Kate has joined Tom at the kitchen table, and she opens the door when she sees me.

"I'll just cool off here for a minute," I say, pointing to the patio chairs.

Kate brings me a chilled glass and a quart of Gatorade, the same flavor I buy at home. She must've noticed it in my refrigerator. The details this woman remembers! I'm glad I stretched myself to buy that expensive bowl. After the Gatorade, I chat with them over coffee, and then I go upstairs to shower.

In the hallway, on top of a narrow bookcase outside my bedroom, is a black leather-bound Bible. I didn't notice it last night or before I left for my run this morning. I open the book and turn the onionskin pages, on which many passages are underlined or highlighted in garish yellow, pink, or green, creating a mishmash of defacements. In the margins, someone—Kate?—has written dates and brief, cryptic notes, as if this were a textbook marked up during classroom lectures. I'm surprised to find this in a tome I assume is beloved. I place the book back on the shelf at precisely the angle I found it.

I clean up and deck out, and I'm feeling pretty good about myself when I descend the stairs in a new sundress and slings. Jake notices, although he says nothing and shyly tucks his gaze back into his motorcycle magazine. He looks pretty good himself in Levi's and pullover.

In khakis and a plaid shirt, Tom looks as stiff as a J. C. Penney ad. "Kate'll be down in a minute," he says.

"Okay. Is there any coffee left?"

"Should be."

I go to the kitchen and take my cup from the collection in the sink. Tom's agency, *D Associates*, is printed on the side. I wonder if the *D* stands for Davis or Dallas. Either way, I'm impressed. The coffee in the pot tastes scorched from being on the burner too long, and even a healthy dose of cream doesn't make it palatable.

I set down the coffee and open the *Dallas Morning News* that's lying on the table. Perusing a local newspaper is the best way to get a feel for a place, and I scan the sections for anything of interest. There's a list of this week's fiction bestsellers, hardcover and paperback. The paperback edition of *Blues* dropped off the list a few weeks ago. I turn the page and find an advertisement for a thirty-five-year JFK memorial exhibit at the Sixth Floor Museum.

"What a great dress." Kate says as she enters the kitchen, fastening her wristwatch. "You'll make your cousins jealous."

"Thanks. Did you see this Kennedy exhibit? Jake took me by Dealey Plaza last night."

"He's fascinated by JFK. Has been since he was little."

"Thirty-five years. It's such a long time. Longer than I've been around."

"That's right. Your birthday is, let's see—I saw it on the chart—September 15. Right around the corner."

Again, with the attentiveness.

"And you'll be thirty," she finishes.

"That's right. Good memory."

"Well, I remember that assassination like it was yesterday," she says. "Our teacher was crying when she told us. Mama had a bunch of newspaper clippings on her dresser, Jackie in that bloody Chanel suit. Mama had a pillbox hat like Jackie's. That's what stuck in my mind."

"How old were you?"

"I was in the sixth grade. Let's see, eleven, about to turn twelve."

I look at Kate's hands, for the first time paying attention to the lines and veins from years of wife duty and mothering. She could be my mother. Somehow the gap between us hasn't seemed as large as seventeen years, but I'm closer in age to her kids than to her.

I help her pack two cardboard boxes with food. Jake heaves them and the red ice chest into the back of Kate's SUV while I stand in the yard watching the muscles of his lean arms flex against the weight. I'm an arms and shoulders woman—always have been. Jake doesn't have the heft of a mature man, but it doesn't make him any less appealing. We make eye contact, and I smile.

"I'm driving," he says, rattling the keys. "You scared?"

"Not of your driving," I shoot back.

Jake and I have a thing going already, a nice tension. Not that it'll go anywhere under the circumstances, but he's a flirt and so am I, and what's wrong with that? Besides, what if something does come of it? Technically he's a grown man, even if he acts like a kid.

Once we're underway, Jake shoots in and out of traffic while Tom peers over to check the speedometer.

"Where's the reunion?" I ask.

"The Botanic Gardens in Fort Worth," answers Kate. "It's a pretty spot."

It's too bad, really, that I didn't see Dr. Wortham again before this little event. I cheated her out of an opportunity to seriously dig around in my past. Who knows? She might've given me a checklist to use. Together, we could've resolved every issue I have. That's just how she'd think too. I suddenly realize that I have no desire to return to Dr. Wortham. It's a waste of time and money, and it does nothing but make me feel tense. The only crazy thing about me is laying out almost $300 a week to be abused. That's sick. No, I won't go back. I'm done.

We enter the park through an iron gate and follow a long, narrow road that gives the illusion we've left the city to meander down a country lane. Through the oaks along each side, I catch glimpses of well-groomed gardens and lawns. Eventually, the trees part at a parking area adjacent to a large pavilion. We step out of the car into the oppressive heat, even though it isn't yet ten o'clock.

The picnic tables under the pavilion are crowded with food and people. Kate introduces me to her parents, who are younger than I would've guessed, perhaps younger than mine. Kate's sister, Renee, is here too, with husband and daughter in tow. The daughter, Karah, is a cheeky little blonde who turns into a mass of giggles in Jake's presence.

Kate is more polished than her mother and sister, and meeting her family, I realize her old money isn't old at all. It must've begun with Tom's success. Like me, she's affected an image that could only have come with some effort. Her perfectly styled gray hair, her perfectly applied makeup, the casually chic but expensive clothes—all things that don't flash dollar signs but radiate quality to those in the know.

After our drawn-out, carb-laden lunch, I watch Kate work the crowd, fascinated by the way people light up in her presence. It's easy to see why. She gives each person her undivided attention, holding eye contact while she listens to every word they say. She's warm, always making a connection with a hand on the arm or a squeeze of the shoulder. I still haven't figured out the motives behind all this charm.

"Have you met your uncle?"

I start at the sound of Tom's voice beside me. "No. I have an uncle here?"

"Well, great uncle, I suppose. Kate was going to introduce you, but I see she's gotten sidetracked." Tom shakes the crushed ice in his red Solo cup. "Want me to do the honors?"

"Sure."

I follow him to an old man sitting by himself in a lawn chair pulled up close to one of the picnic tables, a concrete slab that bristles with abandoned Solo cups. As we draw near, I see the guy's liver-speckled head bobbing in an afternoon snooze. Enormous, greasy hearing aids protrude from his ears.

Tom leans over him, hand on his shoulder, and shouts, "Raymond? Ray!"

The old guy rouses, confused. "Huh?"

"There's someone here who wants to meet you. Don't you have a nephew named Patrick? Out in Arizona?"

"Patrick Earl," I say.

"Your brother's boy, Ray. Patrick Earl. This is his girl."

"What? Who's girl?" Uncle Ray adjusts his hearing aids and asks Tom to say it all again. When he finally understands, he chuckles like he's just heard a good one. "Patrick Earl? Why, I ain't seen him in over forty years."

"I'll leave you two to catch up," says Tom. He makes himself scarce before I can stop him, leaving me alone with my ancient uncle.

"Hi," I say, sitting on the bench beside his chair. "I'm Cami." I extend my hand.

He gives my fingers a shake. "What's that? Tammy?"

"No. C-A-M-I. Short for Camille."

He chuckles again. "Uh-huh. You're Patrick Earl's girl? All the way from Arizona?" He peers at me through cloudy eyes and smudged glasses. "Ain't that what that feller said?"

"Yes sir. Patrick Earl is my dad. He and my mom live in Phoenix."

Uncle Ray wags his fleshy head. "Well, I sure never figured to see hide nor hair of that boy again. Not after all this time passin'. Your daddy has a temper, hot as a red pepper. He ever tell you that?"

"I figured it out," I shout, leaning forward.

He laughs well at this, a worn-out cough of a laugh. "I reckon you did. Well, he come by it honest. My brother was a firecracker too. Them two fought like cats and dogs. 'Course, wasn't no surprise when Patrick Earl took off first chance he got. Don't reckon he ever looked back."

"Doesn't my dad have an older sister?"

"Eloise," says Ray, "She passed a few years back. Cancer." He leans back and regards me. "Imagine this. Nothin' in more than forty years and here you are, Patrick Earl's growed-up daughter. I'm proud I got to meet you, Cami." He pats my hand. "You got a family of your own out in Arizona?"

"No sir."

He nods. "Well, a pretty thing like you won't have no trouble finding a good husband. You just keep lookin'."

"Thanks. It was nice to meet you." I start to get up.

"Is your daddy doin' okay?" he asks quickly.

I settle on the bench again. "He's fine. He plays a lot of golf, and dominoes lately."

"Dominoes? Well, how 'bout that? My brother used to like to play dominoes. You tell Patrick Earl his daddy liked to play dominoes when he got old, will you? You tell him Uncle Ray says dominoes is an old man's game."

"Sure, I'll tell him."

"I used to take him fishin' when he was just no bigger 'n that." He waves his knobby hand toward the ground. "Had a little old wooden boat. Wasn't worth nothin', but that boy did love to go out in that boat. You tell him I said hello. He'll remember me."

"I'll tell him."

"Sure wish I could see Patrick Earl. You favor him, though, near as I can tell." He points to my face. "Around the eyes."

"Yes sir. I'm my father's daughter."

He nods again, almost sadly, I think. "Well, you tell your daddy his Uncle Ray sends his love."

I stand, then make myself lean down and hug him, forcing my arms around his flaccid old body in spite of the feel of his moist, doughy skin under the thin cotton shirt. "You take care of yourself, Uncle Ray."

"I will, honey. Nice visitin' with you."

I leave, thinking the old guy would've been better off without his trip down memory lane. I'm sick of the crowd, so I sneak away with my sweet iced tea to have a cigarette. There's a rose garden across the meadow from the pavilion, and the bushes in it are loaded with big American Beauties and delicate hybrids and tiny crimson clusters that look like bouquets of crinkled velvet. I follow the pea gravel path until the reunion is out of sight and out of earshot. I'm sticky from the day's heat and irritable from the day's crowd, and nothing sounds better to me than a cool shower and some peace and quiet.

The sound of male voices drifts through the garden. I round the end of a hedgerow and find Jake and a half dozen other young guys playing football on the lawn. They're soaked with sweat, running and laughing in the zeal of their indefatigable vigor. Jake waves when he sees me, and I watch him and the other guys exchange words as they glance my way. I linger to watch them a while before continuing along my peaceful garden path.

When I return to the pavilion, I'm grateful to see the crowd has thinned and the cars that remain in the parking lot have gaping trunks awaiting cargo. I find my group gathered around a new addition— the grandmother, sitting in a lawn chair. She's a little gray mouse of a woman with a cotton sweater buttoned up to her throat, despite the heat. Apparently, her hearing is good, but her vision is shot. Her eyes are slits inside folds of skin, and only the left one is open enough to reveal a sightless, milky pupil. She cocks her head to give each speaker the attention of her ear.

"Mamaw, this is Cami," Kate says. She grips my elbow and pulls me close. I kneel in front of Mamaw's knees, setting my cup and cigarettes on the concrete beside her terrycloth house shoes.

"Cami?" the old woman screeches, her voice as harsh as a crow's. "Cami who?"

"Cami, our cousin from the other side of the family. She's visiting all the way from New York City."

"Where is she?"

Kate takes Mamaw's hand and places it on my shoulder. Her fingers immediately come to life, and both her hands take a journey up my neck and over every inch of my face, reading me like braille. Her palms smell of fried chicken and some flowery scent. She pats my cheek gently and places her hands back in her lap.

"It's nice to meet you, ma'am," I say too loudly.

"Are you saved, honey?" she shrieks.

"Saved from what?" I ask. I look to Kate for help, but find her as taken aback as I am. She shakes her head and laughs, and then motions to her sister to take our place. Renee drags Karah over, and we rise and step back.

"I'm sorry about that," Kate says when we're clear. "Mamaw speaks her mind."

"Don't worry about it."

Kate finishes putting the leftover food in the boxes we brought. "I need to run over here for a while tomorrow afternoon. I hate to leave you, but Mom needs help getting her to the doctor, and Renee can't do it. It'll just be a few hours."

"That's no big thing," I say. "You don't have to entertain me every minute, Kate. You've already been a great hostess."

"Well, as I said, it won't take long."

Chapter Eighteen

*Y*oung Jake is as lithe as a cat.

I lean on the windowsill of my upstairs bathroom and watch him swim laps. Watch him spring onto the side of the pool as if gravity were someone else's problem. Watch him shake the loose water from his taut flesh and stretch out on the chaise lounge. I should tear myself away from this window, return to my room, and find something to occupy me until Kate gets home. I know this, yet I don't move. Instead, I knock my forehead softly against the beveled glass, rest it there, and sigh in resignation.

Moments later, I'm in my swimsuit, towel and sunscreen in hand, descending the stairs two at a time. Jake doesn't notice me until I dive in and swim the length of the pool. The afternoon is very hot, and the pool's surface feels as tepid as a bath, but the water underneath is cool enough to be refreshing. I come up and begin a backstroke. Jake's watching me, and I smile.

"Hi," he says.

"Hi, Jake."

I keep swimming, letting off steam, swinging my arms and legs smoothly, gracefully, so that the water hardly burbles as I slide through it. Finally, I climb the ladder, grab my towel from the diving board, and walk to the chaise next to his.

"You're a good swimmer," he says.

"I grew up in Arizona. Kids out there spend summers in the water."

He looks away but then glances back at me furtively as I towel off. I sit down.

"So how'd you get to be a writer?" he asks.

"One word at a time. It's what I always wanted to do. I worked really hard at it, and I guess it paid off."

"What do you think of Dallas?"

"I like it. It isn't what I thought. I halfway expected the cliché. You know, cowboys driving herds through the streets." I laugh.

He seems to relax. "You have to go to the stockyards in Fort Worth for that. Not here, not in Highland Park."

He's darkly tanned under the blond down that covers his body. A single bead of sweat makes its way down his cheek from beneath that crown of thick sun-bleached hair. I can imagine him close, his clear gray eyes fixed on mine. His full lips. I look away and begin smearing the suntan lotion on my arms.

"How do you like college life?" I ask.

"It's a blast." He lies back on the webbing but cocks his head to one side to squint at me. "I like the freedom. It's totally different from high school."

"You got a girlfriend in Austin?"

"Nobody steady."

"That must take some effort."

He smiles and shakes his head, charming me with his modesty.

"You're smart, Jake. You have your whole life to settle down."

"Yeah, that's what I figure. Right now, I just wanna have some fun, you know, before I have to grow up." He laughs at this, and I laugh with him.

"Having fun is good," I say.

"Yeah."

"No strings. No . . . complications."

"Exactly."

"Jake, would you rub some of this on my back?"

"Sure."

He sits up and takes the tube from my hand. I turn around, and he smooths the lotion on my shoulders. At first, his touch is timid and quick, as if he wants to hurry and be done with it. I can guess the reasons behind his shyness, given what I've seen of this family. He doesn't know me. I'm older. I'm his mother's friend. I'm his cousin, for God's sake. But, as I yield to the gentle massage, he slows down.

He squeezes out some more and applies it to the small of my back where the swimsuit scoops low. Ironically, I began wearing one-piece suits *after* I got in shape, and I still believe they're sexier than bikinis. The tips of Jake's fingers graze the lower edge of the suit just above the swell of my hips, then reverse direction and glide up the firm muscles covering my ribs and spine. I close my eyes and imagine him enjoying the feel of a woman under his hand, as I'm enjoying the sensuality of balm over warm skin. His palm flattens against me, as if he's no longer just spreading the lotion but really feeling me.

"You have a nice touch, Jake."

His hand pauses, and then keeps going. I turn around quickly, causing his fingers to brush the underside of my breast.

"Sorry," he says.

There's conflict in his eyes, but I don't give him a chance to back away. I cross to his chaise and put my mouth on his. His startled resistance gives way to the pleasure of our lips together. He's young and inexperienced, but also young and ready, and I'm sure he's thought about what it would be like to kiss me. I've seen it on his face.

It takes a while, but finally he puts his hands on me, exploring what's beneath the spandex, and I ease back onto the chaise and pull him on top of me. Our combined weight forces the crossbar into my back, but the feel of him on me is worth that small discomfort. I'm caught up in a vision of us upstairs in my bed.

"Let's go inside," I whisper.

"What?" His question is a reflex. He knows what I mean.

It hits me that he might be a virgin. I hadn't considered that possibility, not with him being in college. Not at his age. I wonder if it matters. Surely, he won't hold onto his virtue much longer, and he could do a lot worse than me for his first conquest.

I caress the nape of his neck with my fingertips and kiss him deeply, and then I move my mouth to his ear. "Let's go inside for a while," I breathe. "Don't you want to?"

He wants to. He definitely wants to. Oh, yes, Jake, I can teach you a thing or two to take back to school.

His mouth searches my throat, my cheek, my ear. "You scare me, Cami," he whispers.

"It's no big thing, baby. There's no one here but you and me."

He's losing control. His chest is heaving. His heart is pounding. He's already past the point of no return. It's a fool's wager to pit chastity against rip-roaring testosterone.

That supple brown body between those crisp white sheets is all I'm thinking about, and my breath comes faster too. It's been a long time, and I'm even more eager than he. I grope him gently.

"We're just getting to know each other a little better," I tell him between kisses. "There's nothing to worry about. We're having fun, is all. No strings. No big thing. You feel so good to me."

His hands and mouth are all over me, and his leg moves against the inside of my thigh. I push him off enough to slip out from under him. I grasp his hand. "C'mon, baby. Let's go."

He looks up at me, and the innocence in those gray eyes sends a sharp arrow right through my heart.

Everything this boy believes to be good and right has caved under the weight of my carnal experience. He's a young bull to slaughter, and I'm the butcher. This is how I repay Kate and Tom. This is how I thank her for welcoming me into her family, for spreading those fresh, snowy sheets on my bed.

Jake is on his feet. He has committed.

"No," I say. I put my hand against his hot chest and take a step back, still breathing hard, maybe harder now. I look at him in the agony of this passion I've stirred. "This isn't right. No. I'm sorry. I'm so sorry." I flee into the house, run up the stairs, and shut the bedroom door behind me.

In the bathroom, I grip the sides of the antique sink with white knuckles. I'm shaking so violently that the pedestal rattles against the floor tiles. Whatever I bring with me, I can't bring it to these people. I wrench on the cold water and splash my face repeatedly. Rivulets run down the surface of the mirror and my reflection.

I have to get out of here.

Still trembling and damp, I go into the bedroom and pull my suitcase from the closet. I jerk open the dresser drawers and begin throwing their contents into it. At some point, I peel off the swimsuit and put on a pair of jeans and a tee.

There's a knock at the door.

"Cami?" Kate calls.

I stand there, silent, and she calls my name again.

"Yes?" I say.

"May I come in?"

I go to the door and open it.

"What are you doing?" she asks, looking past me.

I stare at her. She would've walked right in on us.

"Why'd you come back so early?" I ask.

"I forgot something. Are you packing? Were you going to leave without saying good-bye?"

I stand there with a lie on my tongue. My editor called, and there's a crisis with the book. My mother called, and there's a crisis with my father. For God's sake, my shrink called, and I'm having a crisis.

Instead, I say nothing. I watch her look at my wet hair, then at the swimsuit wadded on the bed. She walks to the window and looks down at the pool, where Jake is swimming laps again. She turns to face me. She knows I've been after him. It's uncanny how they know, these mothers.

Now I'll see Kate come out. Now all that gentle grace can turn to something that cuts. But she looks more hurt than angry, as if she can't believe I would betray her.

"Nothing happened," I say quickly.

There are tears in her eyes. "Excuse me," she says, and she walks out of the room.

I stand motionless a while longer, trying to sort things into the patterns I'm used to. When I finally lay the blouse I've been holding into the suitcase and look around to see what's left, I'm crying too.

◆ ◆ ◆

I descend the stairs with my suitcase and carry-on. It would be so easy to slip out the door and never look back, but I can't leave like this. For some reason, I want to smooth this over. I set the bags in the foyer and walk through the house, looking for her. I find her in the living room. The afternoon sunlight filters through the shutters in long white bands that fall across the hardwood floor and onto the sofa where she sits. Her back is to me, and she's talking to someone.

"Don't ask this," she says. "It's too much."

I walk around the sofa, expecting to see a phone in her hand, but it's lying on the table in front of her. Her face is red and shiny from crying.

"Who are you talking to?" I ask.

She glances my way, and then looks out the window, but she doesn't answer.

I sit across from her. "I'm sorry, Kate. There isn't much more I can say, but it's important to me that you know nothing happened."

She sits in silence, staring out the window, refusing to look at me.

"Well, again, I'm sorry," I repeat. She isn't budging, so I might as well wait for the taxi outside. I stand to go.

"Who stopped it?" she asks. "Jake?"

I sit down again. I can give her a kindness, a little white lie that her virtuous son resisted my advances. "Of course," I say. "You raised him right."

She searches my face for the truthfulness of it, staring at me so long that I have to look away.

"It wasn't Jake," she says. "It was you. You started it, and you stopped it."

"Yes."

"Why, Cami?"

"I don't know. At first, it seemed like nothing. Sex is nothing to me, you know? But then, there was this look on Jake's face, like sex *was* something for him. That look made it into something different for me too. It felt like I was betraying you. You and Tom."

"You were."

"But, I didn't."

"No . . . I guess not," she says slowly and without much resolve.

"So maybe we can part as friends," I say. "Is that too much to ask?"

"Friends," she repeats. "Do you want us to be friends?"

"Sure. I could use a friend sometimes."

Her expression softens then. "I had planned to invite you back for an extended visit. Before this."

"Oh."

"Would you have come?"

"I want to write a novel set in the South," I say. I don't say with a crazy protagonist based on you, Kate. "So sure, it would be nice to spend some time in Texas. But I don't expect to be invited here again, under the circumstances."

"But would you have come here if I'd asked?"

"Probably. What about Jake?"

"He's going back to Austin next week."

From what I hear, Austin's a lot livelier than Dallas. That's where I should go, even if I don't hook up with Jake. As it turns out, even I have boundaries now.

"If you're planning to come back to Texas," Kate says, "this is as good a place to stay as any."

"You don't have to worry, Kate. I'll leave Jake alone."

"I can't afford to worry. I can't possibly protect my children from everything and everyone."

That stings, but I let it pass. I had it coming.

"Consider it an open invitation," she says.

"Thank you. That's really, really good of you, all things considered."

It's a better parting than I hoped for, whatever I decide to do later.

Chapter Nineteen

Christopher greets me with rheumy, bloodshot eyes, the product of too much reading and probably a little too much cognac. Chris's complexion is ruddy, and his hair is snow white. I've always imagined him as a pale, redheaded youth whose coloring turned to a negative image with age. When he busses my cheeks, I smell tobacco and expensive cologne.

"Are you ready for a nice surprise?" he asks, handing me the contract.

"Sure am, but you know I'll want some time to look this over."

"I waited for a call from your agent to take care of that."

"You know I don't have an agent."

"You need one. You're the only major author I work with who doesn't have an agent, and that just isn't done."

"Why should I pay an agent to do something I enjoy doing? Besides, I have you to take care of me, Chris."

"Midway is growing, and so are you. I need to focus on editing, and you need to focus on writing."

"Keep talking and I'll get the idea you don't like doing business with me. Besides, I'll turn into a hermit if I spend all my time writing."

"Just think about it," he says.

"Sure. I'll think about it."

I flip to the clause every writer wants to know first, the one I'm sure holds the surprise Chris mentioned. The advance is a hundred times what I got for *Blues*, much more than I dared hope for, especially given my secret fear that this book isn't as good.

"That's really, *really* nice."

"You like that?"

"I like it a lot."

"We have a big marketing budget this time. Come over here and sit with me a minute."

I follow him to the saddle-colored leather sofa, where we settle next to each other like two old pals.

"You're my career maker, Cami," he says. "You have the talent and the discipline to build an incredible body of work over time. I've watched you grow with every piece you've turned out. I have it all, right there in my files. You're getting comfortable with your style and your voice. You're stretching yourself, taking risks. That's what I like so much about *Rachael and Jerome*. But I don't like the title. We have to change it."

"I don't like it either, but nothing else has come to me."

"We'll put our heads together and come up with something that pops. Soon. I'm saying all this because I don't think you realize what your future holds. When you do realize it, you might be tempted to look for greener pastures."

"This feels like career counseling."

"It is, love. Just think of me as your older, wiser brother, and let me give you some brotherly advice. You're a sharp kid, but publishing is a cutthroat business, and I don't want anyone stealing you away from my house. We'll treat you right. We have in the past, and we will in the future, at least, as long as I'm around."

"Thank you, Chris."

"Now, I'm going down the hall. Use my desk and read your contract. If you have any questions, pick up the phone and the assistant will track me down. Take your time," he says, rising. "Do you want some coffee?"

"No, I'm fine. I'll call for you when I'm done."

The contract with all its legalese isn't a puzzle to me. I practically memorized my first one, researching the terms until I understood what every clause meant. Of course, that was after I'd signed, too late to do anything about it if I'd been sold a bill of goods. All I cared about then was seeing my book—*my* book—that I'd written in coffee shops, the break room at the casino, and my garage apartment, on the shelf at Barnes and Noble.

But Chris is right. Midway has taken care of me. The royalties are good, and they handled the foreign rights for me. Besides a decent contract, Midway gave me a book tour and a publicist. I don't think I'd have gotten either of those at a large house. No one, least of all me, expected *Blues* to hit the bestseller lists. Somehow, though, the novel sparked and caught, like a slow-burning grass fire that I kept thinking would die out, but it didn't. It still hasn't.

I study the legal instrument in my hands. I spent the last couple of years watching the conditions of my first contract play out, and I'm grateful for the comprehension experience brings. I'm grateful for the distraction of negotiating this deal too, which keeps my mind off the phone call I got before I left the apartment. The nurse or someone in Dr. Kuri's office called to ask if I could come by the office today to talk about my test results. That's pretty much all she said, but I felt a bloodred flag snap to attention.

I stick my head out the door and ask the assistant to find Chris.

"I'll take that coffee now," I tell him when he returns.

He buzzes the intercom. "Please bring us a couple of coffees, Nina. One with cream."

"Good memory, Chris."

"Good basic salesmanship. Are we ready to sign?"

"I'm not happy with the foreign rights."

"Seventy-thirty. Same as you got with *Blues*."

"This book will do better overseas. You know as well as I do that it's a perfect premise for European readers. I thought about it the whole time I was writing."

"All right. As I said, I want you to be happy. I can go eighty-twenty. That's an excellent offer."

"I want ninety."

"Not a chance, Cami. It isn't going to happen."

The assistant, Nina, brings our coffee in mugs with the house logo. She's a serious young woman whose intense demeanor, pulled-tight ponytail, and trendy eyewear say she has designs on the editor's desk someday.

"What was that about keeping my loyalty?" I ask when she closes the door. "Was that just so much talk? Authors get those kinds of deals. I read the trades too, you know."

"I meant every word I said to you, love." Chris's voice reveals no emotion whatsoever, but the hue of his inflamed skin deepens, as if he's being boiled in a pot. "But you aren't getting ninety-ten at Midway. Whatever you've seen others get, they didn't get it here. Or anywhere else in New York."

I didn't expect more, but I had to make a run at it, mainly to create some leverage for something else I want.

"I'll settle for eighty-twenty on one condition," I say.

"What's that?"

"I want some input—some real say—in the cover design."

He shakes his head and sets his coffee down, untouched. "I don't want to slow this down. You know it's in the book's best interest if we can get it out before the holidays. There isn't time to screw around with a dust jacket."

"I won't slow it down. I really liked the cover on *Blues*—simple and straightforward. But I've been watching what's coming out of your design department the past year, and I get the feeling they're trying to cram as much as they can on the front cover. Every book is too busy."

He laughs. "What if I told you that's my sister's work?"

"I'd still say the book covers are too busy. Sorry."

"Well, my sister doesn't work here, but I'm not going to squabble over cover designs. How about I give you my word that we'll keep it simple and to your taste? Acceptable?"

"All right."

"It's a done deal, then?"

"Yes. We're done."

I grin like a fool.

"Can I take you out to celebrate? I'm thinking old school. Tavern on the Green. Wasn't that where we celebrated *Blues*?"

My mind returns to the doctor's phone call.

"Can I take a rain check? Maybe later in the week?"

"Sure, just give me a call."

We each sign our names, creating a binding agreement between Midway Publishing and me. I sip coffee while Chris's assistant makes a copy for me.

When I leave, young Nina is back at her desk typing about a million words a minute. She pauses and glances up. "Congratulations, Ms. Taylor."

I thank her, noticing the envy in her guarded brown eyes.

Chapter Twenty

When I leave Christopher, I waste no time taking a cab to Dr. Kuri's office. The stone-faced receptionist escorts me into the doctor's study right away, past a dozen waiting patients, and my stomach tightens into a hard knot. Dr. Kuri doesn't leave me to fidget long.

"Good afternoon," he says as he comes in. The nurse—Sharon is her name—follows him through the door, which he closes carefully and quietly behind her. All of Dr. Kuri's moves are methodical, as if he's not about to cut a corner. He's holding a manila file and sits behind the desk, and Sharon takes the chair beside me. I glance at her, wondering what she's doing here.

Dr. Kuri opens the file and looks up at me, his dark eyes impenetrable over his reading glasses. A shock of coarse black hair hangs low on his forehead, giving him the look of a young rogue, despite his buttoned-up demeanor. "There isn't an easy way to tell you this," he says. He pauses, takes off his glasses, and leans back in his chair, which creaks loudly in the small space.

"Yes?" I say impatiently.

"Cami, your test results came back positive for HIV."

The words don't sink in. It's clear that the doctor is talking *to* me, but I can't quite grasp that he's talking *about* me. Sharon places her warm hand over mine, where they're folded in my lap. I pull away and rub my forehead. "Could it be a mistake?" I ask, my voice thin.

Dr. Kuri leans forward again. "No. We were looking for HIV, specifically. We ran tests at two labs, independently, just to be certain. I'm sorry, but there's no mistake." He looks at the nurse and then back to me. "We talked about your weight loss, the nausea, the fatigue. Have you noticed any other physical changes recently, or at any time? Any fever or night sweats? Perhaps you can remember thinking you had the flu and it passed. Anything such as that?"

"Looking for it? No. I don't know." My heart sends a pounding pulse to my ears. I have a sense of watching the conversation from outside my body.

"I understand from your therapist that you're struggling a bit. Is this a recent development, or have you had emotional, um, challenges before?"

I shake my head, but not in response to the question.

He continues, "From blood tests alone, it isn't possible to determine how long you've been infected. Your weight loss may or may not be symptomatic, but your T-cell count and viral load lead me to believe it is."

I imagine dingy clinics with scuffed linoleum and cheap, soiled furniture. I imagine bottles of pills filling my cabinets and my body growing flaccid for want of exercise. My mother's life, a life I can't tolerate.

It's a singular feeling—like nothing else I can think of—to be told a savage squatter has taken up residence in your body, with no hope of eviction. I would've gotten this scene wrong if I'd ever thought to write a character who received a diagnosis of terminal illness. Terminal illness belongs to cue-ball-headed children and shuffling, emphysemic old men. I would've stereotyped such a character. I'd have written her as weak and sniveling and whiny, without much to live for in the first place. I would not have written me.

"Advances in fighting HIV are being made almost daily," Dr. Kuri is saying. "We'll begin a protease inhibitor regimen immediately. That should bring your blood levels closer to normal parameters. You must eat a healthy diet and continue your current level of exercise. I recommend you quit smoking."

Diet and exercise? He's talking about children's toys against thermonuclear destruction.

"Cami, you must use protection at all times during sexual intercourse. I recommend polyurethane condoms, rather than latex, but if you use latex, you must not use petroleum-based lubricants. They compromise the barrier."

Sexual intercourse? Is he crazy?

"There's a lot we can do to hold autoimmune disease at bay. It's important that you understand this because your frame of mind has an impact on your ability to stay healthy. You're a strong young woman, Cami. You can fight this, and you don't have to fight it alone."

I need to fall back and regroup. That's all I know. Somehow, I have to get control of this thing. "I'm leaving for Texas in a couple of days," I say. "I'll decide about the drugs when I get back."

His eyebrows shoot up. "Decide what? We have to begin treatment right away. I've worked up—"

"No. I'll make a decision about all of that in a couple of weeks, when I get back. I've waited this long. A few more days won't matter."

"That is incorrect. Days *do* make a difference. The virus establishes a set point, and we can influence it with antivirals."

"Dr. Kuri, once I begin drug therapy, I'll be on it for the rest of my life. I'm going to take some time before I do that. That's it."

He looks at me, seeming to consider my resolve. "Very well," he says finally. "I can't force you. You need to contact anyone you might have exposed. They should be tested. We can make the contact, if you prefer."

"How far back are you talking about?"

"As I said, it's difficult to know. When did you become sexually active?"

I remember a coed dorm and hasty rabbit sex under a thin blanket. Does that really count? "About ten years ago," I say.

"Your exposure was probably more recent, but you should err on the side of caution."

Impossible. "I'll contact them myself," I say.

"The past three to five years are the most critical time period."

"Okay."

◆ ◆ ◆

The cab ride home is a blur. I run through the lobby and up the stairs to the safety of my apartment. When I toss my oversized purse onto the table, the book contract slides out. So do the HIV brochures. The apartment reaches out to comfort me with its oak and wallpaper and light. I sit on the sofa and watch the afternoon pass. The colorful spines of my books darken and become indiscernible in shadow.

I assumed the events of my life would coalesce into something profound someday. I believed that, at some point, I would gain an understanding, a wisdom, and all the puzzle pieces would fall into place, and I would say, yes, there was a reason. But my life isn't a novel. There is no nirvana. There isn't even a climax. There is only this day, then another and perhaps one after that, but you can never be sure.

I call Joel's machine and leave a message for him to call me back, that it's important.

I have a desperate need to hear another human voice, so I call Hillary to get her nephew's number.

"Paul's married now," she says. "They live upstate."

"Good for him," I say.

"Yes, she's a darling girl, and they have two beautiful daughters. By the way, how's the book coming along? We're all looking forward to it."

"It's good, Hillary. It's off and running."

I let her chat at me a long time, instead of cutting the conversation short as I usually do. She rambles on about the office and Ethan's recent interest in sailing and renovations they're making to the Bar Harbor place.

"You have to come back for a visit," she says.

"Sure. I'd like that."

Her chatter fills the void, the one HIV left when it sucked the future out of me. Impulsively, I thank her for the way she handled *Blues*. I tell her that she made the experience measure up to all my dreams.

"Why, thank you, Cami."

"I just wanted you to know."

Paul answers on the third ring, and I can hear a baby crying. In fact, he has to tell me to hold on while he deals with the child. "She's mad about the peas and carrots," he explains. "Now who is this?"

"Cami Taylor. Remember? New York?"

A pause. "Oh yes. Cami. How are you?"

"Well, that's what I'm calling about. I just found out I'm HIV positive. There's a chance you were exposed, so . . . you need to be tested."

"Oh, Cami, I'm sorry to hear that." There's an angry scream. "Just a sec."

The phone clunks against a hard surface. When Paul comes back, I can hear his little girl whining, and other muffled sounds too, as if he's juggling her and the phone. "I get tested every time I donate blood," he says. "Wait a minute, sugar. Sorry, not you, Cami." I hear a woman say something in the background, and everything on the other end of the line settles down.

"I donate blood all the time," Paul repeats, "and I'm negative. Geez, I'm real sorry to hear this."

"Good. It's good that you're negative."

"Well, let me know if there's anything we can do for you. I know a couple of great doctors up here."

"I'm all set with that, but can you do me a favor and keep this to yourself?"

"Of course. That goes without saying."

"Thanks, Paul."

I hang up and think about New Mexico. Doubtless that's where it happened. Thanks a lot, Jackie. Too bad I was more naïve than you. Thinking back now, trying to come up with a tally, my recklessness presents itself in face after face after face. There are so few I might actually track down, and so many who might have fetched me this curse. All those good-looking suits who blew through the casino, until I could tell you every amenity offered by every hotel in town, which was a lot more than I knew about the men. All those guys are lost to time and geography.

I knew a few longer than a night or two. The Zuni guy who dealt poker for a while. He might still be in the phone book. Another dealer, the one who was so crazy about me, on whom I based the character Hank. Doug Griffith came after—or was he before? Doug's Auto Parts. I groan, remembering. And Miguel, who had a gallery in Santa Fe. He was kind of shifty. Miguel probably wasn't even his real name.

Things slowed down after New Mexico, but I remember a Barnes and Noble manager in Minneapolis, when I did my book tour. And afterward, in New York? Well, habits die reluctantly if they die at all. There were a few before Joel, men disconnected from such bourgeois technicalities as last names and telephone numbers.

Dear God, what was I thinking?

I rub my forehead. What once felt like notches on my holster now more closely resembles a stack of indictments convicting me as white trash. Jake Davis's face pops into my head, and my heart skips a beat. That was so close! The thought of calling Dallas brings a cold chill over me. Guess what, Kate. I may have infected your boy, the pride of your life, with AIDS. And, oh, by the way, don't guess I'll be coming down for that visit after all.

The phone rings, and I jump.

"Hello?"

"Hi, Cami. It's Joel."

"Is it that late already?"

"It's after one. What's up?"

I open my mouth to speak the words I've rehearsed again and again, but they catch way down deep. All that comes up is a racking silent sob. Joel's beautiful voice uncorks all the afternoon's pent-up emotion, and I can't do anything but cry.

"Are you okay? Cami?" Then, "I'll be right over."

I pull my knees up to my chest and rock, the telephone still gripped in my hand.

Joel lets himself in with the key I never got back. I'm calm by then, and when he sits beside me on the sofa, I look at him through hot, dry eyes.

"I'm HIV positive."

A shadow sweeps over his face. "Are you sure?"

"I'm sure. You have to be tested, Joel."

He nods, takes me in his arms, and holds me close. I can relax now. We don't say another word, and I love him for the comfort he brings.

I awaken slowly, reluctantly, from dreaming about the smell of his musk and the familiar taste of him. I've had many such dreams over the past weeks. The difference this morning is that he's still here when I'm fully awake. I roll over so I can get my arms around him. His beard scratches my chin and cheeks like sandpaper, but I don't mind. We are one again, as if no time has passed. I've missed this so much, and I don't want it to end. Still, when his fingers slip within the veil of that well-trespassed sacred place, I pull away abruptly.

"I can't, Joel."

"It's okay. We'll use a condom."

He puts his mouth on mine to hush me, but my insides are roiling. I want him in the worst way, but not like this.

"Stop. I can't." I lay my cheek against his. "Not with this thing inside me." I raise up and look into his face. The morning sun illuminates those crystal blue irises and exposes the tiny lines his face is taking on. "Promise you'll get tested."

"I will."

"I mean soon. Right away."

"I will. What if I gave it to you?"

I sit up to consider this. I never for a minute thought it came from Joel.

"Do you think that's possible?" I ask.

"Sure, it's possible."

"How many were there before me?"

"Two," he says. We've never exchanged this information before. "You?"

I'm embarrassed to tell him the estimate I came up with. "One too many," I say.

He cocks his head in that way of his. "What did the doctor say?"

"He wants to start drug therapy. I told him I'd have to think about it."

"What's to think about?"

"Nothing, really. I just need some time to get used to the idea. I'm leaving for Texas in a couple of days. I'll try to sort things out while I'm down there."

"Texas?"

"Yeah. I don't know, it's an escape, I guess."

In that moment, I realize that I've decided to retreat to Kate's house, to hole up there and lick my wounds.

"Have you told your folks?" Joel asks.

I shake my head. I won't either. What would be the point? "It wouldn't do them any good to know."

"They have a right to know."

"Where my life is concerned, they have no rights. I don't want them to know."

"Baby, you make everything so much harder than it has to be."

"Do I? Maybe you're right." I rake my fingers through my hair. It's time for Joel to go. Too many old, conflicting feelings when I don't want to feel anything at all. "Thanks for coming over last night."

"What'd you expect?"

"My expectations are a little unreliable lately."

He takes my hand. "Let me know if there's anything I can do. I mean it. Anything."

"I will."

He gets up to leave, and I'm thinking I still have to find a way to get the word to Willie, which means going to the theater on Joel's night off.

"Are you still off Sundays?" I ask.

"Most weeks."

"Call me when you get the test results back. Call my cell phone, in case I'm gone."

"I'll call as soon as I know."

We hug in the open doorway of the apartment, and I lift up a plea to the ether that Joel's tests come back clean. I linger on the landing until I can no longer hear his footsteps on the lobby's marble floor.

Chapter Twenty-One

D r. Wortham calls later in the morning, while I'm sitting at the kitchen table looking through the literature Dr. Kuri's nurse gave me. "I just found out about the results," she says. "How are you holding up?"

"I was a wreck yesterday. Joel came over last night and stayed with me. Today, I don't know. I feel . . . today, I feel nothing."

"I'm glad Joel was there for you."

"Now I'm looking through all this crap they gave me. I have to track down some people. It feels like I have a lot to do."

"You haven't rescheduled any appointments."

"I'm going out of town. I'll call when I get back."

"We can work it out if you want to talk before you leave. Also, I want to give you my private number so you can reach me after hours."

"Okay, I have a pen." I copy the number.

"Cami, this isn't as bad as it feels right now."

"It's pretty bad."

"Yes, but not as bad as it was ten years ago, or even one year ago. HIV isn't the death sentence it once was. Dr. Kuri told me you're postponing treatment. I'm concerned about that."

"Not indefinitely. I just need some time, that's all."

She pauses as if searching for a chink in my determination. "I know it's soon after receiving the news, and I can only imagine what you're feeling."

"Like I said, nothing. I feel numb."

"Of course. I can tell this knocked the wind out of you. I hear it in your voice." She waits for me to come back at her. When I don't, she presses on. "It's normal to be stunned by something like this, but don't let yourself sink. This is the most difficult time, and it's okay to accept help getting through it."

"I just need some time to sort things out."

"It's this sorting out that bothers me. What are you sorting out?"

"My feelings about it, I guess. I have to get used to the idea of being someone with HIV. It changes my whole identity. I don't feel as if I'm the same person I was twenty-four hours ago."

"That's a normal reaction, but you're still very much the same person."

"There's something I've been wondering, Dr. Wortham. Did you suspect this when you ordered all those tests?"

"I have to say I did, yes. Cami, I'm so sorry. I'm extremely displeased with Dr. Kuri. I was called away unexpectedly and couldn't be reached. He should've waited for me to return. I suppose he felt a moral obligation to let you know as soon as possible, but I wanted to be there for you. Again, I'm very sorry."

"How? I mean, why?"

"I do pro bono work with HIV and AIDS patients, so I'm very familiar with the diseases. Your weight loss was a clue, but there could've been many reasons for that. It's hard to say what else. I suppose I'm sensitized to certain signs. I inferred from your characterization of Jackie that you were at risk. You confirmed this, if you recall."

"My alleged promiscuity."

"About that, Cami, research has indicated heterosexual transmission of the virus is more likely male to female than the reverse. Levels of concentration are highest in blood and semen. What that means is, unless a woman has an abrasion, a tear, or an open sore, she's much less likely than a man is to pass it on.

"Dr. Kuri may not have mentioned this because he wants you to contact your previous partners. But I want to ease the burden of guilt you're feeling. There's a decent probability that you haven't infected any of your partners, even Joel. I'm not suggesting you don't contact them. You must. But I do want to give you some peace of mind."

She has given me a precious gift, just now. Oh God, I don't want to get sick, and I don't want to die. But more than that, much more than that, I don't want to make others sick, perhaps even to kill them, to murder Joel with a slow death. I press my fingers against my eyes to stay the rush of tears. "Thank you."

"Please keep me updated. Joel's agreed to be tested?"

"Yes."

"Call me when you get his results."

I wipe my hot, wet face. "I will."

"Good. You have a lot of things going right in this. You have access to the best medical care on the planet. Dr. Kuri and I have discussed your referral to an internist whose experience with the disease is unparalleled. You're young. You're stable. You're strong. You're a survivor, Cami. These are the right ingredients for success in fighting immunodeficiency.

"However, delaying treatment is a poor first step. Your blood tests indicate progression. If you don't begin antivirals, if you don't take care of yourself, physically and psychologically, you could acquire"—she pauses—"something worse."

I say nothing, but I read her loud and clear.

"I'll call you in a few days," she says.

"I'll call you."

"All right. I'll wait to hear from you."

I switch off the phone and go into the bathroom to undress for a shower. From what I can see, my body is unchanged. It should show *something*. The mirror should reflect the disfigurement, with my sick parts brought front and center, like in a Picasso. I open the medicine cabinet to get something for my headache. My birth control pills perch on the second shelf in their little round plastic dispenser. Innocent, they are, as if nothing has changed.

Between these pills and my lame judgment, I thought I was covered. How could I be so stupid? So naïve? How could I think I was in control? Oh, I never went for guys who looked like they got around as much as I did. I went for the shy ones—they stuck out like sore thumbs—figuring they'd be grateful lovers and STD-free. I didn't worry if the condom tore, or if the guy objected to using one. I was cool. Stupid! So stupid!

I jerk the dispenser off the shelf and rip the plastic apart, letting the pills scatter on the floor and into the toilet. When I'm done, there are bits of plastic all over the bathroom and smears of red across my hands from thin cuts on my fingers and thumb. I suck the blood, and it grieves me to the pit of my stomach to know that I'm the only one who can.

♦ ♦ ♦

In the afternoon, when I've finished lying on the sofa, counting and recounting the ceiling squares, I drag myself to the telephone. I call Doug and Miguel. Amazingly, neither of them sounds overly concerned, as if maybe they've heard such news before. When I call the River Bend to get a lead on the lanky Zuni poker dealer, no one knows him. The same is true for Hank's muse.

"Look, I never heard of 'em," the manager says. "They ain't here."

I call information and try the internet, but both searches are equally unfruitful. These men will have to fend for themselves, I decide, and I soothe my conscience with Dr. Wortham's words. I make one last call to the Minneapolis bookstore manager. He's off today, they tell me, but he'll be back on Saturday. "Can I take your name?" the woman asks. No thanks, lady. I'll call back.

I call Kate Davis. No one's home, so I leave a message saying I'm taking her up on the invitation to visit, and I'll be there Monday afternoon. "If that's okay," I add, knowing she's too polite to say no.

Over the next few days, I scour the internet for information about HIV and AIDS. The online medical journals tout advances, but the "Hi, my name is Cami and I'm HIV positive" testimonies are pretty discouraging. I know it's foolish to delay treatment. Why wouldn't I prolong my life? A cure might be right around the corner. I can't defend digging in as I have. It's ridiculous. But I've worked so hard to create myself as I create characters. This image, this version of me, is all I have, and no matter how hard I try, I can't make HIV fit into it.

On Sunday afternoon I take a cab to the Winter Garden and make my way to the box office. I know the girl who's counting receipts. I've chatted with her many times while waiting for Joel.

She looks up and brightens at seeing me. "Hi, stranger! Where you been hiding?"

"How are you, Wendy?"

She sticks her left hand through the ticket slot. "I got married!" she beams.

"Congratulations. Anyone I know?"

"Nah. He's a bartender. Makes martinis to die for."

I force a smile. "How's the crowd?"

"So so. Still payin' the bills, unfortunately. I'm so ready for something different."

"I was going to drop backstage for a couple of minutes. Should be pretty close to intermission, huh?"

She checks her watch. "Oh, about ten minutes. Just a sec. I'll walk you back." She puts away her paperwork and comes out of the ticket booth. "You know Joel's off today, right?" she says as she locks up.

"Yeah, I know."

We make our way down the side aisle in the darkened theater. Grizabella stands center stage. The other cats approach her curiously, but then they shrink from her when they see her torn and shabby coat, her infirmity. She's all used up by life, as they will be one day. This frightens them, and they hate her and shun her because of it. I stop, transfixed, as if I'm seeing the scene for the first time.

The petite gray cat tries to pull off a few of her old moves, but all of her glamour is gone. The actress's face contorts. Everything is there, in her expression—the frustration and heartache at finding herself at this place. The desire to turn back the clock. The longing to be accepted again, instead of being a pariah. My eyes brim with tears, which I hastily wipe away as Wendy tugs at my sleeve.

"C'mon," she whispers.

I follow her backstage, where she gets caught up flirting with a couple of stagehands, leaving me to wait for the cast.

The curtain comes down, and I stand to the side, watching for Willie among the cast members hurrying offstage. The smells of sweat and spirit gum pour off their overheated bodies, reminding me of better times. As they pass, some of them nod or say hello. None stop to chat. The break is short, and they covet every minute. Then I see the broad orange and black shoulders of Rum Tum Tugger coming toward me.

"Willie," I say as he passes.

"Hey, girl. What's up?" I'd forgotten the sound of his voice, that resonant baritone.

"I need to talk to you," I say.

He puts his hand on the small of my back, just as he did that night at the Essex House, and guides me to his dressing room. "In here," he says, opening the door.

When we're alone, I immediately cut to the chase. "I'm HIV positive, Willie. I just found out."

He swears foully and throws a bottle of water that he just picked up. It hits the wall with a hollow, smacking sound, the water arcing from the neck. "Man, oh, man. I don't believe this!" He glares at me. "You gotta be kiddin' me."

His painted Rum Tum Tugger face and furry ears are absurd in contrast to his anger, but I don't laugh because nothing in this room is funny. I want to look away in shame, but I force myself to meet his rage. He has every right to be furious.

"If it's any consolation, my doctor says the odds are really slim that I passed—" I stop, remembering my night with him in light of Dr. Wortham's comment about the abrasions, the blood. If I infected anyone, it's likely to be Willie.

His shoulders slump, and he sits on the stool heavily. "Man, oh, man," he moans. "I knew you were too easy to be a good idea."

This brings a hot flush to my face. I take a notepad and a pen from my purse and lean over his dressing table, scribbling like a madwoman. "Here's my number," I say. "Get tested, and for God's sake, let me know the results." I rip out the page and slap it against his chest. He doesn't try to catch it as it flutters to the floor. I open the door. "My name's there too," I say.

I walk out of the room and begin to breathe again.

Chapter Twenty-Two

K ate hugs me at the airport. The smell of her is familiar and comforting. New York and the past few days are as far away as last night's bad dream. There's no discussion of a rental car. "You can use one of ours," she says. I readily agree, not caring whether I leave the house or not.

"We're having company tonight," she says on the drive to her house. "Well, he's hardly company. We've known him for years, and we get together for dinner once a week to catch up. Anyway, I thought about canceling, but I know David would enjoy meeting you. It isn't a fix-up, even though it'll probably seem like one. David's a professor at SMU, and he travels all the time, so he's way too busy for a relationship right now."

This is a lousy turn. I don't feel like being social. "Well, I'm glad you aren't fixing me up, even though I wouldn't blame you for wanting to put me out of circulation."

"Water under the bridge."

"Is that so?"

"It took me a while, but yes, it is."

"Why'd you bother?" I say.

She looks my way. "That's an odd thing to ask."

I turn away to the window as all kinds of crazy emotions threaten to push through to my face. I thought I was done with all the crying. I have to get myself together or I'll never make it through this. I dig in my purse for a lipstick. It's time to detach, to jettison all these feelings and sail away, unencumbered, into the vacuum of my personal wasteland.

"Anyway," Kate says. "I imagine you get more than your share of fix-ups. Have you been dating since you broke up with Joel?"

"One date. I suppose you'd call it a date, but really it was just a one-night stand."

She doesn't respond to that for a minute.

"It seems to me that a one-night stand might be a very lonely thing," she finally says.

"Trust me, it is. Don't worry. I won't come on to your friend."

"I'm not worried about David. He's a big boy who can take care of himself. Cami, I don't want there to be this thing between us while you're here, this perception that I'm thinking of you in some way that I'm not."

"You mean, that I'm a little bit trashy?"

"That's not what I think."

"How could you not?"

"No human being is trash."

"Oh. Okay."

She pulls onto her street and then into the driveway. After she parks next to the big magnolia tree, she turns off the ignition and faces me. "We don't have to be defined by the things we've done. There's more to us than that." She places her hand on her midsection, and then she actually reaches across the console and puts her other hand on mine. I stiffen.

"Inside, there's more," she says.

"More what?"

"More than we can imagine, even those of us who make up entire worlds." She removes her hand and opens the door. "Besides, you shouldn't be too hasty about David. He's charming *and* handsome."

"Well," I say, "it isn't the best time for me to start a relationship either."

◆ ◆ ◆

In the old days—which is to say, last week—I would've been all over David Nathan Shackleford III. His hair is dusky blond, and so is the fur on his forearms. His ruddy complexion shouts virility, and his green eyes would melt any girl. He's confident too, which is the sexiest quality a man can have. Or a woman, for that matter. I've worked hard to develop it. But the old days are gone, and tonight I must content myself with stimulating conversation.

"It's good to meet you, Cami," he says, taking my hand. "Kate has talked about you for weeks."

"Is that right?"

"It isn't every day we have a successful author among us," he says. "In fact, I have a colleague who's crazy about your work. If she finds out you're here, she'll pester me for an introduction."

"I'm always up for meeting a fan."

"Well, maybe we can work that out."

"Are you two hungry?" asks Kate.

"As a horse," says David.

The three of us move to the kitchen, where Kate has put out a spread of deli meats and cheeses, artisan breads, and all the makings for serious Dagwood sandwiches.

"Kate always feeds me at the kitchen table," David laments. "We never eat in the dining room."

"I'm just trying to make you feel at home, sweetie."

"No, that would mean standing at the sink, eating out of a can."

"I'm familiar with that," I say. "Only for me it's standing in front of the refrigerator eating grapes and cheese."

"So that's your secret," says Kate. "I'll have to try that diet."

The two of them banter about everything and nothing, and neither of them seems to mind that I pick at my food and listen in silence. After dinner, I open a bottle of cabernet that Kate bought for me, the same vineyard she saw at my apartment. Neither of them is interested in drinking, so I have the bottle to myself. I carry it and a glass out to the patio, along with my cigarettes. The backyard shadows are long and the hues have deepened in the evening sun. I don't make it through my first cigarette before David opens the door and comes outside. He settles across the table from me, obviously intent on staying a while.

"It's nice out here," he says. "The best time of the day."

"Sure is," I say and take a drag.

"Kate tells me you just finished your second novel."

"Do you read much fiction?"

"No, not much. Most of my reading is research, but Kate bought me a copy of your book. It's at the top of my to-read stack."

"I hope you enjoy it." I snuff out the butt. I smoke every cigarette down to the filter these days.

"I'm sure I will. It must be quite a high, to finish a novel."

"It is. Finishing *Blues*, well, getting a contract on it was an unbelievable high. This time was nice, but not nearly as intense. Maybe it's a little like sex that way."

He laughs politely.

"Bad joke. Sorry."

"No worries."

I light up again and toss the match into an ashtray that was waiting for me on the patio table. I lean my head back and exhale a rocket of smoke. "Kate says you're a professor at SMU. What do you teach?"

"Ancient Greek. I also teach a couple of days a week at a Bible college in Oak Cliff. They're a completely different group of students."

"Greek's off the beaten path."

"It's fascinating."

"I always thought Greek mythology was cool."

"Everyone loves the mythology, and it's amazing, really, how much of our culture is rooted in beliefs that are similar to those of the ancient Greeks."

"I guess there's nothing new under the sun."

"Right, but that saying happens to come from the Old Testament. 'What has been is what will be, and what has been done is what will be done, and there's nothing new under the sun.' It's in Ecclesiastes."

"That's beautiful, really beautiful."

"Are you familiar with the Bible?"

"More than I thought, I guess. But no, my family isn't religious at all. I do have a housekeeper who's a nut about God."

"What do you mean by nut?"

"Oh, she used to leave Jesus pamphlets all over my apartment, and she had this weird, mystical dream about me once. I think she's a little superstitious. Don't get me wrong. I'm not saying you're a nut. Or Kate."

"Thanks. So is your family in New York?"

"Phoenix. I've only lived in New York since *Blues*. What about you? Did you grow up here?"

"About three blocks that way." He points past the swimming pool. "We Shacklefords were among the original settlers, toughing it out in Highland Park. It was an arduous pilgrimage from Oak Cliff, but someone had to be the pioneers."

"You're old money," I say. It's a compliment, not an accusation.

He laughs. "Not by old money standards. But yeah, by anyone else's we're a pretty privileged bunch."

"Are your parents professors too?"

"Oh, no. The Shackleford men are lawyers. The women tend toward medicine."

"You broke the mold."

He nods slowly and looks off into the middle distance. "It's tough on my parents. Right after college, I took off for Sierra Leone for a couple of years."

"Africa?"

"The west coast. Beautiful country, but the poverty and violence, well, you can't imagine it unless you've seen it. Even then, it's hard to take it in. My parents thought I was wasting my time there. My father said I might as well be pouring water in sand."

"But they must be proud of your academic position."

"It helps, but they don't believe I'm living up to my potential. It isn't hard to understand that, when I look at it from their point of view. They could accept an academic career if it had a bit of luster, but mine doesn't. I haven't published, and I'll probably never be tenured at SMU."

"Why not?"

"I have other irons in the fire."

"Hmm," I say. We fall silent, and I fill my wine glass yet again, even though I'm a little drunk. "Does one of these other irons have a name?"

"No, I'm not seeing anyone."

"A good-looking guy like you? You must beat them off with a stick."

"Not so much." He breaks eye contact and gazes at the white garage wall on the other side of the pool, at the rippled light drifting across it. "I was married before, but it didn't work out."

"Oh?"

He leans back. "I was twenty-seven and Carolyn was twenty-five. We were immature, though. Neither of us had any idea how to make a marriage work."

"Kids?" I ask.

He shakes his head.

"What happened?"

"Oh, we were going different directions, almost from the beginning, but I was too oblivious to realize how far apart we were. It was a disaster. Anyway, Carolyn's a woman of sudden moves. One day, she made up her mind it was over, and she moved on to someone who'd give her the life she wants. And he has."

"How long ago was that?"

"About five years now."

"That's an awfully long time, Professor. Maybe I need to give you the same advice my hairdresser gave me. It's time to get back on that horse. Get back in the game."

"I hate dating. It's a lousy way to meet a soul mate."

"Do you really believe in soul mates?"

"Sure. Don't you?"

"I don't know. Maybe. You're not saying you haven't seen anyone, even casually, since Carolyn, are you?"

"Yeah, that's exactly what I'm saying."

"You have some willpower, Mister."

He laughs. "I play a lot of tennis."

"No, seriously."

"I'm serious. I'm as red-blooded as the next guy, but there are choices to be made in life. This is my choice, given my current circumstances."

"Doing without."

"I don't think of it that way."

"Like a priest."

"I'm not a priest. This isn't a vow of celibacy." He leans forward again, elbows on the table. "It's just my choice, until I marry again." It's a statement, not an explanation or a defense, and I don't believe for one second that Professor David Nathan Shackleford III cares what I think about it.

"That's amazing," I say. "I don't know how you manage it."

"I fill my time with other things, and God gives grace to help."

"I get that it's your choice, and my hat's off to you, but you're wrong if you believe you'll get a gold star for following the rules. Following the rules doesn't make your life any better or worse. The same cruel luck happens to bad people and good people all over the world, no matter what they believe. So what's the point?"

"It isn't about rules."

"What isn't about the rules?"

"Loving God. Your housekeeper. Kate. Me. We love him."

"Good for you," I say. I stand and gather my things. "Look, I'm sorry, but it's been a long day, and I'm exhausted. I think I'll call it a night."

"I enjoyed the visit," he says. "I hope we can do it again."

"Sure. Me too."

I go inside and tell Kate goodnight, and then I carry the rest of the bottle up to my room.

Chapter Twenty-Three

The next morning I wake up early, thinking I'll go for a run, but my body has other ideas. I spend a long time in the bathroom before I stumble back to the bed and collapse on top of the quilt, my energy spent. I stare at the white ceiling, thinking about viral loads and T-cell counts. Dr. Kuri said my viral load is—what? Hundreds? Thousands? I can't remember, I was in such a state.

I imagine those viruses as specks of lint floating in a ray of sunlight, only they're much smaller, and they're in my blood. They aren't floating at all. They're cruising like piranhas and feasting on my lumbering white blood cells, which are too slow to outrun them and too outnumbered to survive. It frightens me to think about all this—this war happening inside me while I lie so still on the bed.

In the quiet of the morning, a distinctly unhouse-like sound falls on my ears, a faint melody. When I slip off the bed and open my door, it gets louder, so I step into the hallway and walk on tiptoes toward Kate's door. She's in there, and she's singing, making such an intimate murmur that I feel as if I'm trespassing. I hold my breath and listen. It's a minor key, and soothing, like spa music. I can't make out her words, so I put my ear to the crack between the door and jamb. Whatever it is, it isn't English. Weird. These people are so strange. I tiptoe back to my room, climb back into bed, and pull the covers over my head.

Kate wakes me late in the morning. "Are you okay?" she asks, jostling my shoulder. "I knocked and knocked."

I groan. I ache all over, as if I have the flu. "What time is it?"

"It's almost noon. Are you feeling okay?" She sits on the bed and puts her hand on my face. "I think you have a fever." She gets up and leaves the room.

I need a day in bed. I haven't been sleeping. I've hardly eaten. Coming off the birth control pills in the middle of my cycle tore up my hormones. I'm a wreck. I'll just give myself a break, time to rest, and then I'll be fine.

Kate comes back and hands me a glass thermometer. "I'm sorry. This is all I have."

"As long as it isn't a rectal thermometer."

She laughs. "No, I promise."

I put it under my tongue, and Kate sits on the edge of the bed. She reaches over and pushes my hair back from my face, like a mother. "Your hair is great," she says. "The color and cut are perfect for your face."

"I have a great hairdresser," I say through clenched teeth. "Gus. He's a whiz."

"Hair and makeup . . ." she says.

". . . are everything," I finish.

"Well, when it comes to looks, they are." She takes the thermometer and holds it up to the light. "It's over a hundred. You must've caught a touch of something."

"I'm gonna take it easy today and get over this. Don't worry about me. Just go ahead and do whatever you had planned."

"Do you want some juice? Maybe something to eat?"

I should eat, but I can't face food right now. "Some juice sounds great. Thank you."

"I'll bring you a glass. And something for the fever."

I stay in bed the rest of the day. In the evening, Kate brings me a bowl of chicken and rice soup that's so delicious I eat all of it. She pulls a chair beside the bed to chat a while.

"Your friend David is a super nice guy," I say.

"He is that."

"Naïve too."

She laughs. "Naïve? Why would you say that?"

"Just the way he looks at life. His expectations, I guess. They're high, and high expectations have a way of disappointing."

"That's true if they're unrealistic, but that all depends on your reality, doesn't it? Personally, I think David's expectations are firmly rooted in his reality."

"There's only one reality. Any other ideas on the subject are just existential crap."

"So wise, at twenty-nine years old," she says. "But I agree. There's only one reality."

I set the empty bowl on the nightstand and scoot down in the bed. Surely, she'll put it into the dishwasher, especially if she thinks I have a bug. I have a compulsive, unreasonable desire to clean up after myself, even though I know the virus doesn't spread through spoons and bowls.

"He won't be disappointed," Kate says. "I'm sure of that."

"Sure of it? Whatever. It doesn't matter. Let him hope. There are worse things."

She pulls the quilt up around my shoulder. "There's a big difference between hoping something will happen and arranging your life in such a way that it will happen, inevitably."

Don't talk to me about arranging a life, lady. I'm the queen of arranging and rearranging, creating and recreating. I wrote the book.

She must read the skepticism on my face. "Do you have a different opinion?"

"I suppose twenty-nine is pretty young," I say, "but I don't feel very young, and I've experienced more than many people who are twice my age. And my experience has taught me that no matter what you do, you never know what's around the corner. Whether you live thirty years or a hundred, in the big scheme of things, it's like—"

"A wisp of smoke?" she offers. "A vapor?"

"Exactly. It's the old cliché. Life is short, and it's uncertain. Anyone who doesn't know that is a fool." I prop myself on one elbow. "God knows I've played the fool. I've read too many well-crafted novels. I used to think life would all make sense one day and have, you know, a beginning, a middle, and an end. But it won't. It never will because there's just one day on top of another until you have a whole string of them, a lifetime of them.

"And that's if you're lucky, because your future can be wiped out in a heartbeat. No warning required." My voice has risen. Come on, Cami, settle down. I measure my remaining words and let the emotion dissipate. "We're all one bad hand away from disaster," I say quietly. "Every single one of us."

"Whew!" Kate says. She leans forward, propping her elbows on her knees. The light from the bedside lamp reflects in her gray eyes, and I can't read what she's thinking. "What makes a successful young woman so jaded?" she asks.

"I'm not. I'm a writer. This is how writers think."

She straightens her back, her gaze unwavering, considering me. I have an urge to lay the HIV out there, like a trump card that proves my point, but do I really want to confess to this woman? No, I most definitely do not. Besides, it would only prove her point, not mine. It's time to back out of this.

"Look, Kate, I've seen a lot of bad stuff. You don't live around the people I've known without noticing that life can be cruel. When I hear the things David says, I think, 'Don't be so sure, buddy boy. There might be an unpleasant surprise waiting for you around the next corner.'"

"So what's your conclusion? How should we live?"

"Well now, if I knew that, I would be the smart one, wouldn't I? Just do the best you can, I guess. Go with what you know."

"Why not eat, drink, and be merry?" she says, "for tomorrow we die."

"My point, exactly. Why not?" After a minute, I add, "I imagine you have an opinion about that."

"I do, but not tonight." She picks up the bowl from the nightstand. "Don't you be naïve, Cami. You aren't the first person to question the injustice and pointlessness of life, nor will you be the last. 'For who knows what is good for a man in life, all the days of his futile life which he passes like a shadow?'"

"You should put that in the dishwasher, just in case this is catching. Who said that?"

"Someone who's been dead a long time, but he was very, very wise."

"Did the wise man say what we should do about this futile life?"

"He did, indeed. Let's see if I can remember." She looks away, thinking. "Wait. Yes, I have it. 'Let us hear the conclusion of the whole matter: Fear God and keep His commandments. Um, the rest is, for God will bring every work into judgment, including every secret thing, whether good or evil.'"

"They're beautiful words. They just aren't very useful to someone like me."

"Someone like you?"

"Keep God's commandments? That's predicated on the belief that, one, there is a God, and two, you know what his or her rules are. There are hundreds of opinions out there about all kinds of gods, but I'm not convinced enough to subscribe to any of them."

She nods.

"So, no words to convince me?"

"Are there any words that could? Tonight?"

"Not that I can think of."

"Me either," she says.

I look at the clock. We've been talking almost an hour. "You know, my shrink gets $275 for a session like this. You should hang out a shingle."

"Is this what it's like?"

"Pretty much. Well, she argues with me more, tries to provoke me more."

"Why is that? Do you know?"

"Oh, she's drawing me out." I straighten the pillow and lie down again. "It's a technique they teach in shrink school."

Kate laughs at this. She stands up, and then she leans over and kisses my cheek. "Goodnight, sweetie. Hope you feel better tomorrow."

"Thanks. I'm sure I will."

She closes my bedroom door, leaving me to mull over our conversation.

◆ ◆ ◆

I do feel much better in the morning. Not well enough to run, but definitely well enough to get out of bed and function. I decline the bacon and eggs Kate offers to cook in favor of a bowl of cereal and some fruit. It's 100 percent more breakfast than I've been eating the past week. I leave the cigarettes upstairs so I won't be so tempted to relax on the patio with a smoke. Instead, I sit at the table with Kate and drink coffee. She says that she—and Tom when he's home—read the paper at the kitchen table every morning. It's their domestic ritual to start the day. I imagine him reading the *Chicago Tribune* in the hotel restaurant at this moment.

"When will Tom be home?" I ask.

"He'll come home for the weekend, but he'll have to go right back on Sunday night. It's a big project."

She glances up at me over her tortoise-shell reading glasses. I used to look forward to wearing cute little half glasses in middle age.

"It's just you and me," she says, "so what would you like to do?"

"I need to check my email. I promised Chris I'd get right on any revisions. Other than that, whatever. I'll help you if you need it, or just hang out. Don't feel like you have to entertain me. I'm happy lying out by the pool all day."

"Well, in that case, I promised my sister I'd help her with some school shopping for Karah, and today's probably a good day for that. You're welcome to join us, but don't feel obligated. I can be back early enough for us to go out for a bite to eat, and maybe see a movie or something. How does that sound?"

"Sounds good."

"The keys to the SUV are in the drawer next to the washing machine in the laundry room. Feel free to use it anytime. You don't have to ask."

"Thank you."

"Make yourself at home, Cami."

"I will."

Kate shows me how to work the security alarm and how to turn on the pumps for the pool and the whirlpool. She writes down her cell phone number and her sister's number, in case anything comes up. "You're on your own," she says as she gathers up her things to leave. "I'll be back by five or so."

I go upstairs and fire up the computer. I need a shower—it's been two days—but if I spend the day in the pool, it can wait. I have two messages from Chris, the second an urgent repeat of the first because I didn't answer him promptly. Checking email was the last thing on my mind yesterday. He has attached files for revision. It'll be a morning's work, but I suppose I should be grateful for the distraction. At least I have something to do with myself.

I download the files and work on my edits. It's a good thing Chris had the manuscript before my little crisis blossomed, or he never would've seen it. Every word of this book now seems trivial and pretentious, and the whole thing has nothing to do with anything that matters. My emotional ties to the story are as withered as severed vines. I rely solely on my writerly skills and professionalism to give him some decent revisions.

When I finish working, I make a sandwich, hardly putting a dent in the food Kate has stockpiled in the refrigerator. Then I take to the pool and swim laps. My body responds, and I begin to relax, even though I hadn't realized I was tense. Afterward, I doze on an inflatable raft, my leg trailing in the warm water.

Here, lazing in this Texas swimming pool under a late summer sun, the complications in my life evaporate, and nothing much matters anymore. There's no one with whom to compete—not even myself—and nothing to prove anymore. There are no feelings to be sorted through before I can actualize my potential. I'm as transient as a flower, and to be honest, it's a relief.

I shower before Kate gets home, and she finds me in the bathroom putting on makeup. She leans against the frame of the open door. "David called this afternoon and left a message for you," she says. "You must've been outside."

"What about?"

"One of his colleagues at SMU is asking if you'll give a lecture to her literature class. They're undergraduates."

"The fan," I say.

"I imagine so. He asked that you call him back tonight."

"I don't know about that. I've never given a lecture." I don't say the rest of what I'm thinking, that I won't waste my time talking to a bunch of privileged, smartass college kids.

"You'll have them eating out of your hand," she says.

"I doubt that."

"Well, if Jake's any indication, you will."

A flush rises to my face, and I look down and twist the lid onto the mascara.

"You're everything they want to be, Cami. Attractive. Sophisticated. Successful. My son was completely smitten. Why do you think I came back early that day? I got to thinking I'd left the matches too close to the gasoline."

I look at her reflection in the mirror. "You knew?"

"I suspected," she says. "The way a woman carries herself tells a lot about her history. I knew you were experienced. Jake isn't, but he's impulsive. Anne takes after her father so much more. She thinks everything through, but Jake's like me, going off on a whim."

I turn around and face her, leaning against the vanity. "Why did you invite me back here, Kate? Come to think of it, why'd you ask me here the first time?"

"I just want to spend time with you, to get to know you."

"Why me? Am I a project?"

"A project?" She processes this for a few seconds. "You can't think of any other reason why I'd want to spend time with you?"

"Not really."

"I don't know what to say to that, except why'd you come if that's what you think?"

"It's a good time for me to be away from New York."

"Why? What's going on?"

"Just"—I wave my hand— "a situation I want to avoid." As if I left my diagnosis in New York.

"It would've been nice to hear that you came because you want to get to know me too, but I'll try not to have my feelings hurt about that."

"I'm just being honest, Kate. I like you, and I think you're an interesting person, but I don't like staying with people, not even my parents."

This is a perfect time for her to ask why I didn't get a hotel, but she doesn't go there. Maybe she's afraid I'll pick up and leave, and she'll lose her project.

"Well, I'm glad you're here, whatever the reason," she says. "I'm starving too. Ready?"

"Sure."

As I follow her downstairs, I tell myself that I don't really care whether Kate's made a project of me or not. If she's bent on saving me from myself, she's too late.

Chapter Twenty-Four

I have a forkful of chicken poised midway between the plate and my mouth when Kate asks if I mind if she gives thanks for the food. "Of course not," I say. I put the fork down and take the hand she extends across the table. She closes her eyes, but I keep mine open to watch the sideways glances of the diners around us.

"Father, we thank you for this time together and for this wonderful meal," she says. "I ask you to bless it and the sweet fellowship we'll share, in Jesus's name. Amen."

At least she kept it short.

I begin eating, and the food tastes pretty good. I haven't had a cigarette since the night before last. I'm dying for one, but if I pick up the ciggies again, I won't want to eat a thing. Kate offers a roll from the basket, which I take, break open, and slather with butter. What abandon! Eat like a pig, Cami. Eat with the lust of a glutton. It can only do you good.

"Are you going to do the lecture?" Kate asks.

"I don't think so," I say. "Giving talks isn't my thing."

"It would mean a lot to David."

"Yeah, but I really don't want to. . . ."

". . . and it would mean a lot to me."

Crap. Okay. Just bite the bullet and get it over with.

"Well, if it's that big a deal, sure. Why not?"

"Oh, good! Thank you, Cami." She picks up her fork and begins to eat, her other hand resting in her lap. I remove my elbows from the table.

"I never told you what I thought of your book, did I?" she says. "Would you like to hear?"

"Are you kidding? We can talk about *Blues* all night."

She laughs. "Well, I can see why it was a bestseller. You have a gift for pulling the reader into Jackie's world. I felt as if I was right there, looking over her shoulder."

"Thank you."

"And your readers experience a life through Jackie that's probably completely foreign to many of them."

"That's an important thing about fiction, not only telling a story, but helping the reader see and feel things. Maybe even understand things, they wouldn't—couldn't—otherwise."

"You hit the mark on that. While I was reading, my mind kept going back to your comment at the bookstore in New York. You said you revealed yourself in the book."

"I said that?"

"Yes, you did. So naturally, I expected Jackie to reflect you. But now that I'm getting to know you better, I don't think she does, and it makes me wonder what you think of Jackie."

Kate's right. Jackie never imitated me. I imitated her, and I don't feel the same about her as I did when I so lovingly formed her in the womb of my computer. The truth is that I blame my HIV on my admiration for Jackie's recklessness. I didn't write her truly in that respect. She got off scot-free.

Kate waits patiently for me to answer.

"I'm thinking," I say.

"Take your time."

"In *Blues*, I wrote a lot about relationships between people, about how they—how *we*—manipulate one another and use one another in every way we can. Jackie understood the relationship game for what it is, a game, and she played the hand she was dealt. At the time I wrote the book, I thought she played it well. I still believe she played it well, but I'm not so sure I should've let her walk away unscathed. The game always costs us something."

"Did Jackie walk away unscathed?"

"Yeah, I think so. At the point when I ended the story, anyway."

The waiter comes by and tops off our glasses of iced tea. When he leaves, Kate absently runs her thumb along the rim of her glass, gazing into it like a crystal ball. "I can't stop thinking about the last scene," she says. "Jackie comes out of a house trailer at sunrise. It's a cool morning. Crisp, I think, was a word you used. She looks across the valley at downtown Albuquerque, and at the river winding past it. She looks at the casino where she works. She sees the hotels she's been in. She stands on the trailer's cinderblock steps, thinking about all of it. Behind her, the sun rises over the Sandia Mountains, throwing light across the mesa west of town. Inside the trailer, the guy she met the night before is still asleep on a pullout sofa bed, amid the empty bottles and full ashtrays from the night before."

"You have a good memory."

"That scene made an impression on me. Jackie stands in the doorway, thinking about her future. I believe she knows her life can't stand up to the years ahead. She knows she'll end up with nothing."

"She does. At that moment, she's also looking at the neighborhoods, at the houses of the people who've chosen lives that are different from hers."

Kate nods slowly. "Yes, I thought so. You didn't write it exactly that plainly, but it was there, between the lines." Kate smiles, but there's no amusement in her eyes. "Then Jackie says, 'Ah hell, double down.' She skips off the steps and gets into her old red Mustang"—Kate stops for a beat—"and she drives away."

"That's it," I say, leaning back.

Kate leans back too. "I've thought about that scene over and over since I read the book, about what it reveals about Jackie. She's like a wild horse. She's used to living wild, sniffing the wind for whatever she wants. In her season, which is all the time, she can't be held back, and no lover who seeks her has to weary himself to find her."

"That's beautiful," I say. "Are you making it up?"

"No, someone else said it."

"Another wise man?"

"A prophet."

I pick up my iced tea, sip it, and wait for what Kate will say next. She leans forward again, her elbows on the table this time.

"If we plead with Jackie to pull back from danger and come into the fold, where it's safe, she gets angry. 'No!' she cries. 'There's no hope for me!'"

The man at the next table turns and gawks, and Kate lowers her voice. "Jackie says, 'It's no use. I love strangers, and I will go after them.'" She stops talking and searches my face, knocking at a door I won't open. When I don't react, she says, "Cami, the end of your story haunts me. It breaks my heart to think about a young woman who's determined to go after a life that will destroy her."

So she is trying to save me from myself. "Kate," I say, "Jackie is who she is, and she can't do anything about it. I wrote her that way."

"God rewrites hearts, just like an author. He'll give her a new heart, if she's willing."

"People don't change."

"Yes, they do. Sometimes they are changed."

"Well, I haven't ever seen it happen. Ever."

"Maybe you haven't seen everything yet."

I shake my head. "No, Kate. I appreciate that you're devoted to your idea of God, I really do, but the thing I've appreciated the most is that you don't try and push your beliefs onto me, to convert me."

"Like now," she says.

"Yes, like now."

And just like that, she backs out of it. I don't think she'll bring it up again.

◆ ◆ ◆

I lie in bed the next morning, listening to Kate's song. It drifts to me from her room, barely audible amid the chirps of the neighborhood birds. I lean over and reach into my oversized travel purse, which slouches on the floor, and fish my cell phone from its black hole. I call the answering machine at home and find eight messages since I left New York. All but two are hang-ups. One is from Dr. Wortham, so carefully choosing her words. She says she's thought of a couple of options that might interest me. "Give me a call when you're back in town, or before, if you get this message." I press seven to delete.

The last message is from Joel. His results came back negative.

"Yes!" I say aloud.

I turn off the phone and roll over. I can sleep until noon and spend the afternoon floating in the pool. I'm addicted to this lazy routine of rising late and doing nothing. There's no fire in me to write, no urgency to make the days productive. I've discovered that no effort is as good as my best effort. I've never known such freedom.

Joel's message reminds me that I still haven't talked to the bookstore manager in Minnesota. I'll try and reach him this afternoon, if it doesn't fly out of my mind again. Who knows? Maybe he's the one who gave it to me.

◆ ◆ ◆

My week in Texas stretches into an extended holiday, thanks to Kate's bottomless hospitality. I settle into a routine that centers around floating on an air mattress in the pool. Tom shows up on the weekends, usually late Friday night, and leaves again on Sunday afternoon. He and Kate make the most of their time together, going out to eat and to church, and I stay out of their way. During the week, Kate and I take meals together, but otherwise we go our separate ways.

I eventually finish reviewing the proofs for the new book. Well, I don't actually read them or even open the files, but I tell Chris I did. I don't give a rat's ass about the book anymore. I put off the lecture for David's colleague, blaming Chris's deadlines. I pretend to be working—not sleeping—during the hours upon hours I spend in my bedroom. Sometimes, I lie in bed and try to figure out what to do when I leave here. Should I go back to New York and start treatment? I can't bear tarnishing Cami Taylor's promising literary reputation with this plague, not that anyone has to know, except my lovers, which might as well be everyone. The word's probably all over town already because of Willie.

I even go as far as imagining a new life in a new town, somewhere out West, maybe Denver or Seattle—with a new name of course—living off my royalties. Thinking about all the details of making that happen makes me so tired I can't see straight.

Kate asks questions about my work from time to time, enough to show she's interested in my interests. "Have you started writing the new novel yet?" she asks.

"I'm ruminating," I say.

If she's on to me, she keeps it to herself.

One morning, she asks if I'll come along and help with her Meals on Wheels deliveries. I'm as lethargic as a sloth, but it would be too rude to say no. We drive to a Catholic church in a run-down part of town, and Kate pulls into a shattered asphalt parking lot, where the volunteers meet to pick up the meals. We get out of her Mercedes, and she hands me the smaller of two ice chests she keeps in the back. The larger chest has Meals on Wheels handwritten on the lid. "This one's for the hot meals," she says. "I have cold packs in the small one for the pudding and milk."

Inside the church's paneled foyer, volunteers chat in knots of two or three, drinking burnt coffee in paper cups. Kate introduces me around, and I make small talk with a couple of people until I get a chance to break away and go into the empty sanctuary. The church is old, but clean, the walls freshly painted, and the scarred wooden pews polished. Tables with candles line the side aisles, and some of the candles are burning. I suppose they represent a thermodynamic theology, in which pious prayers are given a boost up to heaven on thin columns of heated air.

As I stroll down the side aisles, an enormous, garishly painted Virgin Mary watches over the place and me. I came in here to see the stained-glass windows. I noticed them from the parking lot, but the sunlight coming through really sets them off. Each window tells a story. They always do. One depicts Jesus embracing a lamb, surrounded by children: Jesus the gentle. Another shows Jesus breaking bread: Jesus the breadwinner. Yet another shows the crucifixion: Jesus the tortured. I hate the crucifixion scenes. Every church has them, even though they're sad and disturbing. Why Christians memorialize their savior's brutal execution is beyond me.

"They're beautiful, aren't they?"

I turn to see the man whose voice echoes across the sanctuary. He's wearing a Meals on Wheels tee shirt and carrying an ice chest, which I judge to be empty from the way he handles it. He's elderly and not too many years from being on the other end of this charity.

"The colors are so vivid," I say, "especially on a sunny day like today."

"Enjoy," he says, "and make yourself at home."

The foyer is quiet when he opens the door to leave, my cue to reluctantly drag myself outside. A truck has pulled into the parking lot, and the volunteers load up their carriers. I find Kate and help her pack a dozen or so meals, pudding cups, and half pints of whole milk. Then we all disperse, carrying our wealth of nourishment to the four corners of the neighborhood.

Chapter Twenty-Five

One meal remains in the back of the SUV, and we've left ten sated old people in our wake. Their wrinkled faces run together in my mind, but Kate doesn't have any trouble remembering the details of their shrunken lives. "The last person on my route is Sam," she says. "Sam's special, and I visit him last so I can spend more time there."

"What's so special about Sam?"

"He isn't elderly like the others."

Kate winds through the neighborhood, signaling every time she turns, whether anyone is behind us or not. I watch the houses go by. Many of them are being renovated, the gentrification of another impoverished neighborhood. Of course, all this new blood moving in means the old blood is being squeezed out. Kate pulls to the curb in front of a prairie style, white frame home with green shutters and a steep yard. The house has fresh paint and a good roof. There isn't a rotted board on it, but the grass needs trimming, and so do the hedges.

"How old is he?" I ask.

"Oh, early forties, I guess."

"What's wrong with him?"

"Sam has AIDS," Kate says. "It isn't contagious, at least not from casual contact, but I understand if you don't want to go inside."

I gaze at the house.

"Had you rather wait in the car?" she asks.

I turn to look at her and then follow her gaze to my hand, which is clenched around the door handle like a bird's talon. I splay my death-white fingers and let the blood flow back into them.

"Maybe you should wait here," she says.

"No. I'll come in."

"You're sure?"

"Yes, I'm sure."

I get out of the car and follow her to the porch, with my insides jumping. Kate knocks at the door, and we wait. "It takes him a while to get up," she explains.

I recognize the man who answers the door with a wheezing effort. I've seen him before in photographs of Auschwitz. He's a skeletal, wispy-haired creature, the face of revelation when the death camps were liberated. Except Sam isn't wearing striped pajamas. He's wearing Levi's that hang from his bony hips, and a pullover sweater, even though the day is warm.

"Katie, you brought a new friend!" he exclaims breathlessly.

"This is Cami," says Kate.

I give him the most charming smile I can muster and reach out to shake his hand. His long, thin fingers are dry and cool.

"Come in, please," he says.

I follow the two of them into Sam's home. He has good taste. His paintings, vases, and collectibles are expensive and positioned just so. The house is surprisingly free of dust, but it smells of sickness, and it's stiflingly hot.

"I'll put your lunch in the kitchen," says Kate, and she disappears through a side door.

"Thanks, sweetie. Come on back to my nest, Cami, where we can visit."

He leads me down the hallway, past a stairway to the second floor, and into a large corner room in the back. This is the bedroom where Sam lives. It's cluttered with his books and magazines, and photographs crowd every wall. There's an occasional table between his bed and an overstuffed chair, and on it are an astounding number of medicine bottles. There are a couple of hopeful armchairs for visitors, and a ladder-back chair that sits against the wall at the foot of the bed. The midday sun shines brightly through four tall windows.

"Have a seat," Sam says. He settles into the deep chair next to his medicine stockpile.

"May I look at your photos?" I ask.

"Help yourself. Are you visiting from out of town?"

"Yes."

I study the photographs, one by one. It doesn't take long to pick out Sam in better times. He was handsome, and he's with other handsome men in many photos. The pictures with people who are probably family members seem to be much older.

"Where's home?" he asks.

"New York. I'm just visiting."

Kate comes in from the kitchen. "Cami and I are—what did we decide? Sixth cousins? We just stumbled across each other."

"You stumbled across me," I say.

"Well, yes, that's true."

She sits in one of the armchairs, and I take the other.

"When were you diagnosed?" I ask. If my candor surprises Sam, he doesn't let it show, and I don't think he minds. I suspect his AIDS is like the proverbial dead horse on the dining room table. I'd kill to have an honest, rational conversation about having HIV.

"Eight years ago," Sam says. "It went into AIDS last fall." He rubs his pants leg. "I'm one of those people who thought it would never happen to me, even though some of my friends died with it back in the eighties. I was careful, or at least I thought I was. But it's hard to be careful enough. It's impossible, really."

"So true," I say.

He sighs, a big hollow breath that sounds like it's blowing through a cave. "Unfortunately, my body doesn't have what it takes to put up a good fight." He sweeps his wasted arm over the table. "Twenty-three pills a day, and they wonder why I'm never hungry."

I get up from the armchair and sit on the bed to survey his medical arsenal. Every single bottle is empty, and unlike the rest of the house, dust covers the caps. "Anyone would get sick of that," I say. I get up and go to the bookcase. "Looks like you're a reader."

Sam lets out his breath. "Yes, I love to read. Mostly poetry."

I pull out *The Collected Poems of Emily Dickinson.* "I have this edition at home," I say. I turn to one of my favorites and read:

> A precious, mouldering pleasure 't is
> To meet an antique book,
> In just the dress his century wore;
> A privilege, I think,
>
> His venerable hand to take,
> And warming in our own,
> A passage back, or two, to make
> To times when he was young.

"You read beautifully," Sam says.

"I love words."

I close the book and start to put it back on the shelf.

"My favorite is page one ninety-nine," he says.

I find the page and read again:

Because I could not stop for Death,
He kindly stopped for me;
The carriage held but just ourselves
And Immortality.

We slowly drove, he knew no haste
And I had put away
My labor, and my leisure too,
For his civili*ty*.

Since then 'tis Centuries; but each
Feels shorter than the day
I first surmised the horses' heads
Were toward eternity—

"Yes, this is a good one. I like the line, 'And I had put away my labor and my leisure too.'"

I slip the book back into its place. I'm ready to leave this sad room, this sad man. "It was nice to meet you," I say. I bend over and kiss Sam's cheek. His skin is as dry as parchment.

He struggles to his feet and hugs me, and I hug him back. He feels like a bundle of sticks in my arms. "Thank you for coming," he says.

When Kate and I are back in the car, she thanks me for showing Sam some warmth. "You connected with him," she says. "You made him feel less like an outcast. He's so isolated."

I say nothing in response. Kate pulls away from the curb, and I watch out the windshield, memorizing the route back to her house.

Chapter Twenty-Six

T he next afternoon, I borrow the Mercedes and return to Sam's house. I don't say anything to Kate about it.

"This is a surprise!" Sam rasps when he opens the door.

"How are you today, Sam?"

"I'm fine, just fine. Come on in."

I follow him down the hall. He walks close to the wall, touching it lightly now and again, as if he might topple over. Today he's wearing sweats that hang from his shoulders and hips as if they're empty, as if they're on hangers.

"Would you like something to drink?" he asks.

"Sure. Anything you have."

"Coca-Cola?"

"A Coke would hit the spot."

"Wait here, honey, and I'll bring it."

It's insufferably hot in the house, but I came prepared in a sleeveless cotton blouse, shorts, and sandals. I wait in one of the armchairs until he returns with the Coke in a Waterford tumbler. "I don't have many callers," he says, "so it's a special occasion." He hands me the glass and eases himself into his chair.

"I enjoyed yesterday. I thought we might read some more of your poetry."

"I enjoyed it too, sweetie."

I take my drink to the bookcase and sit cross-legged on the floor in front of it. Right away, I spy a collection of Yeats. Next to it is a volume of sonnets. "You want to hear something from Yeats? Or Shakespeare?"

"The sonnets belonged to my ex. No Shakespeare, and especially no sonnets."

"Yeats, then."

"Page sixty-one," Sam says.

I read:

> When you are old and gray and full of sleep,
> And nodding by the fire, take down this book,
> And slowly read, and dream of the soft look
> Your eyes had once, and of their shadows deep;
>
> How many loved your moments of glad grace,
> And loved your beauty with love false or true;
> But one man loved the pilgrim soul in you,
> And loved the sorrows of your changing face.
>
> And bending down beside the glowing bars,
> Murmur, a little sadly, how love fled
> And paced upon the mountains overhead
> And hid his face amid a crowd of stars.

"Beautiful," I say.

"Isn't it?"

He gives me page after page, which I read. He's as sentimental as a girl, choosing the poignant ones—the ones about lost love and lost dreams. He's choosing the ones with the best rhythm and movement too. Whether he realizes it or not, he's choosing for the sound of the words in his ear.

"Last one," I say. "I'm getting hoarse."

"Page eighty-nine. For you."

I turn to it and read:

> O what to me the little room
> That was brimmed up with prayer and rest;
> He bade me out into the gloom,
> And my breast lies upon his breast.
>
> O what to me my mother's care,
> The house where I was safe and warm;
> The shadowy blossom of my hair
> Will hide us from the bitter storm.
>
> O hiding hair and dewy eyes,
> I am no more with life and death,
> My heart upon his warm heart lies,
> My breath is mixed into his breath.

I read the last two lines again. "That's very nice, and sensual."

"So tell me about the lucky guy in your life."

"Don't have one."

"You do like guys, though, right?"

"Oh, yes, I like men. Very much."

"Are you playing hard to get?"

"No, I couldn't be any easier to get." I put the book back on the shelf. "I was wondering, Sam, how long have you been off the meds?"

He looks away, and I wonder if he'll say it's none of my business. "A few weeks," he says finally. "I'd rather nobody know. It would just cause a to-do."

"Don't worry, I won't tell Kate. As a matter of fact, maybe we can keep my visit today between us too."

"Why's that?"

"No particular reason. How long were you on antivirals?"

"Since I was diagnosed eight years ago. They were miserable, especially back then, but I was buying time, hoping for a breakthrough."

"They say it's right around the corner."

"Promises, promises, but I'm okay with it now. I owe that to Kate."

"Okay with dying?" I blurt, before I can stop myself.

Sam smiles. "I'm on good terms with God, honey, so I'm not afraid of leaving all this. As a matter of fact, I'm just now getting to the good stuff."

"You believe in God because of Kate?"

"Oh, no, I've always believed in God. It never made any sense to me the way some people think the world just happened, just pulled itself together. Things always seem to be going the other direction, you know? Falling apart."

"How do you know you're on good terms with God?" I ask.

"I just know it, in here." Sam points to his chest. "You should talk to Kate. She can explain it a lot better."

I get to my feet. "I need to get going. Can I put this glass in the kitchen?"

"Here, I'll take it." Sam gets up too, which is a bit of a struggle.

"I thought I'd come again tomorrow, if it's okay," I say.

"You know I'd love it."

He walks me to the door, and then waves good-bye from the porch as I drive away.

Something hardened in me this afternoon, seeing what the full-blown disease has done to Sam. I don't know what I'm going to do or where I'm going to go, but I know for sure that I will never go where he is. I will not go into AIDS, no matter what.

When the time is right, I'll know it, and I'll do what's necessary. Not because I have courage, but because I don't.

◆ ◆ ◆

Kate isn't home when I return. She's in and out a lot, going on with the activities of her life in spite of my presence. She left a note saying she'll be home by six and asking if I feel like Mexican food for dinner. It's rude of me to take her car—as I did this afternoon and will again tomorrow—with no explanation of where I'm going or when I'll be back, but I don't feel like listening to her praise me for visiting Sam.

I decide to check my email. The requests from Chris dried up a few days ago, and I assumed the manuscript was going into production, but there's an email from him about the title. "Did you come up with something besides Jerome and Rachael?" he writes. "I need an answer by tomorrow at the latest. I left a message on your cell."

It is a lousy title, but I can't think of anything better.

Chris finishes by saying a doctor named Sylvia Wortham called his office, trying to get in touch with me. "Aren't you checking your messages at home?" he writes. "When are you coming back to New York?!?"

I'm so detached from New York that it's been days since I bothered to check the answering machine at the apartment. I haven't thought about my parents either, if they were trying to reach me. I didn't tell them I was leaving for Dallas, and they don't have the cell number because I don't trust Mom not to broadcast it. I call the machine and cycle through a dozen hang-ups and solicitation calls. There's a message from Joel too. "Just called to see how you are," he says. "Give me a call when you're back in town."

There are two messages from Sylvia. The first is just a how goes it, but the second one bears a trace of frantic alarm.

"I'm concerned about you, Cami. Please call the office or my personal number. You can reach me at one of them." She pauses so long that I'm surprised the machine doesn't cut her off. "Please don't pull away from us," she says.

She must think I've gone off the deep end, which I have. I feel completely trapped, when I let myself think about it, and Sylvia's message fills me with dread at the thought of returning to New York. HIV will take center stage the minute I go back. I can't face it.

I reply to Chris's message: "If Wortham calls again, tell her I'll contact her when I return to New York, which will happen when I'm finished being in Texas. You have carte blanche on the title, Chris. I'm tapped out. Name it whatever you want. You also have carte blanche on any other decisions that have to be made. Just do whatever needs to be done." I press the send button and turn off the computer.

Chapter Twenty-Seven

hen Kate comes home, she asks if I mind running by David's house before dinner. "He's out of town, and I need to feed the cat and check on things," she says.

"Where is he?"

"I think he's in Atlanta this week. He travels almost every weekend, preaching."

"Preaching?"

"David's a preacher, Cami."

"I thought he was a teacher."

"That too."

We pull into the driveway of a house with wood siding and a deep front porch. A couple of ladder-back rockers are on the porch, and I wonder if David ever takes the time to sit and watch his neighborhood. The lawn is freshly mown, and although there are no flowers to tend, the shrubs are trimmed.

Kate unlocks the door, and we enter a small foyer with a living room on one side and a dining room on the other. A huge orange tabby cat reclines atop the bare dining table. When we come in, he stretches and slowly rolls to his back, looking at us upside down and mewing a greeting.

"Get down, cat," Kate says. She starts toward him, and he scrambles up, jumps to the floor, and darts out of the room.

David's house is small, but it still dwarfs my apartment. I see Kate's touch everywhere, but she's made the décor masculine enough.

"Did you decorate for him?" I ask.

"I helped."

While Kate takes care of the cat, I give myself a tour, opening a door to a bedroom that contains only a desk, a computer, and a bookshelf. Haphazard piles of paper and scattered books clutter the room. I close the door again and continue down the hall. The door to his bedroom is open. The bed is a mission oak double, not a king. A matching dresser stands against the opposite wall. Instead of a bedspread, he has a quilt that must be Kate's handiwork, a geometric design in varying shades of brown and tan and blue. He pulled it up over the pillows—slipshod, not neatly. That's okay with me. I hate it when a guy is fussier than I am.

A hardcover copy of *Blues* is on the nightstand. I assume it's the one Kate bought for him. I turn to the title page to see if she wrote a sappy note, but there's only a cryptic reference: Matt 18:19. David is about a third of the way through the book, and he marked his place with an airline ticket stub. Chicago to Dallas, seat 11A. That's a window seat, the same as I always choose. I imagine him looking out the window at the changing landscape as he crisscrosses the country, and I wonder if he notices the same things I do.

Has he seen towering black thunderstorms, with lightning flashing through them like so much pent-up fury? Has he climbed above a dreary winter overcast and thrilled to find the sun shining on white hills and meadows in the sky? I've seen the television antennas in New Jersey poking up through a layer of clouds, looking like so many children's sticks forgotten in the snow.

David stopped reading at a chapter break, which is much better than if he'd stopped at a random place, midparagraph or midsentence. Maybe he's into the story. There's an especially steamy scene coming up between Jackie and a suit from New York. When the guy drives Jackie to his hotel after her shift, he says he's a Madison Avenue mogul, trying to impress her and testing her knowledge of corporate geography. Precious little impresses Jackie, and she doesn't give a rat's ass about corporate geography.

I remember very well my muse for this scene—a good-looking, slick-haired guy who made eyes at me all night from the poker table. When he finally came to my table to play a couple of hands, he flashed his money and his Rolex and his diamond pinkie ring. He fancied himself a high roller, but he was in a two-bit casino, and he didn't fool me for a minute. Later that night, I went to his hotel and showed him how it's done out West. After that, I knew I could handle anything that New York handed me.

I read the erotic scene I penned so long ago. Jackie's pretty— not with Barbie looks, but stunning in her way. She has symmetrical features, green eyes, and dishwater blond hair. Like David's, I realize. I always wanted blond hair. I gave Jackie a prettier face and a more voluptuous figure than mine. She turns men's heads wherever she goes, rising above the end-of-the-line vibe of the casino crowd, as if she could be elsewhere, a much better elsewhere, if she chose to be. I wrote her with options.

Even now, after everything that's happened, Jackie still has the dewy freshness of youth. She's forever twenty-three and not the least bit depreciated by the miles she's racking up. But when I reread this scene, I see an old whore, or something even worse. At least prostitutes are compensated. I got nothing. I wish I'd gotten nothing.

I imagine David reading the scene, in which I included every detail, and wondering how much of me is in it. I imagine him adding this scene to the sum of Jackie's excesses and coming up with someone

I no longer want to be. I move the bookmark past the scene to the next chapter break.

Kate hasn't come to find me yet, so I open the door to David's walk-in closet. As soon as I step inside, his scent overwhelms me—a beautiful, earthy mix of his body and his aftershave, of leather and denim. I press my face into his clothes and breathe in, wondering why I torture myself.

A shiny gold trophy on the shelf above his clothes catches my eye, and I stand on my tiptoes to take it down. First place for wrestling, Highland Park High School, 1983. David has the powerful shoulders and thick arms of a wrestler. I believe I could feel safe in those arms, even now. I lift the trophy back to its place and turn around, and there's Kate, standing in the doorway. No telling how long she's been there.

"Caught me," I say.

"I don't think David would mind." She steps inside and runs her hand down the sleeve of a plaid wool shirt. "I gave him this two Christmases ago." She opens the collar and examines it. "It's getting worn. Might be time for a new one this year. He loves these Pendleton shirts in the winter."

"Tell me about him and Carolyn."

"Come to the kitchen, so we can sit and have something cold to drink."

I take one last look around, switch off the light, and follow her.

"Tom and I used to see the Shacklefords and the Bishops socially," Kate says. "Is Dr. Pepper okay?"

"Sure."

"Sit at the table and I'll fix it. The Bishops are Carolyn's parents. Carolyn and David dated off and on in high school. Nothing serious. He may have taken her out a time or two in college. David stayed here and went to SMU, and Carolyn went off to, well, where did she go?" Kate stops pouring the soda and sets the can on the counter. "You know, I can't remember where Carolyn went to college. Anyway, after college David said he was going to Sierra Leone. What a to-do! Dave and Louise—his parents—were beside themselves. They gave him fits about it, but he needed to go. He needed to get away and figure out who he was, besides David Nathan Shackleford III."

Kate hands me the glass of soda and joins me at the table. Her face is bright red and wet with perspiration, and her hair has frizzed in the humidity. She blots her forehead and neck with a folded paper towel.

"Are you hot?" she asks.

"No, not at all."

"I'm burning up. I must be having a hot flash. Anyway, where was I?"

"Sierra Leone."

"Yes. David came back after a few years and started his graduate work. His parents breathed a sigh of relief, thinking he'd gotten the wanderlust out of his system. By then, Carolyn was back in town, working at her dad's firm. There were some changes in Carolyn's life around that time that brought her closer to David."

"What kind of changes?"

"Spiritual changes."

"She got religious?"

Kate sips her drink and dabs at her neck. "Carolyn grew up in church. The Bishops were there every time the doors were open, but for social and business reasons more than anything else. A lot of business is transacted at First Methodist." She unfolds and refolds the paper towel. "Tom lost quite a few clients when we left."

"So what happened with David and Carolyn?"

"I'll just say this, Carolyn fell in love with Jesus, and then she fell in love with David. He doesn't believe Carolyn ever loved him, but she did. It was obvious to me that she loved him very much."

"What broke them up?"

"Material things. Carolyn was raised with so much, and she assumed so much about what her life would be like. But David isn't into things. You can see that by looking around this house. Choices had to be made. Priorities had to be set. Not that they were going to live like paupers, but they had to decide if they were going to spend time at cocktail parties, playing golf and bridge, and all of that, or if they were going to pursue a different kind of life. Actually, Carolyn had to decide. David had already settled his mind on what he wanted to do, probably in Sierra Leone. I believe Carolyn struggled a long time with it. I imagine she still struggles with it."

"A material girl," I say.

"Like a lot of young women, Carolyn probably spent years fantasizing about what her life would be like when she was grown and married. Social status may not be important to you or me, but it's part of who Carolyn is—at least who she thinks she is. She assumed the lifestyle that goes along with money would be hers. She might not be able to admit it, even now, but she wasn't prepared to give it up."

"Poor little rich girl."

"Well, I'm not going to sit here and defend Carolyn, but I don't think she deserves to be pigeonholed either. David made mistakes too. He assumed a lot. They were young and in love, their courtship was a whirlwind, and I doubt they talked about any long-term plans before they married. It would've been better if they'd taken time to get to know each other."

"Why did you and Tom leave First Methodist?"

"That's a story for another day, but speaking of church, I'm going to a service tonight. It won't be very long. Would you like to come?"

"I guess not, but thanks."

"All right," she says, but she looks disappointed.

Chapter Twenty-Eight

I put off the lecture for as long as I can, but eventually I run out of excuses, and David's colleague schedules a mid-morning session. The day before, Kate asks if I want to shop for a new outfit, which is a good idea. I need all the confidence I can muster. It happens to be my birthday, my thirtieth, but I don't mention that to Kate.

On the drive to a shopping center, she asks, "Do you know what you're going to say tomorrow?"

"I don't have a clue. I can't think of anything that isn't boring and trite."

"But you know so much that they need to hear," she says.

"Like what?"

"Well, you know about working hard to reach your goals. I imagine you burned the midnight oil all the time, trying to write a novel while you were working at the casino."

"I did. I wrote through the night a lot back then."

"You probably faced discouragement too, when you thought you were wasting your time."

"I felt that way all the time. I just tried to push it out of my mind and hope for the best."

"That's a powerful message in itself," she says.

"You think I should talk about perseverance, staying the course, and all of that? Those things have been said too many times before. It's a stale message."

"They haven't been said by you. You'll make the message fresh."

"How?"

She pulls into a parking space.

"You can't always analyze everything ahead of time, Cami. Just get up there and talk. Tell them about yourself. Open up and let them see what's important to you, what motivates you. Show them who Cami Taylor is. You're a bestselling author, a celebrity. If you open your heart to them, even a tiny bit, it'll be more than enough to inspire them."

"Open my heart," I repeat.

"Bare your soul," Kate says. She's teasing me. She knows I won't. She cuts the engine and opens her door. "Those kids don't want to hear about your writing or how your book got published. They want the chance to get to know *you*. You don't have to worry about impressing them. They're already impressed."

"I'll try," I say, opening my door. It's hot as hell, and I'm ready to buy something so I can go home.

"Okay," she says. "I'll leave you alone, but you know I'm right."

"Maybe. We'll see."

I'm so thin and tanned that everything I try on looks great. I settle on a flattering, unpretentious outfit: slender, ankle-length black slacks and a sleeveless white blouse that pops against my brown skin. I'd love to finish it with sandals, but my feet are overdue for a pedicure. I browse the closed-toe shoes but don't find anything that's quite right.

Kate must be reading my mind because she says, "I don't know about you, but I could use a pedicure."

"I'm desperate for one," I say. "I haven't had a pedicure since . . ." I think back to my last trip, when Darla nicked my toe. Oh my God, the blood!

"There's a salon here that takes walk-ins. They probably aren't too busy. How about it? My treat."

"I'm in," I say, even though my stomach is tied in a knot.

We stroll along the sidewalk, with me imagining what I'll say to the tech. I'll tell her I have sensitive feet, so go easy and leave the cuticles alone. I might say I have a low platelet count, so be really, really, super careful not to nick me, okay? Or I could just come clean: Hey, girlfriend, just FYI, I'm HIV positive. Do you mind?

Kate hooks her arm through mine as we walk. She pats my hand, mothering me. "I'm so glad you're here, Cami. Really, really glad."

"Me too."

We reach the salon, and I know the instant I look inside that I can't do it. I just can't.

"Oh, my God," I say. "I just remembered I'm supposed to call my editor." I look at my watch. "Like, right now."

"Oh," she says. "Do you have your cell phone? You could make the call in the car. Or there's a coffee shop around the corner."

"I left it at the house," I lie. "Besides, I need to be on my computer during the call."

"Oh. Okay. I hate you not getting new shoes."

"I can make do."

When we get back to Kate's house, I follow her into the kitchen, forgetting all about my imaginary phone call. I pour a cold cup of coffee and plop at the table, feeling terrible about the pedicure I had in New York and about Darla wiping up all that blood. I hope she didn't have a cut or a scrape. I really should call her, tell her to be tested, but I can't bear everyone at the salon knowing about the HIV.

"Go on and call your editor," Kate says. She opens the refrigerator. "I'll fix some dinner."

"Thanks. I'll help clean up."

Upstairs, I lie on the bed, stare at the ceiling, and think about nothing because there aren't any ceiling tiles to count. When Kate knocks at the door, it seems that no time has passed.

"Cami? Ready for a bite to eat?" she calls from the hall.

"Sure."

The aroma of fresh coffee fills the kitchen, and there's a little box wrapped in gold paper on the table.

"What's this?" I ask, knowing she remembered my birthday from that stupid genealogy chart.

"Open it."

"Anything in a box this small was way too expensive."

"Hush," she says. "I don't want to hear any griping about the money. We both know money doesn't mean a thing."

I rattle the package before taking off the paper. Inside is a black velvet box that contains a single translucent pearl on a thin gold chain. "It's beautiful," I say.

Kate sits down next to me. "I thought about getting the earrings that match it, but I decided you'd prefer your gold hoops."

I put the necklace on. "How does it look?"

"Very pretty. Your tan really sets it off. Pearls are special, you know."

"How so?"

"Well, there's the pearl of great price." She takes the creamy jewel on her fingertips, examining it in the light. "And there's the way pearls are formed, the way a thing as common and irritating as a grain of sand transforms into something beautiful and valuable. They're like people that way." She winks.

"Some people."

"Yes, some people. Your thirtieth birthday is special, Cami, a sort of a coming of age. I thought a pearl was appropriate." She gets up and opens the refrigerator. "How did the call with your editor go?"

"Good," I say after a beat.

"Do you have business in New York next week?"

"Not really. My work with the book is done, for the most part. Why?"

"I thought you might stay on. I've gotten used to having you here."

I don't have any plans to leave, so it's a good thing she asked. I can put off the inevitable indefinitely, as long as I'm holed up here. "Thank you, Kate. That's really generous."

"Good. It's settled then." She smiles and then hugs me. "Happy birthday, little girl."

Chapter Twenty-Nine

I knock and ring the bell, but Sam doesn't answer. I turn the knob on the heavy wood door, painted such tasteful, high-gloss hunter green, and it swings open. "Sam?" I call. "Sam, are you here?"

I find him in bed. "Having a bad day," he mumbles. His lips are chalky gray, his voice a whisper.

"What should I do?"

"Sit with me."

The room reeks of urine, and I can just imagine what's under those covers. No telling how long he's been lying there. I hardly know Sam, but it's hard to see anyone come to this.

"You want me to help you get up?" I ask. "Help you—"

"No, honey. Please. Just sit."

"At least let me get you some water."

I go to the kitchen, toying with calling nine-one-one. Instead, I pour a glass of cool water from a bottle in the refrigerator and carry it to the bedroom. When I hold the glass to Sam's mouth, he only pretends to sip.

"Open these windows, sweetie," he says. "Let the fresh air in."

I raise the blinds on the window nearest the bed and unlock it. The heavy wood frame glides up smoothly. "How's that?"

"All of them. I want to feel a breeze."

"All right." I open the rest of the windows, and the foul stench dissipates.

"That's nice," he says.

"I should call someone, Sam. You need help."

"Shh. Hush now. Sit and talk with me."

"Yeah. Okay." I pull the ladder-back chair to the bed. "Would you like me to read? Maybe some more Yeats?"

"Something different." He pulls one of those mile-long arm bones out from under the sheet and flops it toward the bookcase. Thin, purple veins lace his forearm from wrist to elbow.

I stand and lean over the shelves, scanning the titles. "Which one?"

"On top."

I pick up a black leather volume. "This?"

It's a Bible. This is not good. I'm not qualified to take a last confession.

"First Corinthians," Sam says.

I have no idea where to look, so I thumb through a thousand onionskin pages.

"Toward the back," he says.

"Okay. I'm there."

"Chapter Fifteen."

It's a long chapter. Fifty-eight verses. "All of it?"

"Do you mind?"

"No, it's fine. Here we go." I begin reading. The writer claims that Christ died for our sins and rose from the grave three days later. That he was seen by a lot of people—five hundred, at least—after this resurrection.

"Slow down," Sam interrupts. "I want to think about what he's saying."

"Sorry. Okay. '. . . Christ has been raised from the dead, the firstfruits of those who have fallen asleep. For as by a man came death, by a man has come also the resurrection of the dead. For as in Adam all die, so also in Christ shall all be made alive.'" I stop reading. "Are you scared, Sam?"

"No, honey. Not one bit."

I continue reading the writer's arguments for resurrection, not only Christ's, but ours too. "'If the dead are not raised, let us eat and drink, for tomorrow we die.'"

Wait a minute. I've heard this before. "Kate," I say aloud, more to myself than to Sam. This hope of a resurrection was Kate's answer, the answer she didn't explain.

"What about her?" Sam says.

"Nothing." I search for my place to begin again.

"Don't be angry with her, Cami." Sam's looking at me with those dull eyes of his.

"I'm not."

"Good." He closes his eyes again. "Go on."

I read that the resurrection is like a seed that's been planted. A body goes into the ground as one thing, and it comes out as something different. "'What is sown is perishable; what is raised is imperishable. It is sown in dishonor; it is raised in glory. It is sown in weakness; it is raised in power. It is sown a natural body; it is raised a spiritual body.'"

"Oh, Jesus, thank you," says Sam.

I look up into his face, which is perfectly relaxed, eyes closed. I return to the page and continue reading the escalating comparisons between the earthly, from the dust, and the heavenly, from God. In the end, when everything is said and done and the last trumpet has been blown, our mortality will put on immortality. The horses' heads turned toward eternity, according to Emily Dickinson.

"'Death is swallowed up in victory. O death, where is your victory? O death, where is your sting?'" Powerful words, for sure. It's easy to see why people cling to them in times of desperation.

I look up to see Sam's reaction to this climax, but he is entirely still. I sit and watch him a long time, waiting for his chest to rise with a drawn breath, waiting to see the twitch of a wasted muscle, but he has left me in this room alone.

"Good-bye, Sam," I say.

I close the Bible and put it on the bookcase, and then I pick up Sam's telephone and dial nine-one-one. The gauzy curtains flutter inside, wrapping around the headboard before turning loose again. The sound of kids playing in the yard next door drifts into the room.

"Nine-one-one," says the operator.

"There's a man who's died at this address. You need to send someone."

"827 Ash?"

"Yes."

"Your name and relation?"

I hang up and move my chair back to its place. Then I leave the house, closing the door gently behind me.

I drive around with the radio blaring, trying to decide what to do with myself. This was my first time in death's presence. Watching Sam die was like watching a fellow survivor lose his grip and slip off the life raft. He slid beneath the murkiest water of all, never to surface again. But even though Sam is the one who passed the point of no return—the only true point of no return—I don't grieve for him nearly as much as for myself. Sam couldn't have had a better comfort than the words I put in his ears, words I have no doubt he believed with his whole heart. *You're not dying, boy. It's nothing permanent. Just lie down and sleep for a while, until big brother comes for you. When you wake up, you'll be a new man. No more worries and no more AIDS. No more dying either.*

Oh, man! What I wouldn't give to believe something that wonderful. I wish I had such a safety net to catch me as I'm falling, as I'm falling even now. Some belief—I don't care what, it doesn't matter—into which I could trust myself to plunge without harm. But I'm the skeptic tottering on the edge of a dark, bottomless pit, with no safety net, no lifeline, and nothing below to break my fall. I want to reach out to someone to save me, but this is a journey everyone makes alone, without the comfort of a hand to hold.

"Are you saved, honey?"

No, Mamaw, I'm not even close.

I find myself on a levee that overlooks the Trinity River. It's midafternoon, a Wednesday, and there isn't anyone else around. I cut the engine, stumble from the SUV, and crumple on the grassy ridge. I am gut shot. Painfully. Fatally. I let myself go, really let go, and grieve like an old Jewish woman at the Wailing Wall.

Weep, girl! Weep like you mean it! Cry out and lament for yourself and for every person who has drawn this air, only to exhale the last breath of their allotted number. There's no one with whom to file a complaint. I paid my money, and I took my chances. The wheel is spun. The cards are down. The hand is over. There's nothing left to do but fork over the losses and go on home.

Dear God! God help me.

After I catch my breath, I rise and brush the grass from my palms and knees and wipe my face. I start the Mercedes, resisting an insane urge to throw the transmission into drive, push the pedal to the floorboard, and take a flying leap. I carefully crank the gear lever to reverse and back up to retrace my path down the levee.

At the house, I park in the back but walk around to the front door, the shortest route to my room. I let myself in quickly and quietly with the key Kate gave me. I hurry up the stairs, shut the door, and lean against it.

Kate's footsteps on the stairs. She stops on the other side door. "Cami, honey, are you okay?"

"I have a headache, Kate. I'll see you in the morning."

Silence. I feel her there, on the other side of the door. "Okay," she finally says, and I hear her descend the stairs.

◆ ◆ ◆

Kate deserves to know about Sam, but she doesn't hear it from me. She does hear it though, from someone. While we're having coffee the next morning, she tells me that Sam has died.

"I'm sorry to hear that, Kate," is all I can muster.

If she has cried for him—and I'm sure she has—she did it early. There aren't any tears now. "He'll have a graveside service," she says. "Would you like to go?"

I shake my head. I've never been to a funeral, and my own will be more than enough, thank you. "I can't, Kate," I say. "I'm sorry."

"Well, you only met him the one time. I understand." She rises and refills my cup. Kate drinks her coffee black, but she always has half-and-half on the table for me, in a sweet little ironstone pitcher that I've come to think of as mine.

"Thank you," I say.

"Are you all set for this morning? I wish I could be there to hear what you'll say."

"I'll fill you in."

"Let me fix you something to eat. It would be good to have food in your stomach."

"No, thanks. I'm not hungry."

I take a cigarette from my pack on the table and open the door to the patio. My brief holiday from smoking, during which I enjoyed the appetite of a farmhand, passed with Sam. I strike a match and light the Marlboro, letting the flame burn the tiny stick almost to my fingers before I shake it out. I reach back inside to the table for my coffee, holding the smoking cigarette at arm's length toward the open door. Barefoot in my sleep tee and shorts, I lean against the doorway and release perfect smoke rings, one after another, into the backyard.

Given my state of mind, it was nuts to accept this lecture offer. No telling what will come out of my mouth, and I wish I could just ditch it like everything else.

I glance inside at Kate, who's staring into the backyard, her thoughts elsewhere. I would've been someone else entirely with a mother like her.

Most likely, I'd be happier and better adjusted, and probably a mother myself now. But I wouldn't have been me. In spite of everything that's happened, I'm not sorry that I am who I am. Thanks, Patrick Earl, and thank you, Mom. You did all right by me after all.

"Watch this." I blow an enormous smoke ring, quickly take another drag, and shoot a thin jet through it before it comes apart. "I learned that in New Mexico," I say, pointing.

Of course, it isn't really a talent Kate can appreciate. She nods absently and gets up to put her coffee cup in the sink. Then she stands there looking out the window. Looking at nothing. Finally, she sighs and rinses out the cup.

"Well, I'm going to get dressed," she says. She smiles at me, but she's sad. I've seen that smile before. "I can't wait to hear about today. You'll be great."

"Are you okay?" I ask.

"Oh, yes. I'm fine."

"Is it Sam?"

"I just hate to think about him dying alone," she says. "I was so sure it wouldn't happen that way. I guess I expected to be with him when the time came."

I'd like to comfort her with the truth, but I can't make myself fess up after my lying silence. I put out my cigarette in my cold coffee and throw the soggy butt in the trash can under the sink. Standing beside her, I rinse my cup under scalding water.

"You know he'd quit taking his medications," I say. "He was ready to check out."

"How do you know that?"

I shake the water from the cup and put it into the dishwasher. "Remember, I sat on the bed and picked up one of the bottles?"

"That's right," she says slowly. "I remember."

"Well, the bottle was empty, but it was one of his main meds, Indinavir. It's an inhibitor. I know a guy who's on it." I close the dishwasher. The truth is that Indinavir is one of the drugs Dr. Kuri prescribed, a drug with a list of possible side effects a mile long.

"All of the bottles were empty," I say, "and there was a lot of dust on the caps. He'd been off all his meds for a long time."

She looks at me with wonder all over that guileless face. "You saw all that in one afternoon, and I was completely oblivious?"

I shrug. "You weren't looking for it, Kate. I'm nosy."

"I had no idea. How could I miss so much?"

"Like I said, you weren't looking for it. But Sam was ready. I've had friends go out with AIDS," I lie. "You have to let them find their own way. Sam was okay with death, I'm sure, or he wouldn't have stopped the antivirals."

She shakes her head, as if I've given her too big a bite to chew. "I'm too out of touch with the world."

"Kate, trust me. You don't want to be in touch with that world."

"Oh, that's not what I mean." She takes my hand and pats it. "Thank you, honey. Thank you for seeing so much and for telling me. I know Sam was okay. I know that."

I smile a big Cheshire cat grin, like the hypocrite and fraud that I am.

Chapter Thirty

"**C**an I record your lecture today?" David asks as he's chauffeuring me to the university in his white Ford truck.

"What for?"

"You might want to listen to it later. You know, to critique yourself. I recorded all of my lectures when I started teaching."

"Since I'm not starting anything, no. But thanks anyway."

"Okay. It's your call."

Dallas Hall rises from the live oaks, four stories of red brick and white columns presiding over an expansive mall with a fountain, yards of sidewalk, and acres of grass. The whole campus projects an aura of serious studies and high tuitions. David and I climb the wide steps, and he opens the big wooden door for me. Our heels clack in the rotunda, and I stop to look up at the stained-glass dome, designed to inspire.

David's colleague, the lit professor, greets us and gives me a firm handshake. Her dark hair is pulled back in a tight knot and salted with gray. She isn't worried about foolish vanities, such as buying back a few years with hair color and a flattering cut. She wears flats with no hose, a straight skirt, and a men's shirt with the tail hanging out. This woman is no nonsense all the way. She introduces herself as Dr. Penny Rawls.

Enthralled by my portrayal of the seedy side of human nature, Dr. Rawls doesn't stop talking about *Blues* until we reach her classroom, which is crammed with students. The way she goes on about some of the passages, I feel as if someone else wrote them. She's gleaned meanings I didn't intend.

"Literature, Ms. Taylor," Penny concludes, "at its best, its very best, reveals us."

"Call me Cami," I say.

David has been silent throughout our one-sided conversation, and I wonder how much his opinion of my work differs from his colleague's. On the heels of this unpleasant thought, I get a good case of stage fright while Dr. Rawls introduces me. I'd do well to concentrate on her praise of my wordsmithing, rather than on these good-looking students, whose minds glint like swords in their clear eyes. I search desperately for something, anything, to level the playing field. David stands against the back wall—it's standing room only—and gives me a double thumbs-up. It helps, but not nearly enough.

Then, while I'm standing there beside Dr. Rawls, an unexpected gift comes my way. I remember how nervous I was when I started dealing blackjack, how at first the faces of the people who sat at my table struck terror in my heart, as if they could see right through me. I had to fight down a visceral panic that made me want to run out the back door. But as time went by and I stuck it out, I began to understand that they couldn't see anything unless I revealed it. That knowledge gave me more confidence than I'd ever had, and not just at the casino.

Suddenly, I'm back at the River Bend, tucked inside the horseshoe of a twenty-five-dollar table. A vanload of kids has just arrived, and here they come through the door, boisterous and arrogant. They're gonna show us deadbeats what's up. They have attitude in spades, but not much else. Come on, boys and girls. Belly up. But watch yourselves because I have the cards, and I have the experience, and I'll get the cash. All of it.

Dr. Rawls finishes introducing me to the class: Ms. Cami Taylor, bestselling author.

"First things first," I say. "Call me Cami. We can check our decorum at the door and just relax. So if you want to ask a question, go ahead." I scan the room, sizing them up. "I need to take a minute and get my bearings here. How many of you are actually interested in writing fiction for a living?"

About a third of the students raise their hands.

"So what are the rest of you doing? Sucking up to Dr. Rawls here?" There's a snicker, and I glance at stern-faced Penny, who seems to think literature is the Holy Grail. I turn and select a red marker from the tray at the bottom of the whiteboard.

"Cami, I have a question." A male voice.

"What is it?" I turn and search for the kid who spoke.

"What's your phone number?" he asks. He has brown eyes under beautiful eyebrows, and a smile full of straight, white teeth. He's as cute as a bug. In fact, he looks scrumptious.

The guy next to him, his buddy, punches him. "Cool it, Jason," he hisses. Penny stands up, but I wave her down.

"Are you heckling me?" I ask. "Or do you really want to know?"

"I want to know," he says, but doubt flickers in those brown eyes.

"Then see me after," I say, and turn back to the whiteboard.

A murmur rises, but it's quickly knocked down by Penny, who barks, "Quiet! Or I'll clear the room."

I print the phrase I've come up with in blocked capital letters. The handwriting looks like my dad's, I suddenly realize.

"*GO WITH WHAT YOU KNOW.*"

I turn around and face the class. "Does that mean anything to any of you?"

They're silent. I can't tell if they're scared of Penny or dumbstruck by me. I look at David, and he smiles. He looks worried too.

"Anyone?" I ask.

I study the class. They aren't at all what I counted on. As I envisioned this moment in the days leading up to it, I was filled with disdain for what I assumed would be a bunch of spoiled rich kids. No doubt they are exactly that—some of them anyway—but my attitude was all about my own sense of inferiority in school. My problems weren't their fault.

I was primed to lay into them with my caustic tongue at the slightest provocation, but looking at them now, all I see is their eagerness to find out what life will bring, anticipation untarnished by the disappointments that will come later. They remind me of my own high hopes when I moved to New York, when I didn't think I could ever taste regret after having realized my dreams.

A blond girl, a gum chewer who managed to get stuck on the front row, appears to be self-consciously bored.

"Does that phrase mean anything to you?" I ask her.

"It's pretty simple," she says, glancing sideways.

"Is it? Then I wonder why it's giving me so much trouble. Does anyone else have a thought about it?"

"It's like Shakespeare," says a boy. Buzz cut and black-framed glasses.

"How is it like Shakespeare?"

"You know. 'This above all—to thine own self be true, and it must follow, as the night the day, thou canst not then be false to any man.'"

"*Hamlet*, right?"

"Polonius, to his son, Laertes. But yeah, it was in *Hamlet*."

"What's your name?"

"Randy."

"What else do you know, Randy? That you didn't read in a play or a book."

"I know a lot of things . . . I guess."

"Like what?'

"It's hard to think when you put me on the spot."

"Sorry. Let me ask it this way, what do you believe in?"

"Well . . . I believe in love."

"Oh, yeah," says Jason, "especially when it's free." He doesn't get much of a reaction from the class.

"And I believe in people," says Randy.

"It must be nice to believe in people," I say. "I envy your trust. What else? Who else?"

"I believe in money," says Jason.

"Ah, Jason, I knew I could count on you. So is that piles of money to wallow in, or the things money buys?" The class laughs.

"Both!" he shouts over the laughter.

"Who else?"

I hear a faint, "I believe" under the noise.

"Wait. Who was that?"

"I believe in God," a girl says quietly. She's a shy-faced thing, speaking in a voice so timid that she seems afraid of the reaction she'll draw. But she did speak up, and that's something.

Another girl, a tough nut with hostile eyes, says, "Dumbass parrot."

I glare at her. "What did you say?"

She looks at me and then at Penny. "Nothing," she says.

"That's exactly what I thought you said. Nothing."

"Dr. Shackleford, what do you think about believing in God? Wait—which god?" I say to the girl.

"The only one," she says, without hesitation.

"The unknown God," says David, "but not unknowable. I think believing is a smart move," he adds.

To the timid girl, I say, "*Are* you parroting someone else, like your parents?"

"No, ma'am."

"Why do you believe, then?"

"I just do," she says. "He answers my prayers." She pauses, seeming to search for some proof. "I feel his presence."

"His presence?"

"Yes. Definitely."

"Now?"

"No, ma'am, not right now."

"Me either," I say.

We leave the topic of the unknown God and move on with a discussion that reveals how little any of us know. We're just getting loose with one another when the time is up. The students pump my hand on their way out the door. "You really made me think," they say. When everyone else has drifted out, Jason presents himself expectantly.

"Oh, right," I say. "Do you have a pen?"

He produces one. I push up the sleeve of his shirt, write on his muscled, veined forearm, and push the sleeve back down. Only he sees what I write, and he isn't smiling.

"Think about it," I say.

Dr. Rawls is enthusiastic in her unenthusiastic way. "It was a fresh perspective," she says.

Thanks, Kate. You were right after all.

Chapter Thirty-One

T he restaurant David takes me to for lunch is an SMU hangout, a funky Mexican food place in an old gas station. The hostess leads us past a small dining area with fifties-era chrome and Formica tables, velvet Elvis paintings, and a stream of colorful fish hanging from the ceiling. We step from checkerboard linoleum to the concrete floor of the former garage. Its corrugated metal doors are raised to let the future rulers of the universe watch the passersby while they eat and drink. Ever the gentleman, David holds the Naugahyde-upholstered chair for me to sit. We order iced tea, while the carefree kids around us knock down Coronas and Dos Equis.

"You were good today, Cami. Really good. You had those kids right here." He holds out his hand, palm up. "You could've led them anywhere."

"It was fun," I say, "more fun than I thought it would be."

"I don't think Penny knew what to think of the way you handled Jason."

"Did I go too far?"

"That depends. Professors get canned for fraternizing with students, and you were essentially representing Penny, so if you gave him your number . . ."

"I didn't. I wrote the word 'discretion.'"

"No wonder he wasn't smiling."

"I did him a favor in the long run," I say. I feel inexplicably happy that Jason will never be another notch in my holster.

The waitress brings chips and salsa and about a gallon of attitude to the table. "Are y'all ready to order?" she asks. She's a hot little number who smiles at David like he's a hot fudge sundae. "Hey, don't you teach over at the university?"

"Sure do. You know, we could use a few minutes to look at the menu."

"Okay. Well. I'll come back then." She smiles sweetly at me like I better watch my man with her around. It's a move I instantly promise myself never to make again, if I ever make my old moves again.

David doesn't miss any of it. He winks at me. "I hope you're not feeling too threatened."

"You must have the constitution of Superman to resist these girls throwing themselves at you."

"Not even tempting," he says.

"If you say so."

Apparently, I'm not tempting either. I know why I'm not going after him, but I can't help wondering why he has no interest in me. I tell myself I'm transmitting subconscious signals that say, "Stay Away." I hate to think David doesn't find me attractive. Men always find me attractive.

When the waitress returns, she has trouble looking away from a couple of young guys the hostess seats at a nearby table. "Be with y'all in a minute," she coos to them.

"Taco salad," I say.

David orders beef enchiladas and hands her the menus without looking up. When she leaves, he says, "What did you think about the student who said she believed in God? I like that you defended her."

I break a chip into tiny pieces on the paper placemat, and then I brush them into a pile with my finger. "I didn't think the girl deserved to be ridiculed, no matter what she believes. What kind of tolerance is that?"

"It isn't tolerant at all."

"No, it isn't. That parrot comment really pissed me off."

"But what did you think of her belief, and what she said about God's presence?"

"I'm an agnostic, so I don't know. I guess there could be a God, or a bunch of gods, but who knows for sure?"

"I know," he says.

"Okay," I say. Even if David's right, I can't picture myself taking the coward's way out now, jumping through hoops to please a God I can't even be sure is there. It's definitely time to change the subject before David tries to lead me down the Hallelujah Trail. "Thanks again for setting up the lecture," I say. "It was fun."

"You'd be a good teacher, if you ever wanted to try it."

"No, but I surprised myself today, and that doesn't happen very often."

"Just when you think you know everything about yourself, along comes something new."

"Well," I raise my glass of tea, "here's to the pleasant surprises."

David clacks his plastic glass to mine. "To the pleasant surprises." We both set our iced tea down without drinking.

The fickle waitress arrives with our food. "Hot plates," she says. "Watch your fingers. More tea?"

"Sure," says David. "Do you need anything else, Cami?" I shake my head, and she slaps our ticket down, tops off our glasses, and leaves. "When do you have to be back in New York?" he asks.

"Kate asked me to stay another week."

"It must be nice to be free from schedules."

"Sometimes." I mix the salad thoroughly, playing with it like a kid who doesn't want to eat. "I'm always at loose ends between projects."

"Well, I'm glad you could stay. Kate thinks the world of you."

"She's been very kind."

"She cares about you."

"I know she does."

David is making short work of those enchiladas, but I don't think I'll be able to make a dent in my salad.

"Will you begin another project right away?" he asks between bites.

"Yeah, I'm thinking about a new novel set in the South. That's the main reason I'm here."

The truth is that I can't imagine ever writing another word. I've hit the doldrums, and the winds of inspiration have moved on to some other writer. I couldn't care less. I've reached a steady state of limbo. There probably is a technical name for it, some syndrome or other. I could drift forever, as long as I don't let myself think too hard or feel too much.

"Writing a novel probably takes a lot out of you," David says.

"Yeah, it does."

"How do you recharge between books?"

"I write short stories for journals and the like."

"Do you have any hobbies?"

"I read a lot. I run and work out. I guess those are my hobbies. I like to go out, you know, to dinner and the movies. And the theater. I love the theater."

"It sounds like you have a nice life in New York," he says. "Aren't you hungry?"

"I'm still keyed up. Sorry, this was a waste—the salad, I mean."

"Hey, don't worry about it. I know how you feel. It's a rush, isn't it? Speaking in front of a group, especially when there's a lot of energy like today."

"Yeah, they were lively."

"People are really drawn to you, Cami," he says.

"No, they aren't."

"Sure they are. Don't you see it?"

"No." I put my fork down. There's no point in poking at this food anymore.

"Well, I think they are." He puts his crumpled napkin in his empty plate.

"People like to get inside your head, if they can."

"See, that's what I'm saying. They want to get close to you."

David catches the waitress's attention and gives her a credit card.

"Be right back," she says.

"People are pushy," I say.

"You have to be strong enough to hold your own with them, without putting up walls."

"What are you saying?"

"Just that it's good to stay open to new ideas, and new people, rather than shutting them out. Walling yourself in is the worst thing you can do."

"Me, specifically?"

"Anyone."

"That sounded pointed, David."

"Then maybe it's something to think about."

"I can deal with being Kate's project, but you? You've known me for, like, a minute."

"What? No."

"Thanks for lunch, David." I stand up, and so does he. "I can get myself back to Kate's house."

"Cami—"

I walk out of the restaurant. When I glance back inside through the window, David's looking around for the waitress who has his credit card. He'll come after me, I know it, but I've had plenty of practice ditching guys. I duck into an alley across the street and walk behind the stores, finally stopping at the back stoop of a dress shop, where I sit on the step and have a cigarette.

I'm so angry that I'm trembling. I think back over the conversation, wondering if I overreacted, but in my heart I know Kate and David are in cahoots. My mind goes back to the copy of *Blues* on David's nightstand, to the cryptic message Kate wrote in the front. I'm pretty sure it was a Bible verse, but I can't remember what it was, so I can't find out what it says. Even so, the fact that she wrote it reinforces my belief that they've analyzed me, like Hillary and her nephew Paul analyzed me. It makes me livid to think about it.

I decide to walk back to Kate's house, if I can find it. Anyway, people here ride around too much. No one walks, like we do in New York. I miss New York, and I miss who I am there. Who I *was* there.

My rage dissipates with each block, and I realize there's no point in making a rash decision just because I'm pissed. Of course Kate and David talk about me. Probably Tom too. They're evangelicals, for crying out loud. They've probably been racking their brains trying to figure out how to convert me, just like Estella and her Jesus pamphlets. But I didn't fire Estella for papering my apartment. I managed it, and I need to manage this. There's absolutely no reason I should let them push me out of the frying pan and into the fire before I'm ready.

I'm sweated through by the time I find Kate's street, but at least I feel like a New Yorker again. Her car is in the driveway, and she's in the foyer before I can shut the front door behind me.

"Cami, I was worried about you." She looks worried too.

"Worried? Why?"

"David came by, looking for you. He said you had an argument at lunch, and you left the restaurant."

"I wouldn't call it an argument," I say.

"Oh," she says, and we stand there for a few seconds, looking at each other. Then she says, "David said . . . he thought . . . he was afraid he offended you."

"No, I'm good. The lecture went really well. Did he tell you that?"

"That's great," she says. "I knew it would."

"David said I had them eating out of my hand, just like you said I would. I'm exhausted though. I've gotten out of shape, riding around everywhere here. I think I'll get comfortable and have some wine on the patio."

"Help yourself, honey. Maybe I'll fix us something to eat later."

"Sure," I say. I take my leave and go upstairs to have a cool shower and change into shorts and a tee shirt.

If I have put up walls, so what? It's really nothing more than compartmentalizing, which everyone does to survive.

Chapter Thirty-Two

I spend the next day in the sweet therapy of the sun and the pool. I'm still floating around on my air mattress in late afternoon when Kate comes outside and sits on a chaise lounge.

"My sister Renee's hosting a dinner tomorrow night," she says. "Tom's staying in Chicago this weekend, so it would be great if you could come with me. Renee's been hounding me to spend time with you. She'd be honored if you came."

"That's nice," I say, "but Chris is after me to get some pages to him, so I need to write this weekend. Go ahead and go, though, and pass along my apology to Renee."

"I didn't realize you'd started writing the new book," Kate says. "Good for you."

"Yeah, it's coming along."

"Maybe I could read some of it."

"Sure. Later, when it's ready," I say.

"I hate to ask," Kate says, "but could you spend a few hours tomorrow afternoon helping us get ready for the dinner? We could use a hand."

"Isn't she having it catered?"

"No, Cami. My family doesn't live that way."

"Oh. Sure, okay. I'm happy to help."

◆ ◆ ◆

It takes us half an hour to drive to Renee's modest ranch-style house in a suburb of Fort Worth. I'm assigned the job of working in the kitchen with Renee's daughter, the incessantly giggling Karah. Karah's supposed to mix and bake a cake, and Renee asks me to chop vegetables for an appetizer tray.

Karah's happy to have an audience, even of one, and she performs cheers and dance routines for me, using the flour and sugar and milk as props. "It's my first year on the squad," she says breathlessly between chants. She dances around the kitchen as if she has springs for bones, blond hair and cake ingredients flying all around. I slice carrots and try to tune her out. I hear the push-pull hum of a vacuum cleaner running in another part of the house.

"E-A-G-L-E-S," chants Karah. "What's that spell? Victory! Victory! VICTORY!" She spins around and shouts, "Yay us!" as she heaves a gallon jug of milk skyward like a pom-pom. The jug flies out of her hand toward the ceiling. "Uh-oh," she says.

I turn around to grab it before it hits the floor. Somehow, as I pivot, I lose track of the knife and catch the blade with my left palm, laying in a gash that runs from the base of my thumb to my wrist. The jug hits the floor like a wet bomb, spewing milk.

"Uh-oh," Karah says again.

I rush to the sink and watch bright red blood pulse out of my hand and onto the white enamel.

"Did you cut yourself?" asks Karah. She comes toward me tentatively, peering into the sink. I lower my hand, palm down, to hide the open wound, but she sees the blood and yelps. "I'll get my mom!"

"No! Wait! Just wait a minute. Please. This isn't a big deal. We can clean it up without bothering your mom. Just get me a dishtowel, okay?"

"A dishtowel?"

Is she an idiot? "Yeah, honey, get me a dishtowel to wrap around my hand."

"They're right here." She opens a drawer beside the sink, and I pick up a towel with bloody fingers and wrap it tightly around my left hand. The blood soaks through immediately.

"Ew," says Karah.

"Hand me a couple more." I wind two more towels around the first, one on top of the other, in a ridiculously large bundle. Before I can say boo, spots of blood appear. "Bring me a trash bag too."

Karah finds an enormous black trash bag in the pantry, and I wrap it around the towels. The whole affair is the size of a medicine ball, with my viral palm hidden at its core. I feel myself sway, and I grab onto the sink and lock my knees to keep from going down. I tense every muscle, like a pilot fighting a heavy G-load, and my contracting field of vision expands again. Thank you, Patrick Earl, for all your Air Force trivia. Some of it finally paid off. I raise my hand over my head like a matador, turn on the water, and begin rinsing the sink.

"Get the bleach," I tell Karah.

"Bleach?" she squeaks.

"Say all words twice," my dad used to say when I answered his question with a question. He hated that, and I do too.

"Did I stutter?" I bark. "Find the bleach, kid, and bring it to me."

There are tears in Karah's eyes, but she goes to the laundry room and brings back a gallon of bleach. She sets it on the counter beside the sink with a thud.

"Open it," I say.

She fumbles with the safety cap, but finally gets it off. I take the bottle and splash bleach all over the sink. There's blood on the countertop and the floor, so I splash bleach there too, and wipe and rinse until every trace of red is gone. I turn around and lean against the counter. "See, no biggie," I say to Karah.

She stands there, looking scared.

"Get your mom," I say. "And, listen, this was no one's fault, okay?"

She looks at the milk all over the floor. "Maybe I should clean that up too," she says.

"After. I need you to find Kate. I need to get to a hospital."

"I'm sorry," she says.

"It's okay. No worries. Just go find Kate."

◆ ◆ ◆

"We had a little accident," I say, when Kate and Renee rush into the kitchen. "I probably need a couple of stitches."

"I'll get our purses," Kate says.

Renee stoops and picks up the milk jug. "What happened?"

"I'm not sure what happened," I say. "What about you, Karah?"

Karah shakes her head.

"One minute we were working, and the next minute all hell broke loose," I say. "It was just one of those things."

"I hope your hand's okay," Renee says.

"It'll be fine."

Kate opens the car door for me and fastens my seatbelt as if I'm a child, not that I could've managed it. She's a different driver behind the wheel today. We blow out of the driveway and take off. No turn signals, and no letting the other guy go first. The jerking stops and starts make me nauseous, and it takes all my concentration to keep from throwing up.

"You're as white as a sheet," Kate says.

I focus on not passing out. I absolutely cannot pass out. My hand begins to throb, an escalating, hammering pain. Kate pulls up to the doors of the emergency room and comes around to help me out. She guides me to a chair. Then she goes to the admissions counter and comes back with a clipboard full of forms, which she fills in as I dictate. I fish my insurance card from my wallet and give it to her.

"I'll turn these in," she says. "Then I better move the car."

I wait until she pulls away, and then I get up and go to the counter.

"We'll get you to a room in a few minutes," says the attendant.

"I'm HIV positive," I say.

"Did you note that on the form?"

"No. My friend doesn't know."

"Okay," she says. She finds my paperwork and thumbs through the pages. "How long ago were you diagnosed?"

"About a month ago." I glance back toward the doors. No sign of Kate.

"Medications?"

"Not yet."

She looks up. "Nothing?"

"No. We're still working up a regimen."

"Okay. I'll call you when we have a room."

"Thanks."

I'm in my chair before Kate comes back. She's just about to sit down when a nurse opens the door and calls my name. "That was quick," she says. She picks up my purse and helps me to my feet.

"Wait here," I say. "Watch my purse, and I'll be back in a minute."

"I don't mind going in with you."

"It's okay. I'll be fine."

"Okay," she says and sits down again.

I follow the nurse into one of the examination rooms. She spreads a rubber sheet across the exam table and sets a chair beside it. "Sit here, Ms. Taylor."

I sit and lay my throbbing hand on the table. She puts on two pairs of latex gloves—two pairs!—and a mask.

"The doctor will be along in a minute," she says, "but let me go ahead and have a look at what we've got here. Do I smell bleach?"

"I used it to disinfect everything."

"That works."

She lifts the lid on a receptacle with red labels stamped all over it: BIOHAZARD and DANGER. The nurse carefully unwinds the trash bag and drops it in. The dishtowels are soggy with blood. "I better wait to unwrap this until Dr. Peters comes in. Are you okay? Do you feel woozy?"

"A little."

She snaps off her gloves and drops them in with the trash bag. "I'll get you some juice." She leaves, letting the heavy door close behind her.

In no time, a doctor opens the door. She's shielded from head to toe. Mask. Surgical gown. Gloves. Even her shoes are covered. She looks as if she's here to clean up a radioactive spill, and here I sit with no protection at all. Apparently, I'm Superwoman. I can touch the deadly thing without fear. Wait. That's not right. I *am* the deadly thing.

"I'm Dr. Peters," she says through her mask. "Did you have unexpected DIY surgery today?"

"You know amateurs," I say.

She laughs. "Well, let's see what's up."

The nurse comes back, also covered head to toe, and hands me an open can of apple juice. Dr. Peters carefully unwinds the first two towels and lays them aside. "You nicked the artery," she says. "I don't want to unwrap this last towel until we're ready to stitch. Did you lose much blood?"

"It seemed like a lot. Any was too much."

"Do you need to lie down?"

"No. I'm fine. Go ahead and get started."

"All right. Liz will give you a local anesthetic. It'll take a few minutes for that to take effect." The doctor pulls off her gloves and picks up the admissions forms. "You're not undergoing treatment?"

"Not yet."

"I'll need to conference your physician before I write any scripts. It's standard procedure. Let's see, Dr. Benjamin Kuri?"

"That's right."

"New York? You're a long way from home. Okay, I'll be back in a minute."

Liz injects my wrist while I sip juice. Then Dr. Peters shows up again, wheeling a portable halogen light. "Ready?" she asks.

"All set," I say.

She puts on two pairs of gloves and goes to work on my hand. I look the other way, and she makes small talk to distract me. After several one-word answers, she finally quiets down.

She's finishing up, putting on a bandage, when the admissions clerk opens the door and says she has a call on line two. Dr. Peters snaps off the gloves and pulls the mask down on her chin. It's exhausting, watching the two of them don and doff all their protection. She answers the wall phone. "This is Dr. Peters." Then she covers the handset and lowers it. "Do you know a Dr. Wortham?"

Uh-oh. "My psychiatrist," I say.

"Oh, okay." She returns the phone to her ear. "Yes, Dr. Wortham. Cami has an arterial laceration on her left hand." She stops talking for a minute, and then she says, "Well, no, I didn't get *that* impression. The bleeding is under control, but I need to issue something for the pain, and an antibiotic. What? Just a minute." Dr. Peters covers the mouthpiece again. "She wants to talk to you."

There's no way I'm up for verbal fencing with Sylvia. "Tell her I'll call her later today."

"She's pretty ragged right now, Dr. Wortham. Can she call you later today? Now, she'll need a Class Two, so what do y'all have going already?" Dr. Peters listens, her eyes on me. "I see. Hmm." She turns and faces the wall, lowering her voice. Liz looks at me.

"My doctor doesn't want her to give me a prescription for narcotics," I explain.

"Why not?"

I close my eyes and let the room turn on its axis. "Because she's smart."

◆ ◆ ◆

Dr. Wortham prevails, and I don't get a prescription for narcotics, only antibiotics. Dr. Peters hands me three pain pills in a sample packet. "Call your doctor for something stronger," she says. "You're going to need it."

"Okay," I say.

I go through the three pills Dr. Peters gave me before bedtime, and I still get no sleep. The next day, while Kate is at church, I ransack her house like a thief. I open her bedroom door and go in, intent on checking the medicine cabinet in the master bath, the last place I can think of to look.

Kate's desk sits in front of the bay window, like mine in New York. Unlike mine, Kate's desk is expensive, and it lacks the scuffs and scars of hard use. I sit down and examine the photographs grouped on each side, pictures of Tom and Kate, and of Jake. Other pictures include a young woman I assume to be Anne, and her husband, although I can't remember his name.

Kate has a delicate Limoges piano and an antique desk tray that holds a couple of expensive-looking pens. A big coral rose in a Waterford budvase perfumes the space. I can see the rosebush it came from through the bay window. This desk is a comfortable and comforting space, as mine is at home. "You have a nice life, Kate," I say aloud. "What's it like to want all the right things?"

Her black leather Bible lies open in the center of the desk, a yellow highlighter in the groove where the pages join. This is her home Bible, the one she moves all over the house like a squirrel moves a nut. This mustn't be confused with her church Bible, or with the half dozen others in the bookcase. They line the shelf beneath the beautiful apricot carnival glass bowl I bought for her. "Different translations," she said, when she caught me looking at them.

She has marked a passage in fluorescent yellow.

> Who has believed our message, and to whom has the arm of the Lord been revealed? He grew up before him like a tender shoot, and like a root out of dry ground. He had no beauty or majesty to attract us to him, nothing in his appearance that we should desire him. He was despised and rejected by men, a man of sorrows, and

familiar with suffering. Like one from whom men hide their faces he was despised, and we esteemed him not.

Like one from whom men hide their faces? I know exactly how he feels.

> Surely he took up our infirmities and carried our sorrows, yet we considered him stricken by God, smitten by him, and afflicted. But he was pierced for our transgressions, he was crushed for our iniquities; the punishment that brought us peace was upon him, and by his wounds we are healed.

Stricken by God? Yes, I feel that way too.

I'm captivated, and I read it again and again for the aching beauty of the prose, and for the expression it gives to my own feelings. Who is this writer, who so eloquently voices my pain? I search the text before and after for clues but find nothing I can comprehend. The front door opens and closes downstairs, and I get up and go to my room.

Chapter Thirty-Three

I consider my reflection in the full-length mirror in my bedroom. Messy hair and lots of dark eye makeup, a skimpy tee shirt and faded jeans. It's the toughest look I can manage.

"I'm borrowing your Mercedes!" I shout to the house on my way out the door.

The big SUV lurches out of the driveway as I wrestle its leather-wrapped steering wheel with my good hand. The day is warm, as if autumn has forgotten to come here and summer will never end. I remember someone saying Texas has two seasons: hot and mild.

I cruise around the SMU campus looking for prospects. It's two forty-five, and I'm thinking classes will let out around three. I pull up to the curb to watch the students pass by, waiting for the right one. After a while, a promising young guy crosses the street. I jump out of the SUV and come alongside him.

"You gotta smoke?" I ask.

He stops and looks me over. "Sure," he says. He pulls a wadded pack of Marlboros from his baggy pants and takes out a cigarette. He smooths out some of the wrinkles and hands it to me.

"You gotta light?" I ask.

He lights it with a disposable lighter he has tucked in the cellophane wrapper of the cigarette pack. "You a student here?" he asks, shaking out a cigarette for himself.

"No. Just visiting from out of town."

"Where you from?"

"New York," I say.

"So you got a name, New York?"

"Camille."

He nods and lights his cigarette. "What happened to your hand?"

"Long story. Look, I could use something recreational while I'm here. You look like a man who can point me in the right direction."

"What kind of recreation?"

"You know the kind."

"How would I know?"

"Pharmaceutical," I say.

"No way, babe. You look done up, you know? You look like a fake."

I wedge the cigarette between the fingers of my bandaged left hand and pull a fifty from my pocket. "Take a chance?" I ask.

He looks at the money. "I can tell you where to go."

"For fifty bucks, you take me there."

He shrugs. "I have a class."

"Yeah, right. Tell you what. If you can get me what I want, I'll give you a hundred."

A breeze of pleasant surprise sweeps his face. "Suit yourself," he says. "'Course, if you're a cop, this is entrapment."

"You bet it is." I throw my cigarette in the gutter. "The sorriest lawyer in the world could get you out of it. C'mon, let's go."

We get in the Mercedes and drive east from the campus to Greenville Avenue. "Turn right here," he says. "This is the main drag, where everything happens."

"Everything, huh? Good thing I didn't miss it." We pass bars and restaurants, an organic grocery and a fortune-teller.

"Turn left at the next street," he says.

We enter a midcentury neighborhood behind the commercial property. Every house is in some phase of decay, with no gentrification in sight. A lawnmower and a bucket of paint—that's all it would take to spruce things up. "What a waste," I say, more to myself than to him.

"This house," he says. "The one with the blue trim."

We pull into the driveway behind a faded orange Datsun 240Z. The garage door is raised a few feet, showing junk stacked wall to wall. A sofa and a chair. Big plastic bags filled with God knows what. An old stained toilet. Worn tires.

"You wait here," he says. While he knocks at the door, I prop my bandaged hand on the steering wheel so I don't feel the throbbing all the way to my teeth. A scruffy orange cat and her kitten crouch in the flowerbed, which is overgrown and dry. The boy beckons me to come inside.

The front door opens directly into a living room choked with the fog of tobacco and marijuana smoke, although it isn't smoky enough to smother the foul odor of human filth. Garbage litters every tabletop, the chairs, and the floor. An old black-and-white movie flickers silently on the television, and whatever's on the stereo sounds as if it's being played backward. I step inside and feel the soles of my sandals stick to the muck. On the threadbare couch, a jaundiced couple lie entwined in a stupor. They look at me with uncaring faces.

"What's the lady's pleasure?"

The house has belched up a horrible man who looks like he's in his sixties. His greasy gray hair hangs like vines down to his shoulders, and he has a long, grizzled beard. He's shirtless, and his flaccid belly hangs in a limp fold over his belt buckle. There's a thin strand of barbed wire tattooed in black ink around the sagging flesh of his upper arm. It's a moment before I can speak. I'm disgusted to draw a breath in the room.

"I need some painkillers," I say. "Maybe oxy or something like that. Something strong."

"How many?"

"How strong are they?"

He steps back and puts his slender-fingered hand on my shoulder. "A gal your size? One'll knock you on your ass."

"Fifty, then."

His hand lingers on my shoulder, and then he lets it down slowly, and his fingertips brush my breast. He smiles through stained teeth. "Don't go anywhere," he says. "I'll be right back."

He returns and hands me an amber prescription bottle. "How much?" I ask.

"Usually, it's two dollars a pop, but I'll let ya have 'em for a buck fifty."

I count out five twenties and give them to him. "Thanks." I turn toward the door.

"Hey, what's the rush?" he says. "Why don't you stay and party? I got a keg in the kitchen and plenty of grass." He grins at me. "Got some sippin' tequila too. Nice and slow."

I keep moving, out the door. The guy who brought me here follows me onto the porch, and I hand him two fifties. "I'm staying here," he says, shoving the bills in his pants pocket.

I look at him, thinking he's some mother's son, and I can't stand to leave him behind. "C'mon," I say. "I need you to get me back to the school."

"Nah, you know the way."

"Don't be an idiot. That pirate will just take your money. Isn't there something you want to buy with it?"

"Yeah. In there." He jerks his head toward the door.

"Listen, you stupid punk!" I shove his chest, catching him off balance. He falls backward off the porch and hits the ground flat on his back, the breath knocked out of him. While he gasps for air, I jump on him in a screaming, cursing fit and dig in his pocket for the fifties. When I get my fingers around the bills, I scramble up and head for the SUV.

"You're coming with me if you want this money!" I climb into the Mercedes and start the engine.

He gets to his feet and yanks open the passenger door. Bits of grass stick out of his hair, and his elbow is bleeding. "Whatever," he says, panting. "You need to chill, babe."

"You're so stupid!" I scream. All my unexpressed rage has found vent, and there's no stopping it. "You know what you get from living like that? *Do you?*"

He shrugs.

"You get hepatitis, for one thing. Or the clap. Or worse. What's the matter with you? Don't you want a life?"

"I have a life!" he screams back at me.

"No!" I pound the steering wheel. "You don't! You got nothing!" I jerk the Mercedes around the corner onto Greenville, with the tires squealing and my right arm working hard to keep up. "You're gonna die, kid! You are!"

"Watch the road, lady!"

"You wanna know how I know that?"

He clasps his hands over his ears and yells, "Stop the car! Let me out!"

"Because I'm dying!" I shout.

He drops his hands and looks at me.

"That's right! Human Immunodeficiency Virus, baby. You want some of that? Because if you do, I can unwrap this hand right now and whack you good with it. You might as well get it here as in that pisshole back there."

Suddenly all my rage is spent, and my arms and legs are trembling. I drive the rest of the way to the campus in silence, both of us staring straight ahead. I park at the curb where I picked him up. "Here," I say, laying the money on the console between us. "Don't worry. You can't get it from the money. It isn't like that."

He picks up the two bills. "Why'd you want the oxy? Are you gonna do something stupid?"

"Get out."

He raises his hand and touches my shoulder. "Sorry."

"What's your name?" I ask.

"Terry."

"Take a life lesson, Terry, from a curriculum they don't teach in there." I nod toward the red brick buildings. "Mark this day in your mind, and choose well. Either I'm your future, or you make a different one. It's up to you. Now go." I face straight ahead until he gets out and closes the door, and then I drive away without looking back.

◆ ◆ ◆

I stop at an ATM and replenish my cash, and then I find a liquor store and buy a pint of Southern Comfort. I pull into Kate's driveway a few minutes after six and walk into the kitchen. Kate is putting together a light supper of fruit and cheeses and warm, fragrant bread.

"Are you hungry?" she asks.

"Sure," I say. I sit down and notice a brownish red stain seeping through the bandage. I haul myself up again. "Be right back."

In the bathroom upstairs, I unwind the gauze around my hand, letting it fall into the sink in a pile that I pour bleach over. I've stockpiled bleach and bandages, plastic gloves and plastic bags, hiding them behind my suitcase in the bedroom closet.

The wound is even more painful with the bandage off, a phenomenon I attribute to the power of visual stimulus. The antibiotics aren't working, and the angry flesh around the slash is red and swollen. Puss oozes between the black stitches, wet and thick and disgusting. I wrap my hand in fresh gauze and seal the old bandage in a zippered bag. This is my new toiletry. It isn't quite like any of my old routines, but it's necessary.

Kate is waiting for me in the kitchen. She has arranged the food in the center of the table and set each of our places with good dishes and cloth napkins. There's a glass of wine at mine and a glass of iced tea at hers. She's made it special for no particular reason, except the pleasure of it.

"This is nice," I say. I sit down and wait for her to bless the food, a custom I've finally learned to anticipate.

"Would you ask the blessing tonight, Cami?" she asks.

"Me? I wouldn't know where to begin."

"Just say something from your heart. It's no big thing." She smiles at having coined my catch phrase.

"Right. No big thing." It seems peevish to refuse, so I bow my head, my mind completely blank. I take a breath. "Okay. Here goes. Dear God, bless this food, and bless Kate for making it." I stop. If this Christian God were real, I'd want him to bless Kate for a lot more than making dinner. I'd ask him to bless her for her kindness and generosity. I'd ask him to bless this family and protect them from evil things, such as the things I saw this afternoon. And, finally, I most definitely would ask him to protect them from the plague inside my body. But these aren't words to speak aloud, so I simply say, "Amen."

I look up into Kate's gaze. "Thank you, Cami," she says.

"You're welcome." I put some food on my plate. All meals are force feedings now, but I can manage it. I can manage the pain too, at least until I get upstairs and put an oxy down my gullet.

Chapter Thirty-Four

As soon as the dishes are washed, I go up to my room and break out the Southern Comfort. I sit on the floor with my back against the bed, sipping from the pint and examining my afternoon purchase. The amber bottle brims with round, white tablets. I halfway expect them to smell like that foul house, but they smell only of chemicals.

I pour them out onto the hardwood floor and count them. Fifty, just as I ordered. Almost a month's worth if I can get by on one in the morning and one at night. There are more where these came from anyway. I wash one down with a swig from the pint. "Work your magic, you little rascal." I start putting the pills back in the bottle.

"Why am I dragging this out?" I say, surprising myself. I look at the pills that still lie scattered on the polished floor, and at the half-filled bottle in my hand. Oblivion, pure and sweet—right in front of me. I quickly finish filling the bottle and put it in my purse.

The sharp throbbing that has been with me for two days subsides, and I'm amazed at how good I feel in its absence. The relief is positively euphoric. I get my portable CD player, put in the earbuds, and turn it on. The last music I listened to, before my diagnosis, begins to play. I crank up the volume.

A cigarette would hit the spot, so I head downstairs with a pack and my pint. I feel so good that I seem to float weightlessly down the steps. I open the French doors and go out to the patio, where the overhead fan stirs the warm, wisteria-laden air. Everything is perfect, just perfect. I pull up a chair on which to prop my feet, and that's the last thing I remember.

My next awareness is that I don't feel good at all. A sickening sweet smell fills my nose. Someone calls my name, distant but clear, like the lapping sound of a faraway shore.

"Get back!" I yell, bolting up and stumbling. My feet catch on each other and trip me with a thud onto the flagstone, but I tighten my throat and refuse to puke until I can get to a toilet. I'm up again as fast as I went down, scrambling to the half bath between the utility room and kitchen, where I can let loose. I make it. Barely. I retch as soon as my head is over the bowl.

"Oh God," I groan.

I flush the toilet, and then I'm hit by another wave. It is viler than any episode I've ever had. I flush again and grab a wad of toilet paper to clear the vomit from my nose.

Kate reaches down and sponges my face with a damp washcloth. I take it from her and wipe my chin. "This is horrible, Kate. Don't stay in here."

"Let me get you something to rinse your mouth." She leaves and returns in no time. "Listerine and hydrogen peroxide," she says. She sets a glass on the floor beside me.

"Thanks. In a minute."

She gets on the floor beside me, but I'm too nauseous to protest. I close my eyes and rest my cheek on the cool lip of the toilet bowl. "I'm a mess," I moan. Driving the porcelain bus, Dad would say.

Kate rubs my back with her warm hand and sings softly in that fluid language of hers. I can't even begin to place it. She has a good voice, and the acoustics of the close space amplify it. She taps a slow rhythm on my back with her fingers, and her song progresses, rising to a crescendo that sounds like a plea. She hovers there for a while and then backs off. But then she rises again, stronger than before, as if the song comes from a place deeper than her diaphragm—as if it isn't exactly, entirely her. I open my eyes. Hers are closed, and her head is thrown back. Her palm presses to my back. I squeeze my eyes shut again.

I feel better by the time she winds down. She pats me the way I've seen mothers pat their kids. "Ready to get up?" she asks.

"Yeah, I think so." I pull myself up and gargle with the Listerine concoction. After I rinse the glass under a hot tap, I carry it to the kitchen, bracing myself against the walls along the way. My limbs feel like jelly.

"How about some juice?" she asks, taking the glass from me.

I nod and slump into a chair. My paraphernalia from last night is outside on the patio table. The pint bottle is empty. I stretch out the front of my tee shirt, which is covered with a brown stain.

"You fell asleep and spilled the Southern Comfort," Kate says. She sets a glass of orange juice in front of me. It's weird to hear her say the name of the whiskey, as if she were commenting on something as uncontrollable as the weather. I infer no accusation in it.

"So I see." The guy didn't lie. One hit knocked me on my ass. I stare at the grimy gauze wrapped around my hand. It's still dry. The day's throbbing begins, sharper than ever, and I rub my face with my good hand.

A breeze rustles the rose bushes and hydrangeas and comes through the open French doors. The air has cleared, and I don't feel the humidity anymore. Perhaps this is the first breath of autumn. I love autumn in New York. I sigh, thinking about trying to make my way back to the city, to my apartment. I can't muster the strength to think about it, much less do it. I realize, in this moment, that I don't have the strength to go on.

Sometime this weekend, maybe on Sunday when Kate and Tom are at church, I'll pack up and call a cab to take me and my oxy to a hotel. That will be the end of it. It's an easy plan. I realize that I've been making my way toward this escape, believing that I'll find peace on the other side. But now that I'm here, with my hand on the latch, there's a chill in my soul. I'm damned if I do and damned if I don't. I am afraid to die and ashamed to live.

Kate has the newspaper spread in front of her on the table, and she glances up at me over her reading glasses. "What are you thinking about this morning?" she asks.

"Nothing." I get up to pour a cup of coffee and slosh half-and-half in it. I miss my Jamaica Blue Mountain. "I should go upstairs and take a shower," I say and sit down again.

I drink coffee in silence until Kate finishes the paper and refolds each of the sections, squaring them in a neat stack. "What do you feel like doing today?" she asks.

"I envy you, Kate."

"Do you? That surprises me." She folds her arms. "What is it, Cami?"

"Why do I envy you?"

"No. What do you want to tell me this morning?"

I look into her face, into so much empathy. I wouldn't change places with Kate. I'd never wish for that, no matter what, but I do wish I could taste the sweetness of her life, if only briefly, to feel the satisfaction of knowing I'm a loving person.

"What does it feel like to be you?" I ask.

She doesn't hesitate. "It feels scary sometimes," she says. "Sometimes, it feels sad. Sometimes I feel as if I don't know what to do next. You think I'm different from you, but I'm not. Not really."

"No. You're very different."

The compassion in her face is as welcoming as a hearth on a bitterly cold night, and I think I would tell her all of my feelings this morning if there were something she could do. But it would be pointless because there isn't. Even so, I feel a longing, an unfamiliar yearning, for *something*, and I don't know how to satisfy it.

"I know you're afraid, Cami," she says.

"I am scared. So scared," I confess.

"It's all over you."

She reaches across the table and takes my hand. I grab her fingers, as if I'm grasping for life itself. She comes around and sits beside me, takes me in her arms, and holds me tight.

"Everything that has happened to you has brought you to this moment, Cami. You think your life has come undone, but it hasn't. I know it hasn't. I love you, little girl. I couldn't love you more if you were my own daughter."

"I love you too." I bury my face in her shoulder and wrap my arms around her.

"I have ached for the loneliness you feel," she says. "I have longed to reach out to you, to make you understand how much we love you. If you could only see that the things that make you feel so different are the very things that draw us to you.

"You say you have no God, but that's not true. You don't know him yet, but he knows you. He formed you in your mother's womb, and he has brought you here, to this house at this time, to reveal himself to you. You think he won't accept you, but he made you who you are, and he longs to be near you, not to judge or to condemn you. He wants to love you and make you his own, to be the lover of your soul.

"You are what Jesus came for, Cami, so long ago. You are the reason he was born on Christmas morning. You are the reason he endured Calvary. It was for you that he rose on Easter morning."

For the first time in my life, I doubt my longstanding skepticism. Am I really so arrogant that my opinion about God, to whom I've given so little thought, trumps the faith of so many generations? And Kate's faith too?

"You are Jesus's reward for everything he went through," Kate says. "You are the reason God became a man. Jesus is the arm of the Father reaching down to you. Just you."

The passage I read a few days ago—could it have been that recent?—comes back to me. "To whom has the arm of the Lord been revealed?" Suddenly, all the coincidences of these past months—Estella's pamphlets and dream, Kate's off-the-wall phone calls, and my visit here—don't seem so random. They seem like God reaching toward me.

Incredibly, the words of the passage are in my mind again with such clarity, as if I'm again reading the black print within the smudge of yellow highlighter. "The punishment that brought us peace was upon him." Jesus died for us. For me. My life pivots on the cliché: Jesus saves.

"Jesus is here now," Kate says. "He paid the sacrifice to open this moment to you. All you have to do is say yes. You aren't worthy—none of us are—but Jesus's blood opens the holy place to you anyway. Can you believe this?"

"Yes," I say. "I'm trying."

"That's all it takes. You need to pray now, Cami, and invite the Lord into your life."

"I don't know how."

"Then I'll help you, and we'll say the words together." Kate is still holding me, holding me tightly, and she begins to pray, "Lord, I bring you my life."

"I bring you my life, God," I repeat. I am all in on this prayer.

"I confess that you are righteous, and I am not." She waits, and I say it.

"I couldn't reach you, so you reached down to me through Jesus, who loved me and gave his life at Calvary as a ransom for me."

I repeat this, and she says, "I accept Jesus's sacrifice, and I open my heart to you, Lord. Come in. Forgive me, cleanse me, and make me whole, in Jesus's name."

I open my mouth, but all that comes out is, "Take me, God, please. I'm desperate." This brief plea vents my pressed emotions—loneliness, regret, terror—and I heave them out in sobs so deep they're tearless. The fragments of me that I've tried to lose by shedding names and burning yearbooks go out after them, and I feel emptied. What's left inside this body, this sick body that I'm stuck in, is something new. Something different. Something I don't understand. I become very, very still.

Kate takes me by the shoulders and holds me at arm's length. She's smiling. I wipe my face, which is, in fact, wet with tears. "What now?" I ask.

"You go upstairs and get your shower, and I'll fix us some breakfast. Maybe now we'll get something down you besides coffee and cigarettes."

"Kate?"

"Yes, baby."

I want to tell her that I'm sick, but I wonder if I dare. It would be out there, on the table and in the way. At least, if I don't say the words Human Immunodeficiency Virus, I can push them aside and explore what's happening to me.

"Thank you," I say.

Chapter Thirty-Five

When I come downstairs from my shower, Kate gives me her Bible. "Read Luke first, then Acts," she says. Instead, I turn to First Corinthians. I want to read these words again, these words that might comfort me now, as they did Sam.

Kate looks over my shoulder. "That was Sam's favorite chapter."

"I was reading it to him when he died."

"You were there? With him?"

"I went to see him, to read to him. That's where I was all those afternoons. He was so sick when I went in that last day, the day he died. He couldn't get out of bed."

Kate sits down at the table, and her eyes well up with tears.

"Sam wouldn't let me call anyone," I say. "I guess he knew it was the end. He asked me to read this chapter, and he was gone by the time I finished. I'm sorry I didn't tell you. I don't know why I didn't."

"Oh, Cami," she says, wiping her face. "I just knew he wouldn't be alone. I just knew it!"

♦ ♦ ♦

I spend hours in my bedroom or at the kitchen table or on the patio, reading. The Jesus within the pages of this ancient book is a long way from the sad savior of stained-glass windows and dusty statues. He's strong and in control, confrontational and thought-provoking. He doesn't hang out with the religious crowd, but with common people, with working men and whores. People like me. I'm amazed at the difference between the son of God described in the gospels and my ideas about him. I read hungrily, captivated by the memoirs of the people who were his friends.

My hand gets worse. The pain grows day by day, and the wound oozes odorous pus. I pour hydrogen peroxide on it and change the gauze frequently, using roll upon roll to make a thick bandage that hides the smell. I try not to look, unwrapping and rewrapping it with my eyes averted. Sharp pain shoots up my arm to my shoulder, and it's becoming intolerable. I make a trip to the drugstore for supplies, and I'm exhausted by the time I get back. But I'm not ready to call in the doctors. They'll slam dunk me into the hospital, and I'll be lost in a maze of medical jargon and high-powered drugs. So I buck up. I swallow Advil and Tylenol by the handful, and I hide the oxy in a pocket in my suitcase, saving it in case I still need to make an exit.

The thought crosses my mind, frequently, that I've brainwashed myself and taken refuge in weird ideas because I'm weak and off my game. My mind runs to money-grubbing televangelists pimped-out in garish suits, and in those moments I ask myself what in the world I'm doing.

I don't feel anything, not like I thought I did when Kate and I prayed in the kitchen. Not like the girl in Dr. Rawls's class, who I could tell really believed she felt God's presence. I counter my renewed skepticism by telling myself that it really won't matter if God isn't real. In the end, sweet oblivion still waits for me, even if he isn't, and if some other god besides Kate's is in charge, he or she probably won't mind. None of the others seem to be as jealous.

♦ ♦ ♦

A few days go by, and Kate says David is preaching at the college where he teaches classes. Not SMU, but the other college. "It's tonight," she says, "and we need to go."

"I don't know . . ."

"I insist, Cami. I won't take no for an answer."

"Okay." I wonder where I'll find the energy to make it through an entire evening out, and I feel awkward about seeing David again. "I don't have anything to wear."

"Let's see what we can find," she says. We go upstairs, and I let her sort through the clothes hanging in my closet. She pulls out my sleeveless black dress, which I haven't worn here. "I think Anne left a cardigan that'll look cute with this. I'll go get it."

I can see there's no getting out of this without a fight I'm not up for.

The school's campus is hardly a campus at all, just a few buildings surrounded by apartments and motels converted to dormitories. The school's name, Christ for the Nations, is prominently displayed on the tallest one, a former hotel that rises from the crook where two freeways come together.

Kate eventually finds a parking place in the crowded lot, and we walk to the main building. The auditorium is packed, and people mill in the aisles and between the rows, chatting. Some of them have Bibles tucked under their arms. I feel out of place, and I wonder what I've gotten myself into. I'll never fit in with this crowd. A guy in a sports jacket leads us to the front, where a couple of seats have been reserved at the end of the third row. I don't see David anywhere.

"This is my first time in a church," I say. "Although I don't guess this is really a church."

"We're the church, Cami," Kate says, motioning to encompass the crowd. "All of us together."

We settle in our seats, and soon people fill the rest of our row and the rows in front of us. A woman with a guitar separates from a group of musicians on one side of the stage. She walks to a podium in the center and says into the microphone, "Do you believe the Lord inhabits the praises of his people?"

The entire auditorium explodes with applause and shouts.

"All right!" she says over the roar. "Let's welcome him into this place tonight!"

The band starts playing, very loudly, and the woman with the guitar leads the audience in a song. David appears from a side door, walking swiftly toward the stage. He looks trim and handsome in a charcoal gray suit, white shirt, and black tie. He sees us and comes to our row. He greets Kate, and then he leans past her and says to me, "I'm so glad you came. Thank you."

"I'm looking forward to hearing you speak," I say.

David bounds to the stage, where he takes his place between an elderly woman and a couple of men. He raises his hands and sings, his eyes closed. The singing escalates, and the whole auditorium seems to be washed with a clean sweetness. I feel as if a newly opened spring inside of me is bubbling up, adding itself to a river that's rushing over us, and I wonder if this is the presence of God.

What happens next astonishes me. The orchestra leaves the melody and begins to play an odd harmony that rises and falls on unpredictable notes. The voices of the worshippers rise through sounds of the instruments. It's the song Kate sings in her bedroom every morning, the one she sang in the bathroom when I was sick. I realize, in this moment, that it is worship.

I'm disappointed when this part of the service is over and it's time to sit down. A man introduces David, and he steps to the microphone. "I'm so happy to be here tonight," David says, "to be among the family of God. It's good to see familiar faces in the audience." He smiles at me.

"I don't know most of you personally, but I know you in the Spirit. Thank you for lifting up Jesus in this place. Great things can happen when we're gathered in his name, so let's go to him now in prayer." He closes his eyes. Lifts his hands. "I yield myself as your instrument, Lord, to minister life. Use this tongue and this body as you used your own, in Jesus's name."

David opens his eyes and says, "Let's turn to the second chapter of Mark."

I find it and follow along as he reads a story about a paralyzed man. His friends wanted to bring him to Jesus to be healed, but they couldn't get through the crowd. So they tore open the roof of the house where Jesus was teaching, and they lowered their friend into the room with ropes.

"Whatever it takes," David says.

"Son, your sins are forgiven," Jesus tells the man. The man's a paraplegic, but Jesus thought his most pressing need was spiritual, not physical. I doubt the guy's friends were betting on that when they went to all the trouble to get him into the room through the roof.

The religious leaders criticized Jesus for saying the man's sins were forgiven. They called it blasphemy. I'm not surprised. Their hatred for everything Jesus said and did is a continuous theme in the gospels. The guys with all the power, and supposedly all the answers, scorned him. To be fair, he didn't have much use for them either. I marvel at the irony of their mutual contempt, but I like that Jesus challenged the status quo.

David reads Jesus's reaction to their accusations:

> "Why do you question these things in your hearts? Which is easier, to say to the paralytic, 'Your sins are forgiven,' or to say, 'Rise, take up your bed and walk?' But that you may know that the Son of Man has authority on earth to forgive sins"—he said to the paralytic—"I say to you, rise, pick up your bed, and go home." And he rose and immediately picked up his bed and went out before them all, so that they were all amazed and glorified God, saying, "We never saw anything like this!"

As I think about Jesus proving himself by revealing the intangible through the tangible, every sound, even the sound of David's voice, fades to silence. You can't see a forgiven soul, but everyone can see a healed body. It's a perfect metaphor. I read the story over and over, absorbing the implication of it.

Time passes while I'm lost in thought, and David finishes preaching. The band plays, more softly now, and the woman with the guitar comes back to the microphone. We stand and sing. David paces behind the woman. He has worked up a sweat, and his blond hair is matted to his head. He walks to the microphone, and she steps away to make room.

"The Bible says signs and wonders will follow those who believe," David says. "Miracles follow God's word. Some of you need healing in your bodies. Some of you need healing in your souls. This altar is open. Bring your needs to the only one who can meet them. Bring them to Jesus."

Kate takes my arm. "This is your cue."

She doesn't have to say it twice. I step into the aisle and go to the front. David looks down at me and nods. He paces some more, praying in an unknown language to his unknown God. Kate stands behind me, her hands resting on my shoulders. The space around us fills with people. I close my eyes and lift a silent prayer to the Jesus who healed that paraplegic man so long ago.

"Bring your needs to Jesus," David says from the stage. "He hasn't changed since he walked the streets of Jerusalem. He's the same. Yesterday. Today. Forever."

Tremors spread through my body, and pressure builds inside me, as if I'm caught between tectonic forces that push against each other. Then I hear David's voice in front of me. He says, "Open your eyes, Cami." He's soaking wet, and his eyes blaze with a fire that I've never seen in a man. "Jesus has all the power," he says. "He doesn't bow to anything or anyone. Everything in heaven and earth and hell must bow to him. Do you believe this?'

"Yes," I say, and I do.

"What needs to bow to him, Cami?"

I hold up my infected hand. I don't know why. My hand is the least of it.

"No. No. No. That isn't it," David says. "We both know it's something else." He wipes the sweat from his eyebrow with his finger and rakes it across his pants leg. "Jesus is going to heal you tonight, Cami, but you need to say the name of this thing. Don't be afraid. Confess it for healing, like you confessed your sin for salvation."

I hesitate. I don't want to say the name of the virus in this crowded place. If I'm not healed, it'll be out there, in the open. The woman standing next to me turns and looks, and I don't want her to hear it.

"Trust him. Trust Jesus," David says. "The Lord already knows what it is, and he's the only one who matters. The rest of us don't matter at all. You know that."

He waits, but I can't bring myself to say it.

"Christ is here," he says. "His anointing is here, the same as when he was on earth."

I open my mouth, and then I close it again.

"Now, Cami! Don't wait another minute! Say it!"

"HIV," I say quickly. There. I'm committed.

Kate squeezes my shoulders. "Dear Jesus," she whispers.

David doesn't flinch. "Take your hands off her, Kate," he says, and I feel her palms lift from my shoulders.

"Raise your hands, Cami, and thank him for your healing." I close my eyes and stretch my arms toward the ceiling. It's crazy, but it feels like the right thing to do. David puts his hands on me, front and back, on my stomach and on my lower back. "Be healed in Jesus's name!" he barks. Then, "Lord, fill her."

Some kind of force arcs between his palms and rushes out through my limbs, knocking me to the floor. A language I haven't learned surges up from deep inside me, and I begin to speak it. I lie flat on my back, arms outstretched, unable to lift even a hand under the weight of God.

Jesus's presence envelops me. I can't see him, but he's here, and he's as familiar as if I've known him all my life, as familiar as if I knew him before my life began. It's that primal. In this moment, I fall hard in love with him.

> My heart upon his warm heart lies,
> My breath is mixed into his breath.

The intimacy that all my carnal encounters lacked, I suddenly share with the only one who understands the sorrows of my changing face, the only one who truly loves my pilgrim soul. I'm caught up in the beauty of his holiness. I'm a virgin bride, as white and clean as any woman ever was. All my filth washes away, and my hard heart melts like wax in his presence.

I don't know how long I'm on the floor, but when I get up, I'm as weak as a lamb and have to be helped to a chair. I sit and rock, eyes closed, not wanting to disturb God's presence that so perfectly fills my gaping need.

I don't know how much time goes by before I reluctantly release the moment and open my eyes. Almost everyone is gone and the auditorium is quiet. David kneels in front of me. His hair is still damp, but the fire is gone from him. He's ordinary David again.

"How are you?" he asks.

"I'm good, David."

"You're healed too."

I'd forgotten it started with that. My friend Kate sits beside me. Her eyes are red from crying, and she's wiped off all of her makeup.

"You need to see a doctor now," says David, "and get tested again. Kate, will you help her?"

"Of course," she says.

David puts his arms around me and hugs me tightly. So tightly. "Welcome to the family of God, Cami," he whispers in my ear.

Chapter Thirty-Six

I t's been months since I saw Dr. Wortham, and she greets me warmly. "I wondered if I'd ever see you again," she says.

"There was a while when I wondered that myself. I brought you something." I hand her two papers, reports from a lab in Dallas and another in New York. I take my usual seat, and Dr. Wortham sits in the other chair, the one across from the beautiful vase.

"Negative for Human Immunodeficiency Virus," she reads. "Dr. Kuri and I discussed this at length." She hands the papers back to me. "Of course I'm thrilled for you, but I feel terrible about the mistake at the lab and the suffering it caused you."

"The mistake at the lab? You mean mistakes, right? The mistakes, plural, at the labs, also plural." I suddenly feel stupid for having expected any other reaction, yet I continue. "Dr. Kuri ordered two separate labs to test my blood, *my* blood, drawn by *his* nurse. Both labs reported me positive. Are you suggesting each lab made a mistake, completely independently? I'm sorry, but that's hard to believe."

262

Dr. Wortham starts to speak, but I hold up my hand. "Then, there were the symptoms I had, even before I was told about the HIV. The vomiting. The weight loss. I have to remind you that *you* ordered the tests because *you* suspected I was sick. *You*, the expert."

There. Her turn.

"Labs make mistakes all the time, Cami. It's common."

"The same mistake on the same patient's samples? Really? That's common?"

"Chain of custody issues are common. Techs mark vials incorrectly all the time."

She looks at me impassively, unwavering in her belief that I was misdiagnosed.

"Maybe these test results I just showed you are the mistakes."

"Is that what you believe?" she asks. Just like that, the miracle is dismissed, and we're back to the psychiatric program.

"Of course not," I say, "and neither do you, obviously, but your explanation is pretty far-fetched, in my opinion."

"Do you have a better one?"

"Yes, as a matter of fact, and I'm glad you asked."

She picks up her steno pad and her pen. "Go on."

"I've had an epiphany, Dr. Wortham."

"An epiphany?" she says, writing.

"I found the Giving Tree. His name is Jesus."

Her eyebrows arch. I've surprised her. "This is out of character for you, isn't it, Cami?"

"Very much so."

"Religion can play an important role in our lives," she says. "I'd never discourage it because spirituality goes to our deepest selves, but I think we can agree that a person doesn't have HIV one day and not have it the next."

"I'm not so sure about that anymore."

"You believe, then, that you received a healing? A sort of faith healing?"

"Yes. That's exactly what I believe."

Dr. Wortham puts down her notepad. "This epiphany, this dramatic shift in your personality, is disturbing. Tell me about the people in Texas, the ones you've been with."

"You think I've been brainwashed."

"I don't think anything. I know you've been in crisis, and I know that religious zealots are opportunistic. They prey on people who are foundering, as you were."

I stand and walk to the window, as I've done so many times. Then I turn around and say, "Look at me, Dr. Wortham." She does. She looks right at me, and I go on, "The HIV wasn't the worst of it. I was miserable. You know that. How can you base everything you believe to be true on the few—Oh, Dr. Wortham!—on the so very few things that you've seen with your eyes? Don't you understand that there's more than what you know?"

"Cami, listen to me. What else can we rely on? There's nothing wrong with religion, with finding comfort in the belief that there's some rhyme or reason to our lives, but don't lose yourself in it. Don't lose who you are."

"I don't know anything about religion," I say. "I only know that I used to be so lonely. I couldn't feel love, and I didn't have any love to give. That's who I was. Then I got sick, and I was terrified. I was hopeless. But now I feel love overwhelming me. I have peace, and I'm happy. I'm well too."

"Now." The obvious question being, what about tomorrow?

I open my mouth to argue, but the words of the prophet come back to me. "Who has believed our message?"

"I came to say good-bye, Dr. Wortham."

"Please, sit down, Cami."

"No. We're finished with our sessions. I'm not brainwashed. I haven't joined a cult or lost my individuality. You of all people know how important my independence is to me, but I don't need therapy anymore."

She stands. "How can you be sure?"

"Time will tell."

"Yes, Cami, time will tell."

"I still have your phone number. I'll keep in touch." I pick up her notepad and pen and write my cell phone number, below where she's scrawled EPIPHANY in big letters, with exclamation marks and question marks after it. "That's my cell phone. I didn't give it to you before." I put the pad down and pick up my purse. "Thanks for everything you did for me, Sylvia."

She hesitates, as if considering how to handle me, and then extends her hand. "You're welcome, Cami." I hug her, and she hugs me back.

"I'll miss you," she says. "I mean that. I looked forward to our sessions."

I smile and walk to the door.

"Cami?"

"Yes?"

"If you're happy, truly happy, then I'm very, very glad for you."

"Thank you."

I descend the steps of the granite building, noticing for the first time how lovely it is. How lovely all the old ones are in this part of town. The sidewalks teem with people, the street with cars and taxis. I walk home down Broadway, letting the city sounds roar around me in the brisk autumn air.

Boxes are stacked in every room of my apartment, their contents listed on the tops in bold black letters. I wander from the kitchen to the living room to the bedroom, remembering. I couldn't bear to let the place go, so I leased it to another young writer, a twenty-five-year-old playwright with a show playing off Broadway. I think he'll fit into the neighborhood nicely.

Estella has lost a client, but she gained a convert. She cried when I told her my story. I owe Estella a debt. My life changed because of her prayers, hers and Kate's. Kate prayed all the time for the people listed on that genealogy chart. I found it, creased and dog-eared, in the back of the Bible she gave me.

The knock I've been expecting comes at the door, and I open it to Joel, beautiful Joel. His eyes are so clear, so blue, and he smiles at me. He's wearing Levis and a brown sweater, the neck of a snow-white tee shirt showing under the itchy wool. The cleanness of him. The smell of him that I know so well.

"Hello, stranger," he says.

I hug him tightly, and we exchange a brief, dry kiss.

"I brought you something," he says, and he pulls a tiny Statue of Liberty out of his pocket. It's one of the cheap green plastic replicas they sell in the souvenir shops around town. I want to cry, looking at it. "It's to remind you of home while you're in Texas."

"I won't forget."

"What's the good news?" he asks.

I go to my purse and get out the lab reports. I hand them to him.

He reads them quickly, and then he scans them a second time. He grins at me. "How did this happen?"

"You better sit down for this one," I say. We sit on the floor, and I tell Joel everything about my encounter with his Messiah. He watches me and listens in silence until I'm finished.

"It's hard for me to believe it, Cam, or maybe I just don't understand, but I'm happy for you. I gotta say that you're the last person I expected to go that way."

"I hardly believe it myself." I take a long look at my handsome former lover. My beautiful forever friend. "I miss you, Joel, so much. Thank you for being there when I needed you most."

"I'll always be there for you."

"Are you seeing anyone now?"

"Victoria," he says, grinning.

"That little cat. Is it serious?"

"It is, Cam. We're cut from the same cloth." He cocks his head. "Is there someone in Texas?"

"No. Well, maybe."

"I don't think you'll be alone for long."

"We'll see."

"Willie was negative," he says.

"You knew?"

"I found out after. His girlfriend broke up with him over it. He was pretty upset."

I nod slowly but say nothing. There's nothing to say.

We get up from the floor, and Joel brushes the dust from his jeans. "Well, I better get going," he says. "I'll be late for rehearsal."

"I'll send you my new address. You'll let me know when there's a wedding, won't you?"

"We'll keep in touch."

We hug in the open doorway. My elderly neighbor comes out of her apartment. "It's good to see you two together again," she says as she passes, and we giggle like kids.

"I love you, Joel."

"I love you too. Bye now." He turns and descends the stairs two at a time.

◆ ◆ ◆

I run past SMU's red brick buildings on the route I'm getting used to. Dr. Rawls and David recommended me for a faculty position in the spring. I like the idea of an academic life. It might be a good fit for me. The trees on campus are still full of green leaves. It was eighty yesterday, but a front blew through last night while we slept and left us a cold, blue sky morning.

"This is Texas," Kate says. "The weather here turns on a dime."

I still miss New York most days, but when I think about those icy winter winds whipping through the canyons of Midtown, I'm glad to be down South.

I turn away from the campus and cross Hillcrest. The shops of Snider Plaza haven't opened yet, and the sidewalks and parking lots are empty.

I take a side street—my street—and jog the remaining blocks to my bungalow. I bought it with the advance from *Lessons Lost*. Christopher came up with the title, and I think it fits the story well. Chris plans to have the book in stores by mid-December, which will mean a tour.

"Just don't commit yourself for Christmas," Kate insisted. "Everyone will be home then, and I want you here."

"I'll be here," I assured her. I wouldn't miss it for anything, although I plan to go to Phoenix between Christmas and New Year's. It's been years since I visited my parents during the holidays.

My little house is native stone, with green shutters and flowerbeds filled with azaleas that I expect to be beautiful in the spring. Kate's Mercedes SUV sits in the driveway, a loaner until I decide what to buy. There's a small brown parcel on the front porch, and I sit on the steps to open it.

A middle-aged man jogs by on the sidewalk, his golden retriever trotting at his side. "Hey," he grunts, raising one hand.

"Hi," I say. I watch them lope away, each of them trailing puffs of steam in the cold air.

Inside the box is a brass kaleidoscope, the shiny metal not yet chilled. I raise it to the sunlight and turn its barrel. The colors flow in and out of one another, and I'm suddenly reminded of the beautiful vase in Dr. Wortham's office. It seems like a long time ago that I held it in my hand—a lifetime ago. There's a note in the bottom of the box.

> Welcome to the neighborhood.
> —David

I take the package inside and put the kaleidoscope on my old desk, which faces the street in a front bedroom I've made into a study. I put a CD in the stereo, a recording of live worship from a church in Australia. I can't get enough of this music. I raise my hands and walk through the house, singing in the language God gave me. His Spirit fills me again and again, until I don't think I'll be able to stand it.

I'm working my way through Proverbs this month, one chapter each day. There are thirty-one. This verse jumped out at me this morning:

> The blessing of the Lord makes one rich.
> And He adds no sorrow with it.

I've been mulling that idea over ever since. I know that troubles will come my way again. I'm not foolish enough to think I've seen the end of hard times, but this is our honeymoon, and for now, I'll shut out the world.

I go to my computer and turn it on. I remove the bandage taped to my palm. It's in the way. Besides, the cut is closed and dry, and the stitches are gone. I touch it, remembering other wounds in other hands.

> I will not forget you. See?
> I have inscribed you on the palms of My hands.

"I've missed you, my friend," I say aloud to the computer. I haven't written in a long time, and my fingers hesitate over the keys. I remind myself that it's only a first draft. It's no big thing. Just relax.

I start typing, and the words are there, pouring from my fingers. I write page after page the rest of the day, telling the story of my redemption.

About the Author

L. K. Simonds is a Fort Worth local. She has worked as a waitress, KFC hostess, telephone marketer, assembly-line worker, nanny, hospital lab technician, and air traffic controller. She's an instrument-rated pilot and an alumna of Christ for the Nations Institute in Dallas. *All In* is her first novel.

There are many places to learn more about God's love for you.
Here are a few:

The Word Church, Lloydminster
thewordchurch.ca

Christ for the Nations
www.cfni.org

I Am Second
www.iamsecond.com

Gateway Church
www.gatewaypeople.com

Jack Hayford Ministries
www.jackhayford.org

CPSIA information can be obtained
at www.ICGtesting.com
Printed in the USA
BVHW032344220719
554138BV00001B/1/P